DESPERATELY SEEKING ROOMMATE

USA *Today* Bestselling Author
MICALEA SMELTZER

© Copyright 2019 Micalea Smeltzer
All rights reserved. This book or any portion thereof may not be reproduced or used in any manner whatsoever without the express written permission of the publisher.
This is a work of fiction. Names, characters, businesses, places, events and incidents are either the products of the author's imagination or used in a fictitious manner. Any resemblance to actual persons, living or dead, or actual events is purely coincidental.
Cover Design: Emily Wittig Designs
Editing: KBM Editing
Formatting: Micalea Smeltzer

To Lou and Abel.
It's probably weird to dedicate a book to my characters, but you guys made me see things differently.
One day I'll have a love like yours.
If you're reading this dreaming of finding your Prince Charming, I promise he's coming. We just have to be patient. After all, good things come to those who wait.

CHAPTER ONE

Lou

"I can't believe I have to do this," I sigh, staring at the ad I've typed up.

"It's not like you asked your landlord to be King of the Douchebags and raise your rent," my best friend Miranda chimes. She's lying across my bed on her stomach, swiping madly on Tinder. I don't know why she likes the stupid app. I find it insulting more than anything. The *one* time I used it I got a message within five minutes of a dick with a bow wrapped around it. I immediately replied that that was not the gift I was asking for at the moment, thank you very much.

She turns her brown eyes to mine and heaves a dramatic breath. She reaches past me and pushes the pad on my laptop, sending the ad through to our university's newspaper.

I cry out, hands fumbling toward my laptop. "Miranda, I wasn't ready! I needed to proofread it again."

"You would've been here all day reading it and then talked yourself out of posting it. It needed to be done."

She rolls off my bed and strides over to my closet door, swiping through the clothes on the hangers.

Miranda is the first friend I've ever had who I could share clothes with. I'm short and curvy—or what many would call plus size—and most of my friends growing up were either thin or average-sized. I always felt like the odd duck out, until Miranda and I met during English 101. Neither of us are from Winchester—I came from the southern part of Virginia to here in the north, and she ventured all the way from Delaware.

Somehow, we ended up sitting beside each other in our English class and the rest is history.

She holds up an oatmeal colored over-sized sweater. "Can I borrow this?"

"Sure," I reply with a shrug, shutting the lid on my computer. With a groan, I stand up, stretching my stiff muscles. I'm twenty-one going on eighty. If I'm sitting or in any position for too long my limbs lock up despite my nearly daily yoga routine. It's ridiculous.

"Thanks." She drapes the garment over her arm. Her dark brown curls swing around her shoulders. With her father being Hispanic and her mother Asian, the girl is the epitome of the word *unique*. She's stunning and I tell her all the time, but she never believes me because of her size.

I don't know why us bigger girls are shamed by society. We're *normal-sized*—I'm sorry your media standards are candy-cane stick thin. I'd rather *eat* them than look like one.

"I wish you could move in with me," I whine, as she goes back to flipping through my closet. I've been pouting about this fact for a solid week—ever since I found out rent was going up and I was no longer going to be able to afford my two-bedroom apartment in the historic district. The idea of living with a stranger isn't appealing at all, and since I have no time to spare, I have to be open to a guy for a roommate too.

The prospect of going to pee and falling into the toilet doesn't sound like my idea of getting wet, but desperate times call for desperate measures, and I need a roomie *stat*.

She sighs, her lips twisting downward in genuine apology. "I know, babe, but I just re-signed the lease on my apartment. There's no way I can get out of it. Living here would be so much nicer. My place is a dump."

She lives in an older apartment beside the small airport of privately owned planes. I still don't know how I lucked out getting my cute place downtown—but right now I don't feel so lucky and want to punch my landlord in his smug face. He's young, probably late twenties or early thirties, and inherited this building over the summer when his grandpa passed away. Now, the greedy bastard wants to make more money off broke college students like me.

"Does this match?" she asks, pairing the sweater with a maroon skirt that ends above the knees with buttons down the front.

"Yeah, it'll be cute," I tell her honestly. "But ... what do you need it for?"

Color blossoms across her dark skin. "Charlie asked me out."

"*Charlie?*" I shriek. "Why am I just now hearing about this? I thought you hated him." I jolt upright from this news, in desperate need of hearing the tea on how this came about.

Charlie is in our history class—he's the type who answers every question correctly and then looks around smugly like we all care that he's so much smarter than us.

Newsflash, we don't.

She shrugs. "It happened yesterday. I bumped into him in the library and he asked. I don't really like him, but ... Lou, it's been *forever* since I got laid and I'm desperate. My kitty needs more than some sweet vibrations. I need a man. On top of me. Inside me. All around me."

"But *Charlie*?" I can't get over this. He's not hideous, but if looks were determined by personality he'd be one ugly guy—like Smeagol.

"He's not horrible looking," she reasons, her bottom lip jutting out in thought. "And you never know, he might be cool."

"Well, when he bores you with his vast knowledge of the size of every shit a president took, don't come crying to me."

"I doubt he knows *that*." She spreads the clothes on top of my bed and stands back, assessing how they look together. Glancing at me she adds, "I'm giving him the benefit of the doubt, okay. Can you do that, too? For me?"

I hug my best friend. "I'd do anything for you."

"Thank you." She smiles, her dark slanted eyes looking relieved. Her relief transitions into worry and her lips flatten. "What are you going to do if no one responds to your ad?"

I sit down on my bed, looking out the old dirty window onto the street below.

"Live on the streets, I guess."

"You know I'd never let that happen," she vows. "My place might be small, but I can make room for you somewhere—maybe add a cat cushion in the bathroom."

I grab a pink pillow and toss it at her. "My ass wouldn't even fit on it."

"At least it's a nice ass." She gives it a tap. "Can we get something to eat now? I'm starving, and you bribed me with the promise of dinner only to spend two hours writing a measly four lines for your stupid ad."

It was more like seven, but even that *is* a pathetic amount of time to spend writing it.

"Fine," I grumble. "I do owe you food."

Her eyes roll as she sticks her tongue out at me. "At this point you owe me a whole fucking pizza."

Twenty minutes later we're seated in a booth inside the cozy wood-fired pizza place—aptly named *Woody's*.

The place has a warm and cozy vibe with browns and blacks used for much of the décor. Our booth is beside the bar, packed with people—mostly fellow college students and the random old guy interspersed. I watch one old man leer down the shirt of the woman beside him.

Nasty old bastards.

Picking up my beer glass, I let the warm liquid slide down my throat. Across from me, Miranda texts on her phone, and I don't dare ask to whom, because I don't want to hear the name *Charlie* leave her lips. The thought alone makes me want to gag.

Who knows, he could prove me wrong, but as her best friend it's my job to have reservations about any guy she dates. She's a queen and deserves to be treated as such. A guy will be lucky to get my stamp of approval, and chances are it won't be Charlie.

She sets her phone aside and stretches across the table toward me. "How much longer until the pizza is here? I'm withering away by the second."

"Considering we ordered five minutes ago, I'd say you'll be waiting a while."

"Dammit." She tosses her head back in aggravation. "Good thing I always have snacks in case of an emergency." She rifles through her purse and pulls out a small bag of popcorn. She proceeds to open it and starts shoving pieces into her mouth.

"If you had that why didn't you eat it earlier?" I remark.

She shrugs and answers around a mouthful. "Forgot I had it."

I shake my head amusedly. Miranda is one of a kind.

I wasn't hungry before, but now that we're here I'm positively *starving*. It feels like it's been a whole day since lunch, not hours. I was too busy agonizing over the stupid ad to think about my stomach.

"Give me some of that," I plead, holding my hand out for some popcorn.

She cradles it against her boobs. *"Mine."*

"Miranda," I gripe. "Please?"

"Fine." She drops a stingy three pieces in my hand.

"That's all you get." She grins and shoves more in her mouth.

I glare at her, but at least it's better than nothing. I eat the three pieces slowly, savoring them. The food is on its way, and once it's here all will be right in the world again. I'm pretty sure pizza can solve any problem. Honestly, I'm not sure why the idiots in government haven't just ordered some damn pizzas already. Nobody can fight when ooey-gooey-cheesy goodness is in front of you. It's like, against the laws of nature or something. I'm sure of it.

She finishes her popcorn and stuffs the empty bag in her purse.

"I'm full, let's go."

I narrow my eyes.

"Kidding," she adds. "God knows it takes more than that to fill me up."

As much as I don't want to bring up Charlie again, I have to. "When is this date of yours?"

"Tomorrow." She bites her lip.

Studying her, I narrow my eyes into slits. "If you've never really liked him why are you acting nervous all of a sudden?"

She tucks an errant piece of dark hair behind her ear. "I honestly haven't liked him. He's arrogant, rude, condescending ... but also kind of hot in a dork-ish sort of way. The glasses, the floppy hair." She rests her chin on her hand and gives a dramatic dreamy sigh. I'm friends with a complete and utter nutcase.

"Don't go falling in love now," I joke. "I can't be left alone in my singledom."

She rolls her eyes and fans her hand through the air. "Not going to happen. I doubt Charlie can handle all of this." She wiggles her body. "I have needs that need to be met and I'm not certain he's the guy for the job. It's only a date though—free dinner and a movie? I'm not going to complain one bit about that shit."

"True." When you're a broke ass college student, getting to go out and have a free meal is the equivalent of the Holy Grail. Toss a movie into the mix and you've found Jesus himself.

It's been so long since I've dated I've become a Scrooge. Freshman year I went a bit crazy, going out all the time to parties and on dates with guys that usually only led to sex. Then last year I decided I wanted something more serious, but most guys still only wanted a one-and-done experience and the few looking for a relationship didn't want someone like ... well, *me*.

I never used to be insecure about my size. I don't think anyone at any size should ever be ashamed of their body. You never know someone's personal struggles, so who are you to judge? But suddenly, I *did* start to become insecure and wondered if men didn't see me as the type they wanted to have a future with—that I was only good for a quick lay.

After that, I swore off men, determined to build up my confidence again.

Junior year is supposed to be *my* year, and I won't let myself get dragged down by pining for some ideal that exists solely in my head.

Love will come along when it's meant to. Until then, I'll be living my best life, which includes pizza nights with Miranda, manicures and pedicures once a month, and whatever else I want to do—which let's be real, after I spend the money on the mani-pedis I'll be sitting in my apartment contemplating my life choices and if I *really* had to buy those Cheetos from the campus vending machine two years ago for three dollars and fifty cents, because surely if I had that money today I'd be better off. You might say I don't need the mani-pedis, which might be true in theory, but I don't need that kind of negativity from anyone in my life, so you can kindly fuck off.

"Here you ladies go," our usual waiter Joe says with a smile, setting down each of our pizzas—Miranda's meat lovers and my veggie. Joe is an older guy, probably in his fifties, bald, and has a black goatee. He's awesome and always makes us laugh. "Don't do anything I wouldn't do tonight."

Miranda snorts. "Like devour this pizza whole? You bet your ass that's happening."

He merely chuckles and walks away to tend to another table.

I cut two slices of pizza and set them on the plate Joe brought earlier to cool down.

Miranda stares longingly down at her plate. "I want to eat it now, but I know if I do I'll have severe regrets when my tongue is burnt for a week." She raises her eyes to mine and shrugs. "Eh, you only live once, right?"

Before I can stop her, she grabs a piece and takes a huge bite. *"Regret,"* she cries, pulling a stringy piece of cheese away from her mouth. "Instant. Regret." She pants, spitting out a blob of too hot pizza.

Stifling a giggle, I gesture toward the unfortunate mess of cheese and other toppings in front of her. "Now look what you've gone and done. You ruined a perfectly good piece of pizza."

She frowns. "Such a tragedy. Let's have a moment of

silence in its honor for its service to my mouth." She claps her hands together and bows her head. Lifting it two seconds later she announces, "Enough of that."

She proceeds to pick up the rest of the piece she bit into and blows on it to cool it down.

Once a few more minutes pass and I feel sure my own pizza is green-lit to eat, I take a bite.

Nope! Abort mission!

"Ah!" I cry, as the hot cheese and sauce burns my tongue, bringing tears to my eyes. "Get it out," I plead stupidly, because it's not like a stranger is going to shove their hand in my mouth to yank out the scalding piece of pizza. I manage to spit it out and reach for my beer, but the starchy drink does little to soothe my tongue. I spot Joe walking by and wave madly, nearly falling out of the booth. "Water," I beg when he sees me. "Need. Water."

He chuckles. "Coming right up."

Looking across the table at Miranda, I sigh. "We shouldn't be allowed out in public. We're both walking disasters."

"I like to think my awkwardness brings joy to those around me."

"As opposed to what?" I inquire, thanking Joe with a nod as he sets down a glass of water for each of us. I gulp greedily at the cold liquid.

"Horror at the realization a walking wrecking ball exists, ready to take down anything and anyone around her. I can't help it that I'm clumsy and stupid things happen to me."

"Same, girl." I can relate to that on every level.

When I was six, I fell from the top of the playground slide onto the ground, banging my head into a piece of wood that was a part of the area separating the grass from the mulch. Suffice to say, there was a lot of blood, more than five stitches, and a scar on my forehead that I carry with me to this day.

"Let's try this again," she says, and takes a tentative bite. She gives me a thumbs up. "All clear."

I follow suit, thankfully, it's not scorching hot anymore, but my sore tongue makes it less enjoyable than it should be.

I eat a total of three pieces before asking for a box. After we've both finished our drinks we grab our things and head outside onto the cobblestone road in front of the restaurant.

The sun is only beginning to set, and it's a little before eight, but already starting to get dark earlier every night. I personally love the times when it's nine at night and still light out. Fall and winter are the bane of my existence. I thrive on the energy the sun brings me. If I could hibernate through the winter months I might like them more, but since I have to get out and brave the cold on the daily it's a hate-hate relationship.

We walk a couple of streets over, both of us much more subdued thanks to the pizza and drinks.

If you put food in me, suddenly I'm ready to sleep. It makes eating breakfast and lunch a game of Russian roulette of will I or won't I fall asleep in class.

Miranda and I say our goodbyes as she gets in her car, and then I enter my apartment building. It's a ground floor unit, which I hated at first because it didn't seem very safe to me, but I've come to love it—when I have groceries at least I don't have to walk up any stairs.

I close the door behind me and sweep my gaze around my place, my *home*. I've spent so much time buying things and making it mine. The white and gray décor with pops of pink in the main space brings me peace. The same theme carries into my bedroom. The spare room has been my office, housing a desk and two bookcases that didn't fit in the main room—though I do have bookcases lining the wall behind my couch.

Tomorrow, I'll have to clean out the office. I don't know where I'll put the things in there, but I'll figure it out. Anything I can't keep will have to be donated, or Miranda can have it if she wants.

I stand in the doorway of the room, wondering who on Earth my roommate will be. I hope we get along and that is doesn't end up being a complete and utter disaster.

Though, knowing my luck, a disaster is exactly what I'll get.

CHAPTER TWO

Lou

I manage to get all the books off the bookshelves in the office space and stack them up in piles in my room, planning to go to HomeGoods to see if they have any wire baskets I can put them in or something. I saw something on Pinterest like that and it looked really cute. Granted, Pinterest seems to be full of lies because nothing I ever try from the site turns out decent. But baskets seem like a safe bet since it doesn't involve sugar or flour.

I decide to leave the shelves themselves since my future roommate might have books they'd like to house there. If they want them gone ... well, I'll cross that bridge when I get there.

Pulling my hair back into a ponytail, I prepare to move my desk into my room. I moved things around to make space for it earlier, but I've been avoiding heaving the heavy monstrosity from the other side of the apartment. I'm already a sweaty hot mess and it's not even ten in the morning.

I deserve an award for my dedication to my future roommate, because this shit sucks.

Once all my stuff is out of the spare room—except the bookcases of course—I vacuum every square inch and then go through the entire apartment while I'm at it.

After that, my OCD kicks in and I decide to scrub the entire place until it's spotless. I figure that way when someone inquires about the place it'll be in decent shape when they see it.

When everything is clean, I take a shower and change into a pair of *real* clothes—not my usual fuzzy pajama pants and loose t-shirt attire. It's after one now, and I'm in desperate need of caffeine. Normally I would've had three cups by now, but I was busy enough to keep the urges at bay.

I grab my phone off the counter—the case it's in holds my credit cards and some cash—and make my escape before I find anything else I need to clean.

I walk out the door and walk smack dab into my landlord.

"Oh my God," I cry, my hand flying to my chest.

"Not God, but close enough." He grins devilishly. His reddish blond hair is neatly trimmed but worn messily, his face is lightly stubbled like he didn't have time to shave this morning, and his hazel eyes pop against his tan skin. He's hot, even I'll admit it, but his good looks don't make up for his asshole personality.

"How can I help you, Jamie?" I ask him in a biting tone, knowing there's no *good* reason why he's here.

He gives me one of his signature smarmy smiles and I resist the urge to roll my eyes. It'd be my luck he'd kick me out on my ass based on rudeness, even though he needs to take a good long look in the mirror.

"I was just swinging by to remind everyone rent is due next Friday at the new price."

I give him a mock thumbs up I'd love nothing more than to turn into a middle finger salute. "I haven't forgotten."

"Mhmm, see you around, Louise."

He starts down the hall to the next tenant and I call out, "It's *Lou*."

He knows this, but he doesn't care. As long as his

pockets are padded with our cash, he doesn't care about any of us lowly tenants.

I walk out the main door onto the sidewalk. The nearest coffee shop is only a block away. It's one of the perks of living downtown. I'm in walking distance to so many things, and as someone who has an aversion to driving it's extremely convenient. It's not that I don't drive, I kind of have to, but I white knuckle it the entire way—wherever I'm going, no matter the distance.

The fading green leaves dance on their limbs with the promise of fall, and more people than usual stroll around in the cooler weather. Like them, I'm thankful to finally say goodbye to the ridiculous humidity. Walking outside and immediately becoming drenched in sweat isn't my idea of fun. Boob sweat is a freaking nightmare and impossible to avoid when it's ninety degrees but feels like one-hundred and ten.

Griffin's, the best coffee shop in the world, appears around the corner and I smile. I love the old-fashioned brick building with green trim. It's unique and doesn't quite look like it belongs in this town, but better suited for a cute hideaway place in some foreign country.

I push open the door, the cheery bell signaling my arrival.

I pause for a moment, inhaling the sweet warm scent of coffee and baked goods.

The line isn't too long, and I send up a little prayer for

this small blessing. At times I've had to wait thirty minutes just to order. It's a favorite with the locals, and even the out of towners, for its charm and the fact it frequently hosts music acts and open mic nights. Plus, with the university not far away students flock here to study or hang out, myself and Miranda included.

Finally reaching the counter, I order a latte and banana muffin. There's an empty seat near the windows, which never happens. I run toward it like I'm racing in the Indy 500 only to get there the same time as a guy.

"This is my table," I declare.

"Pretty sure I got here first," he argues back.

I put my hands on my hips. "Nope, it was definitely me."

He grins, and it's a boyish kind of smile, sweet but with a naughty edge. His teeth are slightly crooked, but I think it's cute. Too many perfect teeth in an imperfect world is a bit much for me, personally.

"How about we call it a tie?" he suggests. "We could share? There are two chairs and plenty of space."

My head cants to the side as I think it over. There are other empty tables, but this one is the best with its natural light and people watching capabilities.

"Fine," I agree, albeit reluctantly since I'm not fond of strangers. "We'll share. But if you think I'm going to share my muffin with you, you're wrong." My sharing streak does not carry over to food.

His smile grows wider.

"*Not* the muffin I meant."

He chuckles, and it's a husky raspy sound—almost too sexual sounding to be a laugh. "It was still funny."

My cheeks heat. *Why do I have to be so awkward?*

I sit down, and he follows suit. He looks to be my age, and I wonder if he's going to the university too. Campus is large and it's impossible to know everyone or see every face. He has light brown hair, brown eyes, and a heavy dusting of stubble on his cheeks like he couldn't be bothered to shave for the past couple of days.

"I'm Tanner." He holds out his hand.

I take his hand and shake it before letting go. "Lou."

"Lou?" he repeats, raising a brow. "Can't say I've heard that one."

"It's short for Louise," I explain, tucking a stray piece of blonde hair behind my ear.

"Family name?"

I nod. "My grandmother's. She passed away before I was born, and my mom wanted to honor her." My name is called for my order. "That'll be me," I say unnecessarily. "Try not to give my seat away."

He chuckles, leaning back in his seat to watch me. "It seems like a hot commodity. Someone might buy it from me and who am I to turn down a few extra bucks?"

"Don't even think about it," I warn with a joking smile.

I grab my order and return. Tanner's made himself comfortable. His long legs are sprawled out into the aisle and he's set up his laptop on the table.

He looks up at me and I shake my muffin. "Not sharing," I remind him.

He chuckles, closing the laptop lid so he can look at me. "What about your coffee? You sharing that?"

"Nope." I pull my muffin out of the bag along with a plastic fork.

"So mean to me," he remarks, pressing a hand to his chest.

I notice then he's dressed nicely in a dark blue sweater and jeans that look like they cost more than my rent.

"I guess it's a good thing I already placed an order." His eyes sparkle with barely contained laughter.

I peel the wrapper away from my banana muffin. "That's a very good thing," I concur. I pull off a piece of the muffin and pop it in my mouth. I've always eaten them that way, much to mother's chagrin.

She'd scoff and say, "Louise Myrtle Powell, a lady does *not* walk around with crumbs on her bosoms."

But in my opinion, if you aren't producing crumbs then you're not enjoying yourself. Life's too short to not get messy.

Tanner smirks at me over the top of his computer. "I'm suddenly very jealous of your ... muffin."

I choke at his words and muffin crumbs tumble down my throat, the once soft bites now feel like icepicks digging into my esophagus as I try not to hack up a lung.

His smile widens as I grab my coffee and try to compose myself. "You're kind of adorable."

Adorable.

That word feels like an ice cube dropped down my back—cold, prickly, and utterly distasteful.

Most girls get told they're pretty, or if they're lucky beautiful, gorgeous, or even stunning. I've always been stuck in the cute or adorable category. It's a corner I don't like being shoved into. Is it my size that doesn't make me worthy of more flowery descriptors or am I forever going to be the girl that never is in the starring role, even in her own life?

About that time his name is called. I doubt he even notices the shutters I close around myself. I don't like people-ing, and this is what happens when I do.

Honestly, why do I have to leave the house? Human interaction is overrated. I could survive as a hermit. Me, myself, and I sounds like a mighty fine life to me.

Tanner slides back into the chair across from me with a *gigantor* cup of coffee.

He must have asked for the 'I'm a closet dick' special. Actually, in that case his coffee should be the tiniest cup size imaginable to match his, I'm sure, below average penis size.

"Why are you glaring at me?" He raises one brow, lowering the lid on his laptop.

"You called me adorable." The words tumble out of my mouth before I can stop them. I wouldn't be so hung up on the silly word if one of the horrible guys I went out with last year didn't tell me, "This was fun and all, don't get me wrong you're adorable, but this won't be happening again," *after* slept with him.

I hate myself for letting it get to me now, but let's face it, word vomit is the worst kind of vomit of all. At least if you're sick you can clean up the mess and move on, but words? Once you speak them you can't gobble them back up and swallow them down.

He narrows his eyes in confusion. "What's wrong with adorable?"

I roll my eyes, swaying my hand casually through the air. "Little girls are *adorable*. I'm a woman. I should be can't-touch-this hot, or sexy-and-I-know-it sinful, *not* adorable."

He throws his head back, laughing so hard his whole body shakes with the force.

"Why are you laughing?" I hiss, my palms landing flat on the table to stop it from moving along with him.

Laughter that can only be described as giggles, erupts from him. There are literal tears in his eyes and I feel like a fool. I want to grab my stuff and run far and fast away, but something keeps me compelled to stay in my seat.

Why is it so funny that I think I deserve to be called hot or sexy? Just because I'm a bigger girl, doesn't mean I'm any less than another woman—so why does it feel like I am.

When he finally sobers, wiping tears from his eyes, he leans over the table and motions with his hand like he wants to tell me a secret. I lower my head, my ear tilted toward him and he says, "You're not my type."

I rear back like I've been electrocuted. Any time I've heard that line it's usually followed by, *"Look at me and look at you. We don't match."* It's beyond frustrating feeling like I'm constantly being judged on my weight. I'm happy, smart, and I know I'm pretty. Yeah, maybe I'm not a Victoria's Secret model, but I'm *Lou*. I'm *me*. The most beautiful thing we can be in this world is our own unique self. No one else can ever be you, so I believe in loving myself whole-heartedly. I'm stuck with myself until the day I die. If I hate who I am, and what I look like, it's going to be a long damn ride.

"Because of the extra junk in my trunk, right?" I challenge, raising a brow. I never defend myself when this kind of thing happens, because frankly anyone with that kind of mindset isn't someone I want to associate with, but this time I refuse to let it go.

His eyes widen like saucers and his cheeks redden as he too whips back in his seat. "Oh, fuck, God no. I'm *gay*."

My entire body collapses onto the table, my head in my hands. I don't know whether to laugh or cry so I settle for a combination of both. It figures when I finally decide to call a guy on his bullshit he ends up playing for the other team.

When I finally gather my wits, those pesky little buggers, I sit up straight and hold my chin high.

"If you weren't gay, would I be your type?" I give him my best duck lips and sultry-eyed Instagram model worthy look.

He looks me up and down and a slow grin spreads over his face.

"Most definitely."

I shrug and let out a sigh. "I can live with that."

I finish my muffin, sipping my coffee along. Brushing the crumbs off the table I stand up, my half full cup clasped in my hand. "It was nice meeting you, Tanner."

"Leaving so soon?" His fingers halt against his keyboard and one brow peaks as he regards me with a grin.

I lift my shoulders in a small nonchalant shrug. "I've peopled enough for today."

He lets out a full laugh. "Not much of a people person, are you?"

I let out a small not-very-lady-like snort. "Not really. I only like a few people."

"Well," he drags out the word. "Give me your phone."

"Why?"

"Just do it." His smile never falters.

For some reason I hand it over.

A moment later he hands it back to me, his number added to my contacts under **Tanner-The-Very-Gay-Coffee-Non-Date**, and I can't help but burst into laughter.

"If you ever decide on adding a fun gay bestie into the mix, I'm available. I'm a great time at parties, an excellent study partner, and in case a spontaneous pillow fight breaks out you don't have to worry about a boner taking flight. Pussy doesn't do it for me. I like hotdogs, not tacos."

My laughter only grows. "You know, I think Miranda and I could totally use a new gay bestie."

He smiles. "I'm new in town, so friends would be nice." There's something vulnerable in his eyes, as if he hates admitting it.

"Here," I motion for his phone, "I'll give you my number too."

He slides his Android—*blasphemy*—into my outstretched palm and I add my contact info.

He chuckles when he reads my contact name. "Lou-That-Weird-Coffee-Bitch." He shakes his head and clucks his tongue. "For the record, Lou, I bet your taco is the best one out there ... if one enjoys tacos."

I smile back at him. "Oh, I know. It's time for the

male population to figure that out. I'm amazing. A total catch."

With that, I swish my hair over my shoulder and saunter out the door.

I might have my moments of weakness, who doesn't, but I never let my self-doubt dull my sparkle for long.

I'm a unicorn—a rare, precious thing, and any man will be damn lucky for *me* to choose him.

CHAPTER THREE

Abel

I stare at the ad in the school's online newspaper. School's only been in session a few weeks, but if I don't change my current living situation, I'm going to lose my ever-loving mind.

When my former roommate and best friend—well, he's still my best friend—decided he wanted his "future wife" to move in, I knew it was time for me to get the hell out. They both swore I didn't need to go, but I couldn't stand being around their overly lovey-dovey selves when she *didn't* live in the same four walls. The idea of having to stomach their sickeningly sweet words, glances, and endless fucking was the final straw to get my ass in gear.

Justin and Kelly—throwback to that *terrible* movie with those American Idol winners my sister made me watch when we were little—waved goodbye from the front porch, looking like the idyllic couple; his arm around her waist, as she leaned into him with a hand on her chest.

It made me gag.

Don't get me wrong, I'm happy Justin found someone to love, but I've never been quite as lucky. It's left me with a lot of meaningless hookups, which have become sparse.

Leaving my former abode behind meant moving in with my sister, her husband, and three kids.

The first hour after I moved in—*temporarily*—had me wondering why I thought I'd had to leave Justin and Kelly behind so quickly.

Endless fucking or a newborn screaming?

Both suck, both mean little to no sleep for me, but the former means I get lassoed into baby holding at times and now several of my shirts sport puke stains.

I'm living the life.

This is *exactly* how I imagined my senior year at university going.

I read the ad over again.
WANTED: A ROOMMATE

Requirements

1. **Don't be a smoker. That's gross.**
2. **Don't be a jerk. I have no time to deal with your mood swings.**
3. **Clean up after yourself. Is it really so hard to put dirty clothes where they belong?**

If you meet these qualifications, call me.

Sincerely,
Desperately Seeking Roommate

There's no name, but the way it's worded tells me the poster must be a female. The idea of living with a chick is weird. I've only lived with my parents, Justin, and now my sister and her family. Living with only a woman is a foreign concept. I'm not opposed to the idea, especially if she's hot. But even if she is, I won't be fucking my potential future roommate. I made a vow to stay celibate this year, so I could focus on my last year of football, school, and all the shit that comes after you graduate.

I lean back in the black plastic leather chair in my brother-in-law's home office. I would've been upstairs in the guestroom on my laptop, but I had to escape the gremlins—aka my niece and nephew of talking age. Don't get me wrong, I love those kiddos, but I can only take hearing, "Uncle Abie! Play wif me!" so many times a day before I lose my mind.

The kids are great if I'm just visiting, but living here day in and day out? I never get a break from them.

Feeling like I have nothing to lose I swipe my phone from the desk and call the number.

It rings a few times before I hear a sigh on the other end.

"*Mom*, I'm not giving or receiving oral, nor penetrative sex, you don't have to call every five minutes to tell me you're praying for my soul, okay? I know the fact my hymen is not fully intact, or like at all intact, is a sore subject with you—but you *are* the one who encouraged me to let myself flourish *and* insisted I could tell you anything. The cracking of my hymen falls under the *anything* category."

I clear my throat.

There's silence on the other end and then a squeak, "You're not my mom."

"Nope," I say, stifling a laugh. "I'm *definitely* not your

mom, but I would like to know the story of the ... *cracking* of your hymen as you framed it."

"Oh, the cliché—prom night. Didn't even take my dress off and I rode that tiny dick in the front seat of his car. It wasn't fun, but it did the job. Best night of his life, based on his facial expressions and moans—as for me, I learned guys have *no* idea what to do with the female body. Open a damn anatomy book, already."

I cough to hide my chuckle. "Sounds..."

"Awful—*awful*, is the word you're looking for. For the record, I don't have caller ID and my mom usually calls this time of night and we're close, so I usually answer the phone in some weird way."

"Interesting," I say, despite myself. I should be hanging up. Clearly this chick is certifiable, but I find myself entertained and slightly curious. "How do you not have caller ID? Everybody does."

"On my cellphone I do. This is a landline."

"A landline?" I repeat in disbelief. "Those still exist?"

The girl huffs in my ear. The sound is so loud it's almost like she's right beside me. "Yes, they do."

"Why didn't you put your cell number in the ad?"

"Um..." She begins slowly, her tone implying I'm an idiot. "I'm a single woman living on my own, no way in hell am I posting my cell number in an online ad. I just watched those Ted Bundy tapes on Netflix—I'm not about to hand out my cell number like candy to a serial killer."

"You sound interesting...?" I pause, waiting for her name.

"I'm not giving you my name."

"How do you expect to get a roommate, then?"

"Meet up in broad daylight in a very public place, obviously. I'll be the one with a pink Taser."

"Well," I clear my throat, "you're desperately seeking a roommate, and I happen to be desperately seeking a place to live. I don't smoke, I'm not a jerk—at least I don't think I am—and I'm capable of cleaning up after myself. I also cook, so that should score me some bonus points, right?"

"Possibly," she hedges. "I've never lived with a guy."

"Coincidence, I've never lived with a woman before—well, except my mom and sister. Come on, I really need to find a place to live and nothing sounds promising."

She's quiet on the other end for a beat ... two ... "Fine, meet me outside of Griffin's coffee shop tomorrow at four, does that work for you?"

"Sure. How will I know who you are?" That time of day there are all kinds of people hanging around Griffin's, the surrounding restaurants, and shops.

Another beat of silence and somehow, I know she's smiling.

"Why don't we let fate guide our way? If our paths are meant to cross, we'll somehow know."

"You're crazy."

"I've been called worse. See you tomorrow, Stranger. Or not."

Before I can respond, there's a click and she's gone.

I stare down at my screen flashing *call ended,* completely baffled and slightly turned on by this mystery girl.

I love games, and she's initiated one of the most interesting.

"I'm going to find you, mystery girl."

CHAPTER FOUR

Lou

It's five minutes until four when I finally amble near the vicinity of Griffin's. A crowd is gathered around one of the trees out front, sitting on the stone built around it. Others stroll by, talking on a phone, some walking their dogs.

A breeze stirs the leaves on the trees and the hair around my shoulders with it.

I look at my phone and find it's two minutes until four now.

I'm not going to make this easy for the guy. I said we could meet at Griffin's, but that doesn't mean I have to loiter around the front, making it obvious I'm waiting for someone.

I lean over, perusing the menu in front of one of the restaurants on the walking mall. I know the menu well, having eaten here plenty of times, but being inconspicuous means pretending I'm not waiting for my potential future roomie.

If he can find me.

On the phone, his voice was buttery and smooth with a slight rasp that sent lust spiraling through my body. He could be a total troll for all I know—not just in looks, either.

I knew in my desperate times I had to be open to a guy roomie, but the possibility and the reality are two different things.

I know girls can have weird quirks too, I have my fair share, but guys are inherently gross. It's a fact.

But he did say can cook, which scores him more bonus points than he can imagine.

I don't cook. Ever.

It ends in disastrous consequences.

Last time, I had to get four stitches in my finger when

I nearly cut it off. It was traumatizing and after that, I decided the kitchen is *not* the place for me.

I live off takeout and those frozen dinner meals I get at the grocery store.

Spinning away from the restaurant and facing Griffin's, my eyes connect with brown ones. It's sudden, completely unexpected...

Fate.

All I see is those warm brown eyes at first, then I notice the two cups of iced coffee in his hands, bearing the Griffin's logo, and I think this can't possibly be *Stranger*. A wide smile lights up his face, highlighting his handsome features, sharp cheekbones covered in dark stubble, and tousled dark hair begging for fingers to run through it.

I was taking in each part of him separately, but putting the whole image together—

No. My mind shouts the word at me as he walks forward.

He stops in front of me, his orange Vans nearly touching my white Chucks.

"DSR?"

"Stranger?"

But he's not a stranger.

No, because fate—who I put all my trust in—has fucked me up the ass with no lube. If fate was on my side, we wouldn't have made eye contact.

Abel Russo looks back at me, with absolutely no clue who I am.

On campus, I'm a nobody. But he's a god.

I don't care about sports. Yoga and the occasional game of Bingo at the local fire department where I'm *always* the youngest person in the room, is the most athletic I get.

Despite my lack of sports knowledge, *everyone* on campus knows who Abel Russo is. He's the quarterback of the football team. He's managed to lead the team to the past two championships or whatever they're called and he's expected to do it yet again this year before he graduates and says goodbye to football.

"I got you a coffee." He holds out one of the cups, the one with a pink straw.

I wrinkle my nose and take the offered cup. Pink, my favorite color, is clearly another sign.

Look, Fate, I get it—this guy is meant to be my roomie but I don't have to be happy about it.

"Looks like fate wanted us to meet." He grins and it's a disarming kind of smile. I understand why he's the campus heartthrob, leaving behind a trail of broken hearts everywhere he goes.

"It appears that way," I admit, walking over and plopping my ass on the stone around the tree I was looking at earlier.

He follows and stands in front of me, blocking the

sun with his looming height.

"I'm Abel."

I know.

I swallow nervously. "Lou."

That smile again.

"Lou," he swirls my name around his tongue, "unique name."

I don't comment.

"Well," he begins, shoving one hand in the pocket of his jeans, his other still clasping the other iced coffee, "does this mean we're roommates? You know, since fate made sure we met."

"Why'd you call me DSR?" I've never been good at keeping my mouth shut, even when it would do me good. "And why'd you get me a coffee? You don't know what kind of coffee I like—I could hate this, and that's a waste of money, plastic cups, *straws*. God, the *straws*. Don't you want to save the turtles?"

"Whoa." His hands fly in the air—well, one hand does, and three fingers fly off his cup in a *simmer down* motion. "One at a time ... DSR for Desperately Seeking Roommate, the coffee is my secret order and I've never let anyone have it before, so count your blessings, Blondie." He tilts his head to the side. "Plus, once you taste it you'll be *begging* me to tell you what it is." He drags his straight, white teeth over his bottom lip and dammit if my lady bits don't clench in response. "Thirdly,

I do love turtles, but I left my stainless steel straws at home."

"I feel like you're being sarcastic."

He grins.

With a sigh, I spare a look anywhere at him before my eyes finally meet his again. "Why do you want to live with me?"

"Because, living with my best friend wasn't going to work out once he moved his girlfriend in with plans to propose. I don't want to listen to Justin and Kelly going at it like rabbits twenty-four-seven. I do need to study and I kind of like my sleep. Plus, Kelly uses all the hot water. Not cool."

"Whoa, whoa, whoa," I interrupt, holding up a hand. "Your friend's name is Justin and his girlfriend is Kelly? Like those American Idol winners in that horrible movie? Don't get me wrong, Kelly Clarkson has some pipes, but she's no actress."

He throws his head back and laughs. Something in me stirs because *I* made him do that.

"Finally, someone who gets it."

"You've seen that movie?" I ask in disbelief.

Do you mean to tell me campus's number one hottie has watched the worst movie known to man?

He shrugs, his eyes twinkling. "My sister made me watch it when we were little."

"Admit it, you liked it."

He pretends to gag. "Absolutely not. But that brings me to my current dilemma. After I left Justin and Kelly, I moved in with my sister temporarily. They have a new baby and two other kids. I love those kids, but they never stop blabbering. It's exhausting. I need some peace and quiet."

"How do you know I'm quiet?"

"You have to be better than a newborn crying from three in the morning until six."

"True," I acquiesce.

"So," he rocks back on his heels, "what do you think? Am I suitable roommate material?" He tilts his head to the side, an adorable grin lifting his lips. I never thought I'd be interacting with one of campus's elite, and if I had imagined it I wouldn't have expected this. Abel seems nice, easy going. Living with him couldn't be too terrible, right? He's not bad to look at either.

"I don't know? Depends." I bite my lip, trying to hide my growing smile.

"On what?" He blinks at me, waiting for me to finish.

"You do have a job, right?"

"Excellent question. I do, in fact, have a job. I work as a mechanic part-time, it's how I became friends with Justin actually. I know it's nothing luxurious but I do make enough to pay bills. Come on, Blondie. I really need this."

"You haven't even seen the apartment. Don't you

want to check it out first?"

He brings the yellow straw of his cup to his lips and takes a sip before answering. "I've seen you, that's enough."

I raise a brow. "What does that mean?"

He releases a warm chuckle, his chocolate brown eyes capturing my baby blues.

"Whatever you want it to mean," he replies. "When can I move in?"

"This weekend?" I suggest. "I hope you have furniture and a mattress, because I don't have that in the spare room."

"I have them."

I sigh, seeing this is unavoidable. "All right, new roomie." I hold out my hand to shake his. "Welcome to Casa Louise."

He takes my hand in his and I feel electricity shoot up my spine from his touch. His tanned hand swallows mine whole.

"Thank you, Lou*ise*."

"One more rule," I warn him, pulling my hand from his since he hasn't let go. I wiggle my finger in front of him and blurt, "Don't fall in love with me." It's meant to be a joke, but the words sound serious from my lips.

His eyes darken and fall to my mouth where I realize my tongue is moistening my lips.

"Don't worry, Blondie. I don't fall in love."

CHAPTER FIVE

Abel

I rap my knuckles against Lou's door.

Against *my* door, since I'll be living here too.

Before we parted ways at Griffin's she gave me her cell number and the address information for the location of the apartment.

In hindsight, I should've taken a tour of the place. It could be a total dump, but something about Lou piqued my curiosity and I decided living with her would not only be interesting, but fun.

Not to mention, I'm as desperate to move as she is to have a roommate.

Now that I'm here, the building is nice, so I'm praying she's not one of those people who should be on the television show *Hoarders*.

"Come on, man," Justin grumbles, holding onto my mattress. "Don't you have a key yet or anything? My arms are tired."

I turn around and stifle my laughter as he struggles to hold my queen-size mattress.

"Dude, I told you to lean it against the wall. Stop trying to show off for your girlfriend. She's not even here yet to see your heroics."

Justin and Kelly volunteered to help me move, and since my sister and brother-in-law have kids to wrangle, I took them up on it. Kelly's busy sorting through the boxes in the back of my truck, because apparently things need to be carried inside in a proper order.

Whatever the hell that means.

I'm about to knock again when the door swings open. I have to look down to meet Lou's eyes she's so short, and a grin spreads over my face.

Her hair is split into two parts and done in those space-bun things girls on my Instagram keep posting pictures of, but instead of looking ridiculous like those girls do Lou actually looks good in them.

"Welcome, mi casa is now su casa—but don't think that means you can run a prostitution ring out of this place. I'm not your co-pimp."

Justin snorts behind me and she peers around me.

"This is Justin, one half of Justin and Kelly," I introduce her. "Justin, meet Lou. My new roommate."

"This is Blondie?" he asks, a brow raised in surprise. "She's hot."

"Who's hot?" Kelly chooses now to enter the building.

Justin turns bright red. "You, babe. You."

"You must be Kelly," Lou says politely. "Nice to meet you."

With the niceties out of the way Lou steps aside and allows me into the apartment.

"Holy hell, there's a lot of pink."

"It's not that much," she defends. Her eyes flick around the space. "There's gray too—and cream."

She's not lying, I guess. But there are light pink throw pillows, blankets, vases—hell, pink dotted everywhere like sprinkles on a cupcake.

My eyes land on a pink rotary phone sitting in the corner of the kitchen counters where someone might normally put a blender. Not Lou. Hanging above the phone, on the wall space between the counters and cabinets is a picture that says, *Never let anyone treat you like a yellow starburst. You are a pink starburst.*

"But I like the yellow ones."

"Huh?" She crinkles her nose like some sort of woodland creature.

I flick my fingers toward the picture.

"Oh, ew, the *yellow* ones? Get out, I changed my mind. We can't be roomies."

"Ah, shit." I place a hand over my heart, feigning hurt. "I can't take back the monogrammed towels now."

"But *lemon*—" she sounds entirely offended, "—is blasphemous."

"Strawberries are gross—artificial strawberry flavoring? It might as well be used as poison."

She pushes at my chest; her small hands hardly make a dent against my muscled body.

"Why won't you move?" she huffs out, nearly falling face first on the floor when her feet begin to slip on the rug.

I grab her arm to steady her and as she rights herself I get a shot of her tight white jog bra beneath the cropped sweatshirt she wears.

"Are you guys done having your first roommate spat? I'd like to be able to take my girlfriend to dinner tonight and at the rate we're going, this mattress won't be inside come morning."

I let go of Lou's arm and glance behind me at my best friend.

"Always such a whiner—why didn't I leave your ass a long time ago?"

A strangled laugh leaves him. "Because I keep the fridge stocked with beer." Peering around me, he glances at Lou. "Just a heads up, Abel leaves the toilet seat up."

I shake my head. "Fucking hate you, dude."

He's not lying—but when it's two guys living in the same place, what's the point?

"Since it looks like you guys have it covered, I'll be in my room." Lou points toward her right. "Your room is there." She points to a bedroom on the opposite side.

She pads across the old, dinged up hardwood floor and closes her door softly behind her.

Shaking my head, I fight a smile.

I don't know this girl, only just met her, but something tells me living with her is going to be unforgettable.

CHAPTER SIX

Lou

I stay sequestered in my room while Abel brings his stuff in with the help of Justin and Kelly.

I keep my door closed so I can't be tempted to peek. Normally, I would offer to help, it's the kind of person I am, but when Abel's hand touched my elbow I felt the same thing I did when we first met. The electricity, a sizzle of connection that's unexplainable.

I've never felt anything like it, and I don't want to feel it for someone like Abel.

Yes, he seems nice enough, but I've heard things. College is a breeding ground for gossip, and people like Abel who are on the top of the social chain are the most talked about. He's the kind of guy who dates supermodel type girls and then discards them like they're not worthy of a Wal-Mart greeter position. I can't be dragged into something just because he's possibly the best-looking man I've ever seen, and my body seems unable to not react to him.

He's my roommate—I need him to help pay the bills, so I don't end up homeless.

I don't need to form a pathetic crush on him like some little girl who litters her room with posters from the Jonas Brothers and scribbles *Future Mrs. Nick Jonas* on her notebook—not that I ever did that or anything.

The longer I can stay away from him and his magnetic charm, the better. We've never run across each other on campus before, so that part should be easy enough. It's not like we'll be going out and doing things together because we're roommates, so the only time I should have to avoid him is when we're both here, which hopefully won't be often. I babysit for a few families, that's how I make enough money to live here—or until stupid-face Jamie decided to hike up the prices—and Abel must have a job too. I don't know of any college student who gets to freeload. We work, we go to school, we pay bills—and then live off of Kraft mac n' cheese and ramen noodles.

There's a soft knock on my bedroom door and I snap the lid of my computer closed like I'm about to be caught watching porn.

Wait, does this mean I'm going to have to mute my porn now that I have a roommate?

Everyone needs some self-lovin' now and then. Don't act like you've never twiddled your diddle.

"Um, yeah?" I choke out, straightening my clothes —*again* acting like I was just watching porn moments ago.

I totally wasn't—not that I won't be guilty of it in the future.

"Can I come in?"

Abel's deep, husky, *man* voice sounds behind my closed door.

It's beyond weird to think I have a roommate now. A male roommate. As in, one with a penis.

I wonder what it looks like? Someone as tall and big as him has got to be hung, right?

Oh my God! Snap out of it, Lou! You're worse than a horny teenage boy!

"I need to get laid," I mutter to myself.

"Huh?" Abel mutters.

"Shit." I shake my head. "I said you could come in," I lie.

My door swings open and he steps inside. His larger-than-life presence threatens to swallow my room whole.

"Can I help you with anything?"

Way to sound like a customer service representative, Lou.

He cracks a small smile. His dark hair is damp from a shower and he's changed into loose gym shorts and a gray t-shirt with our University's mascot—a hornet.

"I was going to order pizza for dinner. You want any?"

"Do I look like I'd say no to pizza? Only crazy people turn down that deliciousness."

He chuckles, his eyes dancing around my room as he takes things in. His eyes stop on the lit neon pink sign above my bed that says *Hello Gorgeous* in cursive writing. I've been obsessed with neon signs for as long as I can remember. When I was a little girl I was enamored with all the multi-hued lights at our local carnival, so when I moved out on my own I knew I had to have one. As luck would have it, I found this one at a yard sale for five bucks.

It was fate.

"You're quite ... vibrant," he remarks, pointing at the sign even though he's talking about *me* not *it*.

I shrug, my loose sweatshirt falling off one shoulder with the gesture. "I am who I am."

He shoves his hands into the pockets of his shorts and his brown eyes meet mine. "What do you get on your pizza?"

"Whatever you're ordering is fine. I'm not picky."

He tilts his head. "Why do I feel like that's a lie?"

I smile, because he's caught me. "I like onions and green peppers—but red pepper flakes on the side is a must."

"Cool. I'll call the order in. I thought maybe we could bond over beer and pizza."

"I can't say no to those two things," I reply, even though I know this means I can't hide in my bedroom any longer.

I'm not intimidated by Abel, but having lived alone for so long I don't really know what to do with myself.

He's already pulling his phone out of his pocket as he walks out of my room and I flop back on my bed, letting out a long sigh.

I know the awkwardness will fade with time and I'll get used to someone else being here, but at the moment it sucks.

Like what if he constantly has friends over? Or a revolving door of girls?

I am *so* not going to be a part of that weirdness.

Groaning, I rub my hands over my eyes and sit up. I blow out an exaggerated breath, stirring the hair around my face. Grabbing a hair tie from my wrist I gather up the long blonde strands into a messy knot on top of my head.

Finally stepping out of my room, I nearly haul ass back inside and isolate myself there.

The common living space is now littered with *things*. Things that are not mine but are definitely Abel's. There's a half empty bottle of blue Gatorade on the coffee table, a red sweatshirt tossed on the back of the couch, and a pair of tennis shoes lying on the floor.

Clean up after myself, my ass.

The urge to pick up and straighten the out of place items is strong, but somehow, I manage to hold my chin high and pretend it doesn't matter to me.

There are far more important things in life than the possible water ring forming on my coffee table because he didn't use a coaster.

"Oh my God," I cry, unable to take it. I dive over the couch, and roll off of it, picking up the bottle of Gatorade and rubbing the sleeve of my sweatshirt over the wet spot before grabbing a coaster from the side table and placing it in the same spot.

"That was impressive."

I jump, and the bottle falls from my hand before I can set it down and rolls under the couch.

At least the cap is screwed on tight.

I press my lips together, looking up at Abel towering above me from where I'm sprawled on the floor.

"Um..." I hum, thoughts ticking. "There's a totally reasonable explanation for this ... as soon as I come up with one."

His grin becomes impossibly larger. "I take it you have a thing for coasters?" He quirks one brow, regarding me with amusement.

"I-I like things kept neat."

He tilts his head to the side. "Rule number five, coasters are a must. Noted."

"There were three rules."

"No." That ridiculously gorgeous smile of his grows. "You added a fourth—no falling in love with you."

"R-Right," I stutter. I feel stupid down here on the floor while he stands above me, tall and immovable like a mountain, but at this point it feels more ridiculous to pick myself up.

Besides, his bottle is still under the couch and I can't leave it there.

"Maybe we should make a board with all these rules and amendments." He's still smiling, his tone light, but I already feel like a failure at this whole roommate thing.

Damn, my control freak ways! I blame my mother for this! Heaven forbid there be one speck of dust in her house, and even though I swore to never be like that, here I am. We become our parents even when we say we won't.

"There won't be any more added rules. Promise." I cross my fingers over my heart.

"You gonna get up now?" He holds out a hand to me and I stare at it blankly.

I didn't know a hand could be sexy, but Abel's is. I'm seeing for myself, in the flesh, why he's the talk of campus. His tanned hand is masculine and strong looking. I didn't know a hand could look strong, but his does. His nails are short and rounded, his palms rough looking like he uses them a lot for more than football. The thick veins in his hand rope up into his forearm and—

I'm staring.

I'm staring at his *fucking* hand.

If this isn't proof I need to get laid, I don't know what is.

"Oh, um, I'm quite comfortable down here." I flop backwards, lying down. "See, I can do floor angels." I sweep my arms back and forth like I'm making a snow angel. There's not much room, but I make it work.

He busts out laughing, that beautiful hand going to clutch his stomach. "You're something else, Lou." He wags his finger at me. "Living with you is going to be fun."

He turns his back, and I let out a breath.

He might think living with me is going to be a blast, but my lady parts have decided it's going to be absolute torture. It should be illegal to have to live with someone as gorgeous as him. It's not fair to us mere mortals.

Exhaling a sigh, I roll onto my stomach and shove my

arm under the couch, reaching blindly for the bottle. I manage to get my fingers around it and when I pull it out, I bring an empty pink starburst wrapper and an unopened condom. I quickly shove those two things back under the couch and place the Gatorade firmly on the coaster, glaring at the drink for causing this whole mess.

From across the room the reason for my dancing lady bits meets my eyes.

I gulp.

"Is that pizza here yet?"

Great segue there, Lou. You're the sharpest crayon in the box.

"Are you planning to eat on the floor?"

Jesus Christ! I'm still on the fucking floor!

I place my hands on the coffee table and push my body up. Squaring my shoulders, I raise my chin. "Better?"

"You don't look nearly as uncomfortable," he remarks with a casual shrug.

I exhale a breath, hating that my stomach is in knots.

I blame it on the fact I'm used to being alone and it has nothing to do with his dark brown eyes doing a slow perusal of my body.

My body quakes with a shiver.

"Cold?"

I shake my head.

"Hmm," he hums. "Interesting."

A smug smile tilts his lips and my eyes narrow, wanting to wipe that look off his face. It's not condescending, more amused than anything, but it still irks me.

If I could strangle Jamie Miller for forcing me into this whole roommate situation and get away with it, I would.

It hasn't even been a full twenty-four hours and I'm wondering how I'm going to survive living with campus's star player.

One thing is for sure, I'm going to need a hell of a lot of Starbursts, a venti Pink Drink from Starbucks, and a U-Haul size truck full of patience.

Two of the three sound doable.

I guess it's better than nothing.

Abel

Lou disappears into the bathroom, and I take a seat at one of the barstools in front of the small breakfast bar attached to the kitchen.

Watching her vault herself over the couch because of her mini-panic attack over my bottle of Gatorade resting on the coffee table without a coaster was not only amusing but kind of impressive. I didn't know someone with such short legs could leap like that.

Not going to lie, it was kind of hot.

I hear her mumbling something to herself behind the closed bathroom door and I let out a small chuckle.

She's stayed holed up in her room most of the afternoon. At first, I figured she was giving me space to get settled, but then I decided she was avoiding me.

I'm sure it's awkward as fuck for her, being stuck with a brand new roommate when she's used to living alone, but avoiding each other sounds like a headache. That's when I decided ordering pizza sounded like a great way to bond. Everybody loves the stuff, and if they don't, they're not my kind of people.

There's a knock on the door and it couldn't be better timing because I'm fucking starving. If Lou doesn't get out here I might end up eating the entire pizza by myself.

I sign the receipt and hand it back to the delivery guy before taking the large box from him. Kicking the door closed with the back of my foot, I swipe the lock into place and set the box on the counter.

"Lou," I call, "food's here."

I doubt she doesn't know it, but I figure it's good to remind her she can't hide forever. I don't want her to be afraid of me. We're going to be living together for a while, since I plan on staying here through the year until I graduate. Perhaps even longer if she'll let me, while I figure post-grad things out.

It's crazy to think this time a year from now I won't

be in college anymore. The real world awaits and I'm none too excited for it.

I fix myself a plate and sit down on the couch in front of my Gatorade. I turn the TV on and flip through the channels. I stop on *Full House*, because something tells me if I put ESPN on Lou will strangle me before I even spend one night here.

The door to the bathroom opens and Lou steps out. Some of her blonde hair escapes her haphazard bun, and she looks ruffled.

"What?" I ask, holding a piece of pizza halfway to my mouth.

She blinks at me.

"Are you broken?" I probe.

She exhales a breath. "It's only really settling in with me that there's one bathroom."

"Okay?" I raise a brow in inquiry.

"Well," she begins slowly, wringing her small fingers together. "Contrary to popular belief, girls do, in fact, poop."

This girl.

I can't contain my laughter. I'm pretty sure Lou is the only woman in the world who would willingly bring up this topic. I like her openness and it makes me wonder how we've never crossed paths before. If we had, I know I would've remembered her.

When I manage to sober myself, I meet her wide-eyed

gaze, setting my plate back down, the food far less interesting for the moment. "I assume anyone, male or female, with a normally functioning bowel system does, in fact, *poop*."

"Yeah, and it smells," she says slowly like I'm not gathering what she's saying. With a massive sigh, she sticks her hands on her hips.

"I lived with Justin for the last three years. Believe me when I say, nothing can be worse than the damage he punches the toilet with. Now, can we please move on to a different topic so I can eat my dinner?"

She stares at me for a moment before shrugging. "Fine."

As easily as that one word she dismisses the conversation and her worry seems to ease. She's a peculiar sort of person.

She grabs a plate and a couple of slices of pizza. "You didn't need to get only onions and green peppers on the whole thing," she comments, picking up a packet of red pepper flakes to sprinkle across the two slices she has on a plate.

Finishing the bite I'm chewing, I reply, "It's what I always get."

Her eyes widen and I swear her lips mouth the word *fate*.

Grabbing her plate she joins me on the couch, curling her legs under herself. She's close enough for me to get a whiff of her perfume, or maybe it's lotion, whatever it is smells flowery with a hint of vanilla, like the cupcakes my mom used to make.

"*Full House?*" she asks, noticing what I have the TV on. "I didn't peg you as the *Full House* kind of guy."

I grin around a mouthful. "I always had a crush on Aunt Becky."

"I'd make fun of you, but I'm pretty sure anyone with eyes and a vagina has crushed on Uncle Jesse at some point in time." She takes a bite, chews, and swallows, before her light blue eyes swing my way. "How is it the big man on campus ends up practically homeless and living with his sister? I would think you'd have friends and admirers begging at your feet for you to live with them, yet here you are."

"I have other friends, sure, but…" I trail off, not sure how to finish.

"But?" she prompts in a challenging voice.

I wipe my hands on a paper towel I tore off before sitting down. "Living in a house full of guys partying and drinking every chance they can, well … it gets old fast. Don't get me wrong, I've had my fair share of benders, and parties are fun every now and then, but maybe I'm getting old because I can't handle that scene nonstop anymore. So, I'm here." I stretch my legs out as far as I can, which is difficult with the coffee table, but something tells me Lou would strangle me if I put my feet up there, but with long legs, I need to stretch them from time to time.

She mulls over my words. "That seems like a legitimate reason to me."

"Don't tell any of my friends that," I warn her with a chuckle. "They'll never let me live it down, but I *do* actually need to study and graduate."

"What are you majoring in?" She nibbles on a piece of crust, moving her teeth from one side to the other like a beaver.

"I want to be a physical therapist."

Her eyes widen in surprise. "Wow, that's cool."

"You look shocked."

She finishes her crust and brushes the crumbs from her hands onto the plate. "Not to sound judgmental or anything, but I assumed all football players were airheads."

I chuckle. "Definitely not judgmental at all."

Her cheeks flush with color.

"You know we have to keep our GPA up to be on the team, right?"

"Sure." She turns her body toward me. "But I figured coaches didn't really care about that kind of thing."

"Not my coach." I shake my head. "He's a stickler on grades. What about you? What are you going to do with your life, Lou?"

She snorts, brushing an errant hair behind her ear.

"Does anyone ever truly know what they're going to do with their life?" She exhales a weighted sigh. "I'm studying journalism," she replies. "As for what I'll do with it, who knows." She gives a small shrug, rubbing her lips together in thought. "Hopefully I can get hired at a magazine or something when I graduate. A stepping stone of sorts."

"Into what?" I prompt, draping my arm over the back of the couch. I don't know if she even notices but she scoots a bit closer to me.

"Something that means something. I want to make a difference in the world."

"I think you will."

"Why?" she blurts. "You don't even know me. We're two strangers who've been thrown together because I'm desperate for a roommate so I don't get evicted and you need a place to live."

I laugh, entirely amused by her bluntness. "Some things are easy to know."

She wrinkles her nose. "That makes no sense."

"It makes perfect sense." I stand up then, swiping both our empty plates from the coffee table. She sits there watching as I clean them in the sink and wrap up the pizza before dropping the now empty box in the trash. Facing her where she's curled on the couch, I utter a soft, "Night, Lou."

She inhales a shaky breath. "Goodnight, Abel."

"Sweet dreams," I murmur, edging toward my new room.

I step through the threshold and I've almost closed the door completely when I hear her reply.

"The sweetest."

I close my eyes as the door clicks closed softly.

The sweetest.

It was always my reply as a little boy when my mom tucked me into bed at night. Even now I can picture her dark hair sweeping over her shoulders as she'd lean forward to kiss my forehead before telling me to have sweet dreams.

Fate.

I hear Lou's voice echo through my skull on the phone only a few days ago, telling me fate would guide our way if we were meant to meet.

I never believed in something so trifle, but now, I'm beginning to wonder.

CHAPTER SEVEN

Lou

I present the check for rent to Jamie with a proud smirk. He eyes the slip of paper in my hands before his hazel eyes lift to mine.

"Did you start stripping, Lou? Who'd you blow?"

I shove the check against his chest. "Take it and go, Jamie."

A slow grin tilts his lips and behind him the door to the building opens and Abel enters, shaking rain from his hair and stomping his boots on the rug someone laid out—definitely not Jamie—to keep people from slipping.

"All I'm saying is, if you're shimmying on a pole, that's something I'd like to see."

Over his shoulder Abel's eyes widen, flashing with anger.

Before he can snap at Jamie I meet his eyes and say, "Abel, meet our landlord Jamie. Jamie, this is my new roommate, Abel."

Jamie turns around, holding out his hand. Abel doesn't grab it and he lets it fall.

"Well," Jamie holds up the check I shoved at him, "I have other people to collect from. But I'll be visiting again soon, because *this* is in violation of your lease."

"Excuse me?" I blurt, while Abel's eyes turn deadly.

Jamie's smile grows wicked. "He needs his name added to the lease. Legalities and such. You understand," he says in a mocking tone.

"I'll sign whatever you need me to. Leave Lou out of it."

Jamie rubs his lips together, fighting a grin, and tips his head at me like the gentleman he's not. "See you soon then, *Louise*."

Abel's shrewd eyes watch Jamie disappear up the stairs to harass someone else.

He adjusts his backpack, currently slung over one

shoulder and heads inside the apartment. I close and lock the door behind him.

I only had morning classes today, so I've been home for hours, but I did see Abel on campus today, which I swear has never happened before. He even waved, while I looked around awkwardly wondering if he was actually waving at me. A dark-haired girl, basically clinging to his elbow shot daggers at me.

If she's one of his many admirers I don't know what she's worried about. It's not that she's prettier than me, but I'm done chasing after guys and while Abel is hot, getting involved with my roomie is a big no-no.

When I turn around Abel is leaning against the breakfast bar, his backpack on the floor by his feet.

"Does that guy always talk to you like that?" He crosses his muscular arms over his chest, his plain white shirt riding up a bit and exposing his smooth tan stomach. Abel has ridiculously warm colored olive skin only attainable with the right genetics that can't be replicated in a tanning bed, despite how many girls try.

"Who? Jamie?" I scoff, waving a dismissive hand. "He's an ass-face, but he's harmless."

Abel narrows his eyes. "A man should never talk to a woman like that."

I head over to the refrigerator and grab a Capri-Sun—they might be geared toward children, but I can't seem to stop drinking them. I like the squeezable silver packages and the satisfaction of stabbing them with the yellow straw as much as the flavor. Beside the juice pouches it's obvious there's an invader in my home—or a new roommate, whatever—because there are Gatorade bottles lined up beside them along with newly added Smart Water and Coors Light.

"Honestly, it's not a big deal." I slam my fist down on the counter with the yellow straw clasped in my hand. The plastic breaks and I stab the drink pouch, taking a long sip of the Orange Pineapple Tango flavor. "Jamie's just like that. He doesn't mean anything by it."

Abel sighs and runs his fingers through his dark hair. "Sorry, I'm just ... a little testy about that sort of thing. My sister was in an abusive relationship when she was in her early twenties. Since then, I can't stand when a guy talks to a woman like that. It's wrong."

"But your sister is good now?"

He nods, easing into one of the barstools. "Yeah, she's married to a great guy and has her own family. Trust me, if he treated her like shit I'd do anything I could to get her away from him."

"Well," I say, slurping my Capri-Sun. "I have to babysit tonight, so you'll have the place to yourself."

A slow grin tilts his lips. "Should I add no parties to that list you promised wouldn't get any longer?" I roll my eyes in response and he chuckles. "Kidding, I actually have some studying to do while I can. We have a game tomorrow, you coming?"

I snort. "Me?" I point to myself incredulously. "To a football game? No." I shake my head rapidly.

His smile widens. "Why not?"

"I'd be bored out of my mind. If I want to waste that much time I could do something else with it—like seeing how many licks it actually takes to get to the center of a Tootsie Pop." He chokes and my jaw drops. "I was talking about an actual lollipop."

He stands up and grabs his backpack. "I'm going to study. I'll see you later, or tomorrow, I guess."

Looking at the time, I know I need to throw on some clothes—I changed into my PJs as soon as I got home from class—and head out.

Finishing my Capri-Sun I toss it in the trash, smiling to myself. In the week Abel has been here, he's taken the trash out every time, which is a definite bonus in a roommate. One time, I took the trash out and screamed bloody murder when I encountered an opossum. I don't think it was impressed by my ninja moves or the flailing trash bag.

Closing my bedroom door behind me I inspect my closet for something comfy to change into. I'm babysitting, not going on a date, and I'm likely to be spit up on so wearing my nice clothes is pointless. I settle for a pair of stretchy yoga pants and a Jonas Brothers shirt. I might have a mild, totally not stalkerish at all, obsession with them.

I fix my hair into a ponytail just as someone starts to pound incessantly on the door.

"Abel?" I call out, hoping he'll get it.

The knocking continues.

Uttering an indignant groan I shove my feet into my pair of white Chucks, forgoing doing the laces for the moment, and stomp over to the door.

If it's Jamie again I can't be held responsible for my actions.

I swing the door open in dramatic fashion, but it's not Jamie on the other side.

Instead, it's the dark-haired girl I saw Abel with on campus. She's a Megan Fox lookalike with full lips and slanted blue eyes, pretty but in a mean girl way.

Faking a smile, I ask, "Can I help you?"

She holds a bottle of wine—*ew, what college student drinks wine?*—and waves it around. "Bringing Abe a house warming present."

Abe.

She peers around me as if searching for him.

"Are you going to let me in?" She smiles, but it's fake.

I step aside. "Welcome," I grumble.

I know I can't begrudge Abel having people over, this is his place now too. God knows Miranda will probably be here all weekend, but this chick's attitude ruffles my feathers.

"I'm Lou, by the way," I add, because it seems like the nice thing to do.

She looks me up and down, like she's wondering why I'm still talking to her and would bother to offer my name. "Where's Abe's room?"

"There." I point at his closed bedroom door.

"Thanks." She smiles again and this time she looks like a great white shark ready to take a bite out of me.

I don't quite understand what her issue is. It's not like we know each other, and I'm definitely not friends with Abel, we've not even been living together a full week yet, so there's no reason for her to hate me, except...

Except she clearly wants a piece of Abel, and I'm the girl living with him.

Bending over I tie my laces and swipe my keys from the counter along with my phone.

As I head out, she opens Abel's door and I let out a breath, hoping they're done sexing it up by the time I get back.

Abel

The door to my room opens and I look up from my computer where I'm writing a paper, expecting Lou—

probably saying goodbye before she leaves—but it's Danika instead.

"What are you doing here?" I ask, setting my computer aside and standing up.

I don't like her in my room, in my space. We were partnered up our sophomore year for one project, and run in the same social circles, but she constantly finds reasons to be near me.

She's hot, sure, with a great pair of tits and a nice ass, but she's certifiably crazy and apparently a stalker because I didn't tell her where I live.

"I ran into Justin at the grocery store." She stays by the door, probably picking up on the animosity rolling off of me in waves.

I know she's wanted me to fuck her for a long time, but not because she likes me or remotely cares about me. No, girls like Danika only care about climbing the social ladder. I've been there, done that type of girl in the past, and I'm over it. It's why I vowed this summer to spend my senior year focused on school, football, and graduation. Distractions like sex don't fit into that equation. Deciding to stay celibate for the school year is probably not my best idea, but it seemed like a good one at the time.

When I don't say anything, she continues, "We got to talking and he said you moved out. I told him I'd like to bring you a house warming present, so here I am."

She sets the wine bottle on my dresser beside the door and her tongue flicks out, moistening her lips as her fingers go to the buttons on her shirt.

"But the *real* present is me."

She gets enough buttons undone to show the lace of a hot pink bra and my eyes can't help but stare at her full pert breasts straining against the cups.

I might've vowed to be celibate this year, but I'm still a guy, and Danika is hot. But ... fuck, if I'm going to break this vow and this early into it, it's *not* going to be with her.

"Stop," I warn her.

She takes calculated steps toward me. "Don't you want me?"

The sickeningly sweet scent of her perfume hits me and my stomach roils against it.

"Danika." I grab her hands when they start to trail under my shirt. "Go home."

She pouts. If she means for it to be attractive, it's not. She looks like a pitiful child begging for a piece of candy.

"I've been waiting for you to wake up and see me for two years now." I wait for her to stomp her foot because it seems like the kind of thing she'd do. "And you don't see me, not at all."

"I'm sorry," I say, truly not wanting to hurt her feelings.

I know the rumors around campus, the lies that have

been spread about me. How I use girls and discard them. But any girl I've slept with has known it was a one and done deal. I've never had an interest in dating. My time is devoted to football and making something of my future. It's what my mom wanted for me and I'll be damned if I don't fulfill the promise I made to her.

"I'm not interested," I tell her.

"Whatever, Abe." She backs away, buttoning her shirt again and flipping her hair over her shoulder and out of the way.

I truly don't want to hurt her, but unlike other guys, I won't settle for any girl who throws themselves at me. I have more respect for women than that. It's what I learned growing up.

She leaves my room in a flurry, leaving behind the too strong scent of her perfume and a moment later the main door to the apartment slams closed.

I stand there for a moment before I grab the bottle of wine, toss it in the trash, and return to my homework as if nothing at all happened.

CHAPTER EIGHT

Lou

"God, I love Chinese food," Miranda says, carrying the bag of takeout over to the coffee table. "I could marry the delivery boy."

"Ew, he's like twelve," I laugh, digging into the bag.

"There are a lot of dirty and illegal things I'm willing to do for Chinese food."

She plops on the couch beside me and reaches for the

box of vegetable Lo Mein I've laid out. I undo the lids on several of the containers before digging in.

Miranda and I go out sometimes, even to parties, but most of the time this is where you can find us. Sitting on my couch, eating take-out, while watching *Friends*. We've seen the entire series way too many times to count, but it doesn't stop us from rewatching it over and over again.

I pluck out a piece of chicken and dip it in the red sauce before popping it in my mouth.

"You've been avoiding me about the whole Charlie thing," I remind her. "You can't avoid the subject forever."

She huffs out a breath, stirring the hair around her face. "I was hoping you'd forget."

I slap a hand to my chest in mock offense. "Best friends don't forget anything."

She rolls her eyes at me and dips an egg roll in sauce before taking a monster bite, once again avoiding the subject.

"Miranda," I drag out her name in a whiny plea.

She swallows and wipes her mouth on a paper towel. "Ugh, fine. The date was good. He held the door for me, took me to a nice restaurant, we talked and it was actually nice." She pauses, exhaling a breath and I know something bad is coming. "He drove me home and I invited him up. One thing led to another and suddenly we were going at it like teenagers on prom on the floor of my living room, and it was *great* sex. Charlie actually knows what he's doing..."

"But?" I prompt.

"He never texted after that."

She spears a piece of sesame chicken with a fork and eats it.

"Wow, what a jerk." I shake my head.

"It's not a big deal," she says, and while her tone implies it isn't, I can see in her eyes that she's hurt.

"Miranda," I croon like a mother, wrapping my arms around her. "Guys suck."

"I know." She hugs me back. "It wasn't like I was expecting to ride off into the sunset with him, but I don't know ... I wanted something more, I guess. It's pathetic."

I shake my head rapidly. "It's not. There's nothing wrong with wanting more or expecting to be treated with respect."

"Can we talk about something else?" She flips her hair over her shoulder. "Like the fact that you bagged the hottest guy on campus as your roommate? How come you haven't invited me over to introduce us? Huh? Even now, he's gone." She raises a playful brow. "But seriously, girl, that's some wicked good luck having Abel for a roomie."

"Good luck?" I snort. "Good luck would have been not needing one from the start."

"But still," she argues, going in for some more chicken, "you could've done worse."

"True. He's not bad as far as roommates go. Except..."

"Except what?" she prompts when I'm quiet too long.

"It's stupid." I feel foolish for being irritated over the girl who dropped by yesterday. He's entitled to do what he wants, including her, but her clear disdain for me didn't sit well. She doesn't know me any better than I know her. "His girlfriend, or hookup chick, whatever, came by yesterday and she was just..." I look down at my lap, wringing my fingers together. "Rude, I guess. Like *I* was in her way. Bitch, I lived here first, chill."

She rolls her eyes. "Catty bitches. I bet it's that Danika chick."

"Who?"

She waves a dismissive hand. "I had a few classes with her last year, and she's the type of girl who chases after all the popular jocks. She hasn't figured out yet that dropping to her knees for all of them isn't getting her anywhere."

"Like I said, it was silly," I reply dismissively. "He's only been here a week, and for the most part he's not bad."

"Have you gotten to know him?" She digs into another container of food, but I suddenly don't feel hungry anymore.

"He's only been here a week," I repeat. "We both have

school, work, and lives. So, I mean, it's not like it's been cold, but we haven't really gotten to know each other. He did get us pizza the night he moved in."

"Oh?" She raises a brow in interest. "How'd that go?"

I take a sip of water. "It was nice, I guess."

Leaning against the cushions she pretends to fan herself. "Nice to look at him, right? He's gorgeous, so you definitely scored there."

"Can we just watch the show now?" I grumble, rewinding to the start of the episode.

"Fine." She raises her hands in surrender. "Whatever you want, but if you think this is the end of the conversation, you're wrong."

CHAPTER NINE

Abel

I got in late last night from the game and after party, but like usual wake up at the ass crack of dawn because my body refuses to accept the concept of *sleeping in* on the weekends.

Throwing the covers off I head into the bathroom, stifling a yawn, and put the toilet seat up. I try to see where I'm aiming, but with sleep still clouding my vision I don't doubt some ends up on the tiled floor.

I grab my toothbrush and smile when I see the pink Post-It note stuck to the mirror.

I've been here one week and every day there's a new Post-It stuck to the mirror with some quote, words of wisdom, or random thought Lou has had. She must switch them out at night before she goes to bed, because not once have I woken up to a duplicate.

Today's reads: *Haters gonna hate, potatoes gonna potate, I just want to eat mashed potaters.*

I shake my head, stifling a laugh as I run the bristles of my toothbrush under the faucet and then squeeze a stripe of blue toothpaste onto it. I clean my teeth thoroughly and rinse the white suds from my mouth.

Turning on the shower I wait for it to heat up. I showered last night after the game, but my morning showers are a routine I can't seem to stray from. It's what wakes me up and encourages me to get on with my day.

Stepping beneath the warm spray I wash my body with some smelly shit called *Woods* my sister got me for Christmas. I don't know that it actually smells like woods, but it's not bad.

Around me in the shower are all kinds of signs of Lou. A yellow razor, which always gives me a chuckle since it's not pink, a loofah which is in fact in her favorite color, and an assortment of different body wash scents invading nearly every crevice. At least she only has one bottle of shampoo and conditioner each.

I asked her about all the different body washes after the first time I took a shower here and she said she likes to match her scent to her mood. I think most girls would just pick what smells good to them, but not Lou.

When I finish with my shower I dress in a pair of jeans and t-shirt.

The apartment is dead quiet, and if last weekend is any indication Lou will sleep late, but the idea of sitting around doing nothing for hours doesn't appeal to me and I'm not in the mood to contact any of my friends. After last night I'm sure they're all sleeping away like Lou.

Pacing the small apartment and finding nothing of interest, I hesitantly push the door to Lou's room open.

I feel weird doing this, she could have a guy in here for all I know since she was in bed before I came home, but I don't stop.

She lies in bed curled on her stomach, her face toward the door with her eyes hidden behind a black sleep mask with pink words spelling out *Hot Mess*. Her blonde hair fans out around her wildly and she's kicked her covers away, revealing a pair of gray Calvin Klein underwear hugging her every curve. Her loose t-shirt has ridden up, exposing the side of her tanned stomach and her breasts threaten to fall out of the deep V-cut.

Oxygen has been cut off from my lungs and I can't tear my eyes away from her body.

I'm being a total creeper, I know, but I didn't intend to stand here staring at her like an idiot while she sleeps.

Clearing my throat, I knock on the now open door.

Lou stirs in her sleep but doesn't wake up.

I knock again. "Lou?"

Her ass wiggles.

Sighing, I walk forward a few steps and bend down, shaking her shoulder lightly.

"Wha?" She jerks awake, shoving the mask off her eyes. She narrows those same eyes on me and glares. "What time is it? Why are you waking me up?" She turns her head to face her window. The blinds are closed, the curtains drawn, but it's obvious it's dark out. Her eyes fall to the clock beside her bed. "Why are you waking me up at the ass-crack of dawn? Normal people like to sleep, you know, *Abe*?"

I don't know why she's calling me Abe all of a sudden, but I don't touch on that.

"It's another glorious morning, that's all the reason you need to get up."

She sighs. "I'm never going to go back to sleep now, you jerk." She sticks her tongue out at me. "What do you want anyway?"

She sits up, and the sleeve of her shirt dips down over one arm. My eyes follow it, and then because I'm a guy and can't help it, I take in her breasts clearly visible through the thin fabric. Her nipples peek through and if I'm not careful I'm going to get a raging boner, which I don't need. Not when it comes to my roommate.

"I thought we could get breakfast."

"Now?" Once again her eyes flash to the nightstand as if she's expected the time to change drastically since she last looked at it.

"Yes, now."

She exhales a heavy breath. "You know what, yes. Since you woke me up, I think I totally deserve to go to breakfast, but you're paying, bud." She climbs out of bed, standing in front of me.

The top of her head barely comes to my chin and I fight every instinct I have not to touch her.

It's safe to say I'm attracted to Lou. She's not my normal type at all. She's quirky and unique and I feel like I'm only at the tip of the iceberg of her weirdness, but I like that about her. I like not knowing what to expect and it's only been one damn week. I'm in for a wild ride living with this girl and I'm actually looking forward to it.

Lou sticks her hands on her hips and raises one blonde brow. "Are you going to let me get dressed or stand here all day?"

I grin at her. "If you're offering a show, I'm game."

"Out." She points a stern finger.

With a chuckle, I swipe my tongue over my lips as I give her one last long look before I leave her to change.

I wait in the living room as she flits between her room and the bathroom. In less than thirty minutes, which is a miracle considering the length of time it takes some girls to get ready, she stands waiting to go.

She taps an impatient foot, the long laces of her white Chucks dragging against the floor as if I'm the one who has kept her waiting.

A red hat sits on her head, saying *kind people are my kind of people.* The rest of the clothes she's tossed on are composed of a white crop top and the type of jeans that rest higher on her waist. She's rolled up the bottom of them, exposing her ankles.

I know it's nothing fancy, but she looks fucking hot.

I'm beginning to wonder how I never noticed her before, but sometimes unless things are right in front of your face you're oblivious.

"Ready to go, I take it?" My lips twitch with amusement, much like her foot against the floor.

"I'm dressed," she says in a *duh* tone, "which implies I'm ready to go."

I stand from the couch and swipe my keys off the kitchen counter. "Let's go then."

I lead her outside to my truck parked against the curb. The restored 1980 Ford F-150 truck is my most-prized possession. My dad and I restored it when I was fourteen, and by the time I turned sixteen it was finished.

I thought we were working on it for him, but instead he handed the keys to me.

"Your truck looks like a candy cane," she comments, fighting a laugh.

"A candy cane?" I repeat, looking at the red and white truck.

She tilts her head back, looking up at me. "I like it. It's different."

"Thanks." I reach for the passenger door and open it for her.

"Thank you," she murmurs in surprise, sliding onto the beige leather bench seat.

It's still dark out, the barest hint of sunrise beginning to color the sky.

Getting behind the wheel, I pull away from the curb and head toward one of my favorite breakfast spots. It's a small hole in the wall place most people don't know about. It's a few miles from the apartment, so the drive isn't long.

"Stay here." I move the gearshift into park.

Lou looks at me incredulously. "You're not letting me come inside to eat my breakfast? Rude, much?" I know she's joking and I fight a smile.

"I'm grabbing the food and we're going somewhere else to eat it."

"Surely I should get to pick my own breakfast."

"I was right with the coffee, wasn't I?" She hesitates

to answer so I take that as a yes. "Then trust me with this, too."

Before she can protest, because I already know she's the type who loves to argue, I hop out of my truck, swinging the door closed behind me.

"This better be worth it," Lou calls out the rolled down window. "Breakfast is the most important meal of the day."

I shake my head, but don't look back at her as I open the door to the small café. It's the kind of place someone might deem *Instagram worthy* with its chalkboard paint wall on one side and exposed brick on the others.

Oh, Crepe might not seem like the place to find someone like me hanging out but the food is delicious and the owners are super laidback. It's a newer place I discovered that opened over the summer and it has yet to be overridden by other students from the university.

I step up to the register to place my order and Ines, one half of the husband and wife duo who own the café, comes from the back with a smile on her face. Flour, or something similar, is spread across her nose.

"The usual?" she asks in her thick French accent.

"Yes, and an extra order. Four of those, too." I point to the pink macarons in a strawberry flavor.

"One moment." She holds up a finger as she carefully taps her finger against the keys of the register. The total comes up and I hand over my debit card.

She swipes my card and gives it back.

I move off to the side to wait for my order where her husband, Michel, is already making the crepes.

I like watching the way they're made, how he swirls the batter around.

Outside a horn honks, and I'm not surprised when I look out the glass to find Lou leaned over honking the horn of my truck.

Shaking my head, I hold up a hand telling her to wait while she impatiently taps her wrist where there is no watch.

Within a few minutes Michel is passing me a bag with my breakfast order and two cups of steaming hot coffee in a carrier.

I call out my thanks and head out the door where an impatient Lou leans halfway out her window.

She slaps her hands lightly against the side of my truck in a drumbeat. "Hurry up, Mr. Popular. I could be sleeping right now, but instead I'm awake against my will in desperate need of food and caffeine.

I stop in front of her, standing on the sidewalk. "Lucky for you, I have both."

I hold the bag and carrier out to her and she takes them, inhaling the scent of the freshly made crepes.

Hopping in the truck, I drive toward our next destination. Lou starts rummaging in the bag and I cluck my tongue.

"Nope, not yet."

She groans, flopping back against the seat. "You're no fun. Worst roommate ever."

I suppress a chuckle. "Aren't I the only roommate you've had?"

"No, I lived on campus freshman year." She wiggles her lips together. "Actually, that makes you the second worst roommate."

I press one hand to my chest, the other on the wheel. "I'm honored, Lou."

Turning the truck into the park I wind around the road until I get to my favorite spot on a hill.

"Grab the food," I tell her, reaching between her legs for the cup carrier on the floor between her feet. My arm grazes her jean-clad leg and I swear air hisses between her teeth, but when I look at her she seems perfectly composed.

Jumping out of my truck I lay down the back and hop up onto the bed.

Lou comes around the side, the bag dangling from her finger. She eyes me, then the truck. "Do you really think my short little legs are going to get me up there?"

Taking the bag from her I set it beside me and offer her a hand. "No, but I can help you."

She stares at my hand and I wiggle my fingers.

"You should bring a stepstool next time." She slips her hand in mine and I help her up into the bed of the truck. She sits down, letting her legs dangle off like mine.

I grin at her, passing over one of the coffees. "Does that mean you're going to have a sunrise breakfast with me again?"

She rolls her eyes, her small fingers wrapping around the cup. "I guess it depends on how good it is." Her irises sparkle with a challenge I will gladly accept.

I pull out the two Styrofoam boxes and give one to her as well as a plastic wrapped set of utensils and napkin.

She opens the lid and her gaze flicks to me. "That actually looks delicious."

"You haven't even tasted it yet. It's life-changing," I say in an exaggerated tone.

She rips the plastic and pulls out the fork. I wait, watching her take the first bite.

She closes her eyes and a small moan filters between her lips. Her pink tongue slides out, wiping chocolate syrup from her lip.

"Oh, that's amazing." Her eyes open and she looks at me. Knocking me with her elbow, she scolds, "Stop looking at me and eat."

I don't have to be told twice.

I dig into my breakfast, relishing in the sinfulness. I normally cook my own meals and eat healthy, but I have to indulge now and then. I have a sweet tooth, what can I say.

Beyond us, the sky is now bathed in light, the tops of the trees look like they're on fire from the orange hue.

"Getting up early isn't so bad if I get to eat dessert for breakfast."

"And that's not all." I balance the Styrofoam box on my legs and reach into the brown paper bag, pulling out the small box of macarons. "Two of those are mine," I warn her before she grabs it from me. Strawberry isn't my favorite, but I figure I can give it a try.

She opens the lid and her mouth opens. "You're my favorite roommate," she blurts, and I bust out laughing.

"Elevated from the worst to best in minutes? I feel blessed."

"What can I say?" She grins at me, taking two of the pink cake-like cookies out of the box. "I'm easily pleased. *Not like that*," she quickly adds the end.

I shake my head. "You're something else, Lou." I look out ahead as the blue sky appears overhead, the early morning light growing brighter by the second.

"I'd rather be something than nothing."

Her words hit something deep within me and I grab one of the macarons left in the box.

"Cheers to that."

We knock our cookies together, both smiling before we pop them in our mouths.

She giggles, wiping crumbs away from her mouth.

Her silliness is contagious and soon I'm laughing with her.

"Thank you for letting me move in with you."

"It's not a big deal. I needed a roommate, you responded, here we are."

My smile grows. "It's not fate?"

She shrugs. "Who knows, fate is hard to understand at times."

Her baby blues lift to mine, and I think I know exactly what she means.

Things can seem like they're going to shit, and then work out in the funniest of ways.

Lifting her legs up, she crosses them beneath her, peering at me from beneath the brim of her cap. "Did you grow up here?"

"Are you trying to get to know me?" I can't help but joke around with her.

She gives a small laugh. "We do live with each other now. I figure I should know more about you than you play football and are campus's reigning sex god."

"Sex god, huh?"

She glares at me. "Don't let it go to your head, it's just what I've heard. For all I know it could be lies."

"And what things have you heard?" My head cants with interest.

"Nuh-huh." She pushes my shoulder. "You answer my question first."

I finish my last bite of crepe before answering her. "Well, I grew up in New Jersey. I've always been close to my dad. We spent two years restoring this baby." I lovingly stroke the bed of the truck. "I have an older sister—ten years older, actually. My mom ... she was the best, most loving person ever. She could brighten anyone's day." Slowly, I meet Lou's gaze. "She passed away when I was fifteen. Breast cancer."

Her lips part in surprise. She *should* be surprised. That isn't information I share with just anyone, but I feel strongly Lou can be trusted. Yeah, I've only known her a week, but you don't have to be around her long to realize she's real and genuinely true to herself. She isn't like other people who are willing to stomp on others to get somewhere in life.

"I'm sorry," she says softly, her eyes sad. "That must have been difficult."

"It was." I look straight ahead, staring at the leaves on the trees as they're stirred by the wind. "What about you?" I nudge her knee with mine in encouragement.

"I grew up further south near the Blacksburg area. Only child to a single mom."

"You and your mom are close then?"

She smiles, setting the empty container to the side. "The closest. She was my best friend until I came here and met Miranda." She gives a small laugh. "She's always number one in my heart, though." She flicks a crumb off her leg and raises her eyes up to mine. "What made you move from Jersey to here?"

"My sister." I exhale heavily, wondering how much detail I want to go into, but figure if I told her about my mom this should be no different. "After my mom passed away, my dad slowly started shutting down. He was still there for a while, but by the time I graduated high school I just ... needed to get away. Maybe that makes me selfish, but I couldn't stay there and watch him fall apart any longer. So, I came here for school to be closer to my sister and her family. I didn't want to feel alone anymore."

She's quiet beside me, rubbing her top teeth over her bottom lip as she ponders what I've spilled.

Finally, just when I start feeling embarrassed, she says, "That's really sad. I-I'm sorry, Abel."

"Thanks." I start to gather up our trash and pause, looking at her. "My birthday is next week. My friends are throwing me a birthday party but I have a feeling it's going to turn into a house party where the cops are called. You should come. If you want. Bring your friend."

She looks up at me with a mischievous smile. "Can I bring a date?"

Her words catch me by surprise, and that pisses me off at myself, because I shouldn't care if she brings a date or not. Yeah, I'm attracted to my roommate, but that's it—an attraction. I have my life, and she has hers, and just because we're suddenly living together that shouldn't change. I never knew her before this, and she didn't know me. Things should be simple, easy, but ... *fuck*.

"Yeah," I choke out, "bring a date." I force a smile, and pick up my coffee, taking a long sip. "It's going to be fucking awesome."

CHAPTER TEN

Lou

I finish typing up my article for the school paper and click submit, sending it to the editor. It's dark in the room since I'm the last one to leave, like usual. I'm a perfectionist when it comes to my articles.

Slinging my backpack over my shoulder, I lock up the room behind me—our editor, Arnold, gave me a key last year since he got sick of waiting for me to be done—and head out of the building to the parking lot and my waiting Dodge Neon. It's purple, with peeling paint, but it gets from point A to point B with no problems.

The sun is almost completely down as I get behind the wheel. It's only Wednesday and I'm ready for this week to be over. I don't know how I'm going to survive the rest of this school year, and next.

It's going to take a miracle, lots of Capri-Sun, and most likely papers being submitted one minute before they're due.

I make a pit stop at the bakery before I finally arrive home.

Stepping inside, my nose is assaulted with the smell of spices and food cooking—which *never* was the case before Abel.

"Hey." He greets me in the kitchen, standing over the stove tending to something in a skillet. He's shirtless, a pair of low hanging gym shorts barely clinging to his hips. He looks entirely too sinful and it makes me feel disoriented and slightly grumpy because my lady bits insist on reminding how long it has been since they've been serviced.

But I swore off guys, *especially* ones like Abel who use girls and leave them by the wayside. Yeah, he's been nothing but a gentleman the week and a half we've lived together, but he's my *roommate*. We kind of need to get along or this will never work. Besides, after the day that Danika chick showed up, I haven't seen her, which tells me she's probably one among many he's used and tossed aside.

But all of that is okay with me, because I'm not interested in sleeping with him.

Yes, he's hot, I'm not going to deny that and I'll look all I want, but I have no intentions to touch. Besides, I think we could become good friends. So for now, it's window-shopping only over here.

Dropping my bag on the floor and placing the box from the bakery on the breakfast bar, I ask, "What are you making?"

"Chicken with spinach."

"Bleh, boring." I slide onto one of the barstools, crossing my arms on the counter before laying my head on them.

He gives a small smile over his shoulder. "It's *healthy*."

"I'd rather eat cake, and speaking of cake," I nudge the box, "open it."

He turns away from the stove and eyes the large white box. "What did you do?"

"Oh, nothing major." I bat my eyes innocently.

He uses his finger to break the tape on the sides and lifts the lid on the box.

"Happy birthday, Mr. Popular," he reads, "You're getting old." He lifts his eyes to mine, fighting a smile. "Thanks, Lou."

"It's chocolate cake and chocolate icing, like you said was your favorite."

I asked him yesterday what kind of cake he liked, otherwise I would've ended up buying *my* favorite and not sharing it, which defeated the purpose of being nice and gifting my new roomie with a birthday cake in the first place.

"Thank you," he says again, and there's something in his eyes I can't quite decipher.

"You're welcome. Happy birthday." I didn't get a chance to wish him that this morning since he was gone before I was out of bed, probably at the gym or something equally as exhausting that people who look like him subject themselves too.

Abs, or a piece of cake?

Sorry, but I want the cake.

His party at his friend's place isn't until Friday night and I'm nervous about going. I mean I've been to parties before, of course, but not with his crowd. The popular guys and girls don't usually want us peasants crashing the party, which is cool because I don't want to hang out with them anyway. But when Abel asked I couldn't say no. Especially when it's for his birthday.

I'm clearly a sucker.

"Seriously, thank you, Lou. You didn't have to do any of this. You barely know me." He turns back to the stove and finishes making his meal, sliding it out of the pan and onto a plate. "You want any of this?" he asks me. "There's plenty."

"Yeah, that'd be great. I didn't pick anything up, and since I can't cook to save my life, I'm stuck living on cereal and frozen waffles."

He gives a small laugh, grabbing another plate and dividing the food. It looks pretty yummy and smells delicious.

"I could teach you sometime." He slides a plate in front of me, setting the other beside me. He comes around the counter, pulling out the stool and sitting down.

"Teach me what?" I ask stupidly, cutting into the chicken.

He laughs outright. "To *cook*."

"Oh." I stare at him, my brows furrowed. "Why would I possibly want to learn that when I have you to do it for me?"

"Excellent point," he concedes. "But it's still something you should know."

"True," I agree reluctantly. "I was traumatized from the kitchen when I caught spaghetti noodles on fire in home economics in middle school. The fire department got called and we were out of school the rest of the day."

Abel spits out his food as laughter bursts out of him. "Why am I not surprised something like that would happen to you?"

"I'm an interesting person, therefore, interesting things happen to me." Taking another bite of chicken I chew and swallow before asking, "Your birthday is today, so that means," I draw out, "you're a Virgo."

He shakes his head, fighting a smile. "Are you into that stuff? Astrology?"

"Not really," I admit. "At times some of the things they say about our signs seem to make sense, but I don't believe anyone should ever pigeon-hole themselves into one box they think they *have* to belong in."

"What about this *fate* you seem to believe so steadfastly in?" He challenges with a raised brow. There's a spot of creamy white sauce in the corner of his mouth, and I itch to wipe it away but I keep my hands firmly to myself.

"For me, fate is still freewill. We always have the right to choose. I don't believe fate is not having any choice at all, I feel like it's the guiding light. It leads you in the direction of things you didn't know you needed or stuff that has to happen to make you a better person. The good things in life keep us motivated, but it's the bad things that build us and make us who we are with how we choose to handle them. It's all just ... fate." I'm sure I sound like a lunatic, but that's how I view things. "Fate, for me, is finding a reason for everything that happens."

"So, me finding you ... that was fate, then?" His dark

eyes look at me intensely and suddenly I've completely forgotten about my hunger.

"Yeah, it was," I whisper, my cheeks heating.

Sometimes my obsession with fate sounds silly hearing it from someone else's lips, but that simple four-letter word has been my guiding force in life. I've always believed in its power and I won't stop now.

The landline rings and I jump, my fork clattering against my plate.

"I ... uh ... that'll be my mom," I stutter, sliding off the stool.

Abel nods in response and I blow out a breath, feeling ridiculously awkward.

I answer the phone before it can stop ringing and lean against the counter.

"Hey, Mom." I don't even have anything witty to say after the conversation I just had with Abel.

"Baby, girl," she replies. "How are things?"

"Busy," I answer, stifling a yawn. "I had to stay late to get my article submitted. Like usual."

She gives a small, amused laugh. "You're such a perfectionist with your words."

I stick my tongue out, even though she can't see and Abel chuckles. "If only I could be a perfectionist when it comes to other things."

"How's it going with the new roommate?"

My eyes meet Abel's and he gives a grin as if he somehow knows he's become a topic of conversation. He leans back, crossing his arms over his chest, making it obvious he's listening to everything I say on my end of the conversation.

"Good."

"Is he hot?"

"Mom!"

"What? It's a legitimate question, Louise Myrtle."

"Okay, there's no need to bring out the big guns with the middle name, Mom."

She giggles on the other end. "I take that to mean he's *very* good-looking."

"Is there any point to this conversation or did you just call to be a snoop?"

"Ummm," she pretends to think, "I wanted to be nosey."

"Of course you did. I'm tired, I want to shower and go to bed."

"Fine, but if you think this conversation is over you're wrong. As your mother, it's my responsibility to bug you about all potential suitors?"

"Suitors?" I blurt. "What is this, the dark ages?"

"Might as well be," she snickers. "At the rate you're going you'll never give me grandbabies. I'm afraid I might have to set some kind of arranged marriage up for you."

"Thank you for the vote of confidence, Mom. I feel the love."

"All right, all right," she intones. "I'll let you go. Love you."

"Love you, too."

I hang up the phone as Abel stands up to wash his plate. I don't feel much like finishing mine, but I sit my ass down anyway since he made it and was nice enough to offer some to me.

"I'm digging into that cake next," he warns me, turning on the sink. "Do you want a piece?"

"What kind of idiot would turn down cake?" I scoff. "If happiness had a flavor it would be cake."

"The chocolate-chocolate kind?" He grins, pulling out two small serving plates from the cabinet. I know exactly which ones they are. White, with pastel butterflies around the edge. When my grandma passed away they were the one thing I begged my mom to let me keep.

"You have good taste in cake flavors," I admit. *"But my favorite is actually orange cake with cream cheese icing."*

"Really?" He quirks a brow, removing his chocolate cake from the box. "I don't think I've ever had that kind before."

"I'll make one some time. You know, if I ever get a break."

I've babysat the last two nights, then I was late

working on my article, so most days it feels like I don't have any sort of life to do anything I want for enjoyment.

Finishing my meal, I clean up as Abel expertly cuts the slices. Stacking my plate with his in the dryer rack, I take the one with my cake from him and both of us sit on the couch. He grabs the remote, turning the TV on.

"Anything you want to watch?"

I shake my head. "No, but I've been thinking about starting *Psych*. All the seasons are on Amazon Prime."

"I've wanted to watch that one, too. We could watch it together?"

I stare at him, a forkful of cake hovering near my mouth. "Starting an entire TV show together is a huge commitment. This is bigger than marriage. There can be no cheating and watching ahead. Are you prepared for this?"

He blinks at me. "You're serious, aren't you?"

"Absolutely. The biggest sin in the world is watching a show with someone and then they don't wait for you. I don't care how badly you want to know what happens next, there is no watching without me."

"And that means you can't watch it without me?"

I hesitate. "Yeah, I have to hold myself to my own standards." I give a small shrug and finally take a bite of cake. "Oh my God," I moan. "That's the best fucking cake I've ever tasted."

Abel gives me an amused look before bringing up Amazon Prime to start the show.

"It's eight seasons long," I warn him, pointing my fork near his chest. "You can't bail on this commitment."

He narrows his eyes on the fork in my hand. "Or what? You'll stab me in the heart with your fork?"

"Obviously, and then scoop it out and eat it. It's how I stay youthful. I'm actually a hundred and fifty years old," I whisper, like I'm letting him in on a secret.

He laughs, selecting the show. "Guess I'm in this for the long haul, then."

"You bet your ass you are, Mr. Popular."

The show starts and I can't wipe the smile off my face. Having a roommate isn't nearly as bad as I thought. In fact, with Abel, it's not bad at all.

CHAPTER ELEVEN

Abel

The door to the apartment creaks open and I glance away from the TV to find Lou pushing her way inside, mail cradled in her arms. She kicks the door closed and drops the mail and her phone onto the kitchen counter.

She runs her fingers forcefully through her hair, letting out a frustrated groan. "Jamie is blowing up my phone, despite the fact I told him numerous times I was babysitting. He says he's going to stop by tomorrow to add you to the lease. He's such a giant pain in my ass."

"That asshole needs punched in his face. Repeatedly."

She turns toward the refrigerator, pulling out a Capri-Sun. When her back is turned I conspicuously pick up my bottle of Gatorade and put it on a coaster before she can see that it was on the bare table.

Lou kicks off her shoes before plopping on the couch beside me. "Jamie is harmless, just annoying. He's let his *power* go to his head." She emphasizes "power" with air quotes. "He wasn't so bad whenever he stopped by to help his grandpa out."

"Doesn't matter to me. It's still not an excuse to be a dick."

With a sigh, she slurps down the rest of her Capri-Sun and stands. "I'm going to shower and start getting ready."

"Yeah, I should do the same."

Even a year ago the excuse to get drunk and party would've been welcome, but now I'm tired of it. As the guest of honor, however, I'm required to make an appearance.

I hang around the living room until Lou's done showering. Once the bathroom is clear, I take my turn.

The mirror is fogged up, which makes her pink Post-It stand out even more.

I'm fucking awesome. Do great shit today. No really, take a shit.

Even though I've already seen today's note I can't stop smiling.

Showering quickly, I hop out and scrub a hand towel over my hair to dry it faster before I shave. I leave some scruff, just clean it up a bit. If my sister saw me looking like this I would be berated for looking like a, "goddamn caveman."

Heading out of the bathroom and into my bedroom right next door, I rifle through my drawers for something to wear. Grabbing a pair of dark blue pants I tug them on and swipe a white button down from my closet. Buttoning it and tucking the bottom into the pants, I grab my black leather belt and finish getting ready.

Stepping out of my room I clasp my watch onto my wrist. It's nearing nine o' clock when I stride across the apartment to Lou's room.

I rap my knuckles against the door. "Yeah?" Her voice is muffled.

"Do you need a ride to the party?"

She opens the door wearing a white robe with a unicorn hoodie. Her blonde hair hangs down past her breasts in curled precision.

"My date is picking me up." She clasps her hand to the top of her robe, keeping her breasts from spilling out and I try not to choke on my tongue when I realize she's probably completely naked under it.

"Your date." I chew on the words, not liking how they taste in my mouth. "Right. Well, I'm going to go then. I'll ... uh ... see you there."

She flashes me one of her brilliant smiles. "Text me the address."

"Of course." I duck my head in response and she eases her door closed.

I blow out a pent up breath that puffs my cheeks. My attraction to Lou needs to take a hike. I can't jeopardize our living arrangement just because I want to know what the curves of her body would feel like beneath mine.

In the past, if I was drawn to someone, I pursued it. But between Lou being my roommate on top of my vow of celibacy, I can't act on my infatuation.

I won't ruin a good thing just because my dick is trying to steer my brain.

Shaking my head, I grab my keys and head out, hoping I can get a couple of drinks in me before she arrives.

Maybe, by then, I'll have someone else to lust after. If nothing else, I'll at least be too drunk to care.

Music rages and bodies gyrate to the techno beat blowing through the speakers of the old Victorian home in the center of downtown. Alcohol flows through the veins of almost every person and the small hint of pot permeates the air too.

I keep telling myself I'm not looking for Lou as I down another beer, but I am.

It's pathetic how much I want to see what kind of guy she's with. It shouldn't matter to me. This crush of mine is ridiculous, but I feel irrationally angry at the thought of seeing her hanging onto some other guy.

"Man, you look miserable." Kit Jacobson claps me on the shoulder. He's a linebacker on the team and not one of my friends. I shrug off his touch. "And no one should be miserable on their birthday, not with free booze and hot chicks checking you out. Except Danika," he points her out in the crowd. "What'd you do to her? Tap that and leave her dry? That chick's got it bad for you."

"Didn't give her what she wanted." I lift the red solo cup to my lips, the taste of cheap keg beer sliding across my tongue. "I'm sure she hates my guts now."

"You mean to tell me you turned down that sweet piece of ass?" He pushes his dark hair off his sweaty face. "I'd love to get a taste of that pussy." He laughs obnoxiously and bumps his shoulder with mine like I should be laughing with him. I've never disrespected the women I've been with in the past. I was raised better than that. If

I start spewing the stuff Kit says on a regular basis, my mother would rise from the dead to beat my ass until I join her in a grave of my own.

"I need a refill." I lift my glass, which is pretty much full, not that he can see, and move away before he can respond.

I bleed through the crowd, certain a quarter of the entire university's students are crammed into the three-story home. There's barely any space to walk and I'm sure most of the bedrooms are occupied already.

"Yo, Abel," Laurent King calls out, another player from my team. He pushes his way through the crowd, meeting me at the keg where I pretend to top off my cup. He doesn't even notice. "Happy birthday, man." He claps a massive paw on my shoulder. The dude's hands are the size of dinner plates. At nearly six-foot-nine, it's impossible not to spot him in a mass.

"Thanks for throwing the party, man."

"Not a problem, dude. Any excuse for a party." He smiles, his white teeth stark against his dark skin.

"Tell Hayden, Greg, and Jason thanks from me, too, in case I don't run into them."

"Yeah," he scrubs a hand over his bald head, "pretty sure they've already disappeared into their rooms." He winks, but I already caught his meaning.

Most of my friends and the guys on the team that are seniors have talked about how this is their last year to sow their oats before they settle down. There are a few who've had a serious girlfriend and aren't on the *bang-anything-I-can* brigade, but they're mocked endlessly by the other guys.

I keep my mouth shut so I don't have to listen to the ridiculous bullshit.

Somebody calls out his name and Laurent says his goodbyes before pushing his way through the people swarming the keg in the kitchen.

I head in the opposite direction, several people stopping me for a fist bump, to say hello, or tell me happy birthday. I return each greeting with a smile, appearing completely unbothered.

The hairs on my arms suddenly stand straight up and my eyes shoot across the room, locking on Lou. She hasn't noticed me yet and she's laughing at something the guy beside her has said. Her arm is looped through his and another girl stands at her side, laughing with her.

She looks fucking amazing. Her hair is down like it was earlier when I caught her in the robe, but now she's done her makeup, and changed into a tight pair of jeans with rips down the front, a t-shirt tied into a knot at her hips, and a black leather jacket with some kind of spike things on it.

When she straightens, her eyes find mine in the crowd and she says something to her guests before the three of them move through the throng of people toward me.

I notice several pairs of male eyes trail Lou and her friend as they cross the room and I have the irrational desire to punch every one of them for their lustful gazes, as if I'm not guilty of the same thing.

"Hey." Lou comes to a stop in front of me. "Nice party."

"Thanks." I raise my cup to my lips, swaying on my feet, unsure of what to do.

"This is Miranda." She indicates her dark-haired friend on her right. "And this is Tanner." She leans her head on the guy's shoulder.

He looks vaguely familiar, like maybe we've shared a class before or something. He admires Lou in a way that I know means he genuinely likes her.

I hold out my hand to him. "I'm Abel." I do the same with Miranda, adding, "It's nice to meet you." Stepping back, I clear my throat. "Can I get you guys some drinks? The kitchen is pretty packed but I can force my way through."

Lou shakes her head. "We can find it when we get thirsty. Right now, I want to dance." She smiles enticingly at Tanner and tugs on his arm. "Come on, dance with me."

I watch as she pulls him into the living room where most of the sweaty, dancing bodies are glued together.

She sways her hips, wrapping one hand behind his neck. The way they move is as if this isn't new, but in the two weeks we've lived together, Lou has never mentioned a boyfriend or anyone named Tanner. It isn't like I should know much about her in the short time since we've met, but I know way less than I thought.

"Why are you looking at my friend like you're not sure whether you want to grab her and run away with her over your shoulder or storm dramatically from the room like a scorned ex-lover?"

I swivel to face Miranda in front of me. She's a few inches taller than Lou, just as curvy, with slanted exotic eyes. She stares up at me shrewdly, waiting for a response. When she doesn't get one, she twists her fingers behind her back, fighting a smile.

"You've slept with her, haven't you?"

I blanch. "No." I shake my head rapidly. "No, we haven't. Besides, she has him."

"Who?" Her brows crease. "Tanner?"

"Yeah, who else would I be talking about?"

She looks like she wants to say something, but she glances from me to where they dance. When she looks back, she doesn't say a word.

After an awkward moment of silence, she tilts her head, appraising me. "I have to say, it's awfully interesting that a guy like you would be interested in girls like us."

Now it's my turn to look puzzled. "What do you mean?"

"Don't play dumb. Lou and I aren't model thin. We don't eat lettuce out of a bag, but might be tempted to eat cake with our bare hands if we're hungry enough. Guys like you either treat girls us like we're beneath you, or fuck us and laugh behind our backs."

"N-No, I wouldn't," I stutter, stunned by her words.

"I don't know you. From what Lou has said about you so far, you seem like a nice enough guy. But if you keep looking at my best friend like you want to lick her like a melting popsicle in the middle of summer, and act on it, only to break her heart, I will punch you in the nuts. They don't call me Miranda The-Nut-Puncher Hershel for nothing."

"Does anyone actually call you that?" I move my hands in front of my dick, just in case she decides to blindside me.

"No." She raises her chin, narrowing her eyes. "But they should. I'm going to get a drink."

With those words, she brushes past me and down the hallway.

I exhale a sigh, my eyes darting over in Lou's direction one more time before I leave the room.

It's a party, I should be having fun, but I'm not.

I head outside onto the deck where there are less people and I can actually get a breath of fresh air. Sitting down on the top step, I stretch my legs out. My cup dangles loosely from my fingers.

"Hey," a voice says, and I look over to find Alissa, a girl I went out with a few times last year, leaning against the railing.

"Hey."

She moves away from the railing and joins me on the stairs, smoothing her skirt behind her as she sits down. Her skin is pebbled from the chilly night air.

"Haven't seen you in a while." Her remark is softly spoken. She's always been a nice girl, not like some I've gone out with. She's on the cheer team, blonde, and leggy, but she's never hung out with our crowd much, so I'm kind of surprised to see her here. "I guess I owe you a happy birthday." She smiles, bumping her knee with mine.

I give a soft chuckle, watching lightning bugs flit through the narrow fenced yard. A raucous cacophony of laughter sounds from the house, echoing outside into the night through the screen door.

"Thanks." I push my hair off my forehead.

"You look like something is weighing on you." She pulls her long hair over one shoulder, leaning forward.

"I have a lot on my mind. It's senior year, I have to prepare for graduation."

"It's stressful." She leans back on her elbows, tilting her head toward the sky. "But I have a feeling that's *not* what's on your mind." She turns to give me a small smile.

"It's nothing." I drop my eyes to the step below, staring at the knotted wood and a spot where if someone stepped barefoot they'd undoubtedly get a splinter. Not that any of the guys who live here would care.

"Fine, I get it," her tone is still light, "you don't want to talk about it. That's cool. But if you ever need to, I'm here to listen. I know things between us ended, but I like you as a friend." She stands up, dusting her skirt off, and squeezes my shoulder as she passes me to head inside.

The scent of cigarette smoke invades my nostrils from some guy in a leather jacket hanging over the railing. I've never been able to stand the smell. I have my chain-smoking great-grandma to thank for that, who somehow managed to live until she was one hundred and ten.

I stand and move away from the stairs, heading for the back fence. Draping my arms over it, I gaze across the way at the steep concrete stairs leading up to John Handley High School. It's the kind of school you see in movies, but not real life, with tall columns and multiple levels. The high school I went to looked like a one-floor hospital compared to this one.

I sense movement, my body instantly reacting to Lou's presence.

It's like my body is tuned into the same frequency as hers and when she gets close static rattles my ears.

She leans against the fence, unable to see over like I am, her body brushing mine.

"Why's the birthday boy out here by his lonesome? I would've thought Mr. Popular would be the center of attention." I hear something rattle and look over to find her dumping three orange Tic-Tacs into the palm of her hand. She pops them onto her tongue and closes her mouth. "Want some?"

"Sure." I hold out my hand and she taps out three into my hand. I put them in my mouth, looking away from her.

"You didn't answer me."

I sigh, running my fingers through my hair. "This type of thing used to be fun. Getting drunk, letting go, but now it all seems silly to me. I guess I'm tired of it all. I'm tired of being a puppet. Everyone expects a certain thing from me and I've followed that line, but I feel like it's not my path anymore."

"What is?"

The orange flavor melts over my tongue as my eyes take in her appearance. Her body glows with a light sheen of sweat from dancing, her cheeks rosy, and her hair wild.

"I don't know." It's an honest answer, even if it's no answer at all. "I think I have to discover it in time."

"Do you like football, or is that another thing that makes you feel like a puppet?"

I shake my head, grinning now. "No, I *love* football." I wet my lips with my tongue, trying to think of a way to describe it to her. "I like working hard at practice, building a camaraderie and life-long friendship with my teammates, and *nothing* compares to the feeling of being on the field come game day. You know, people screaming and shouting your name. There isn't a rush like it."

She grins, her eyes crinkling. "I bet it's a lot like the rush I get when I eat ice cream."

I can't help it, I laugh. I think it's impossible to bask in the sunshine that is Lou and remain sullen.

She leans her hip against the side of the fence and she's so close to me that if I inhale deeply I'm pretty sure my body will touch hers.

A shadow cascades across her face, cast from the floodlight on the back of the house.

The moment seems to stretch out endlessly, as if it's waiting for something.

"Your date is probably missing you." My words disappear in a cloud of air in the cool night.

She tilts her lips, fighting a grin and I notice how prominent the dimples are in her cheeks when she smiles like that.

She reaches out, straightening the collar of my button down and then pats my chest before stepping back. "You're right. Try to have some fun, all right?"

I swallow and nod, giving her a tight-lipped smile.

She forces one back. I watch her walk away, dodging empty cups littering the yard and God knows what else as she goes.

I didn't feel lonely before, out here by myself, but now I do.

Lou's presence fills a void I didn't even know I had.

CHAPTER TWELVE

Lou

"Lou! Lou! Lou!"

"Oomph," I cry out, as two tiny humans attack my legs and stumble back upon entering the house.

"We missed you!" Matteo clings to my legs while his three-year-old sister tries to push him over so she can have me to herself.

I laugh, bending to ruffle his dark locks. "I saw you three days ago."

"And that was *forever* ago," he drawls.

"Hold me." Once Isabella realizes she's not strong enough to push her older brother out of her way she shoves her chubby arms in the air, opening and closing her fists.

I scoop her up and she hugs me tight, burying her face into the skin of my neck.

"I'm so sorry," their mother says, rocking her one-month-old in her arms. "They just love you so much."

"It's not a problem." I push the door closed behind me with my foot.

I only started babysitting for the Wilson family two weeks ago, but these kids have already weaseled their way into my heart. Babysitting is exhausting, but I also find it rewarding. Kids are fun, and like me, they don't hold back but say what they want. It's refreshing.

"You've been a lifesaver." The baby begins to fuss and she looks ready to burst into tears.

I set Bella down and reach for the baby, Cristian, taking him into my arms. He fights against his swaddle, fists flailing.

"Go take a shower, get a nap, whatever you need to do. I've got these guys."

"Lifesaver," she repeats, giving me a grateful smile

before she heads up the curving staircase of the large home.

Matteo tugs on the bottom of my shirt. "Can we watch a movie?"

"*Moana!*" Bella clasps her hands under her chin, jutting her bottom lip out. Her brown eyes are wide and begging.

"What do you say, Matty? Are you cool with *Moana?*"

His slender shoulders rise. "Yeah, I guess."

I grin, because I already know it's his favorite movie even if he never requests it.

The two children trail me into the carpeted den area where there's a couch, TV, toys galore, and various items like a changing table and rock 'n play for the new baby.

I lay Cristian in the rocker and put the movie on for the other two.

The two kids scurry onto the couch, grabbing their blankets and lovey's, a stuffed dinosaur for Matteo and a unicorn for Bella. Matteo likes to act like a big boy and I find it adorable how despite that, he always wants his blanket and stuffed animal.

"Popcorn?"

I get two head nods in response and smile to myself as I head into the beautiful kitchen. It's the kind of kitchen I only thought existed in a magazine with sleek marble countertops and black cabinets.

I swipe a bag of popcorn from the pantry and stick it in the microwave, able to keep my eyes on the kids thanks to the open floor plan.

Cristian is getting fussier by the second, and since he's a pretty easy-going infant, I figure he's hungry.

As the popcorn finishes, I fix him a bottle of warmed breast milk. Setting it aside, I grab the popcorn from the microwave and divide it into two small bowls for each kid.

Carrying everything back into the den, I hand Matteo and Bella their snack before gently picking up Cristian.

"Oh, ew, you *stink*." My annoying high-pitched mom voice comes through and I mentally roll my eyes at myself.

"Shhh." Matteo hushes me and I grin, because man does that boy love *Moana*.

I change the baby's diaper as quickly as possible before he can either pee on me or start screaming. Wrapping him back up in his swaddle, I join the other two on the couch while I feed him his bottle.

I stayed out too late last night at the party. Despite the three cups of coffee I've already had, I can feel the effects of not enough sleep. I haven't seen Abel since I left him by the fence looking sad and forlorn. There was something heartbreaking about the fact he was at a party thrown for him, yet he was the only one alone.

When I got home he was already there and in bed, so I didn't bother him.

Looking down at Cristian, I smile. His long dark lashes rest against his olive cheeks. His mouth works against the nipple of the bottle as he slurps at it greedily.

Ever since I was a little girl, I've wanted to be a mom. It's what I've always dreamed of. Babysitting helps fulfill some of that desire because God knows I'm not ready for my own kids any time soon. I need to finish college, establish myself, and you know, find a man. Though, there are plenty of options if the right guy doesn't come along. I refuse to lower my standards just because I want to have a family. I'd rather have an A+ sperm shot into my vagina with a turkey baster than to do it the old fashioned way and end up pregnant by some loser who doesn't know the difference between their, there, and they're.

Cristian finishes his bottle and I grab a cloth, draping it over my shoulder to burp him.

The stairs creak near the front of the house and Giulia appears, dressed now in jeans and a long sleeve lightweight sweater. Her hair has been blown dry and she's applied makeup.

"I know you told me to relax, but I have to stay busy. Let me tell you, it feels *amazing* to feel like a normal human and not like a dirty sock." I laugh at her as she grabs her car keys and purse. "I'm going to run and get some groceries. I might grab some coffee too. Are you good here? I hate leaving them, but we don't have *m-i-l-k*," she spells out the letters, "and Matty will have a meltdown without it."

I wave her on. "We'll be fine. I have your number if I need you."

"Thank you." She smiles gratefully, kissing her three children on top of their heads before leaving.

I hear the door to the garage go up a moment later.

Giulia's husband, Leo, insisted she get some help since a business deal has kept him from taking time off with the new baby. I think he thought she could do with some adult company that isn't him and time out of the house by herself. It's thoughtful and sweet. Anytime I've seen them together the love between the two is obvious. He looks at her the way I hope a man will look at me one day.

With thirty minutes left to spare on the movie, two little bodies fall against mine and soft snores fill the room. Cristian snoozes peacefully on my boobs—I swear he thinks they're snuggable and not the massive weights they actually are—and I can't help smiling to myself. Children are a handful, babysitting has taught me that, but there's nothing more rewarding than being loved and trusted by a child. Children don't judge like adults do. They don't see color, or weight, any of it, they just see a person and I think that's a beautiful innocence that's lost too easily in our world.

An hour later, Giulia returns with several bags of groceries and a half-empty Starbucks iced coffee.

"Oh my." Her hand flies up to cover her mouth, stifling a laugh, as she finds me covered in her sleeping children. "How long have you been like that? Your legs must be asleep."

"More than an hour," I answer in a whisper. "I didn't want to disturb them."

"Can I take a picture?" She's already pulling her phone out.

"Yeah, sure."

I smile as she snaps the photo before laying her phone on the counter.

"Here, let me help you." She crosses the room and takes the baby from me so I can slip out from under the other two without waking them. "You're the kid whisperer, I swear. They never act this well behaved."

I laugh, shrugging off her praise. "Some people are good at sports. I'm good at communicating with gremlins."

She laughs at my term. Rocking Cristian in her arms she pulls her checkbook out of her purse and writes a check, passing it to me. "Can you come next Saturday as well? The whole day?"

"Absolutely." I've been accepting every babysitting job

I can get right now, as long as it doesn't interfere with school, so I can put money into my savings. Having a roommate and splitting the costs evenly has freed up some money already, but knowing I only have a year of school after this one is a scary thought. The more money I have saved up the better off I'll be.

"Thank you. I really appreciate having a chance to feel human again. Leo asked me out on a date for next week, but I told him I couldn't accept until I knew for sure you could watch them." Her cheeks are flushed with excitement and I find it absolutely endearing that despite the years they've been together, and three children, she's still excited by her husband asking her on a date.

"That's so sweet."

"He really is the best husband." She sighs dreamily and then shakes her head. "You better get going. I'm sure you have much more important things to do than hang around me. Go do young people stuff."

I roll my eyes as I pick up my bag from the floor—Miranda and I made plans to go to a yoga class after I finished here, so I brought a change of clothes—and say, "You're not old, Giulia."

"I'm going to turn thirty-one. That's ancient compared to you."

"Man," I fight a smile, "way to scare a girl away from aging."

She smiles back as she walks me to the door. "I guess it's not *that* bad."

"Too late, Giulia. The fear already has me quaking."

She laughs and opens the door. "See you next week."

I wave as I step off the porch and head to my car. I call Miranda, letting her know I'm leaving and to meet me at the yoga studio in town.

I've only been doing yoga for two years, since Miranda introduced me to it, but I've become addicted. It brings me peace, and my body has become much more flexible.

One of the skinny bitches who recently started coming told me she couldn't believe I could move my body like that with all the extra fat I have. I replied with, "Well, Susan, I don't know how you manage to talk with all that Botox in your face."

Now she gives me angry eyes every time she sees me. I don't know why she thinks it's socially acceptable behavior to comment on my weight, but I can't say anything about the chemicals she injects in her face.

Pulling into the lot I spot Miranda sitting in her car, jamming out to whatever she's playing.

I'd bet you anything it's Hannah Montana, though she'd deny it until her dying breath.

I found a Hannah Montana CD under her car seat once and she turned as red as a tomato, grabbed it from me, and tossed it in the backseat before taking the steering wheel in both hands. In a deadly voice, she whispered, "We will never speak of this."

I've been sure to keep my lips tightly sealed, because I honestly wouldn't cross murder off the list of things Miranda is willing to do to keep her secrets quiet.

I park beside her and she climbs out, sliding her sunglasses into her hair.

She has her hair in two braids, hanging down her shoulders, and she's already in her yoga pants and a jog bra with a loose tee over top. Grabbing my bag, I join her, and we head inside. After signing into class, I go to the bathroom to change.

A few minutes later I join her. I pull my yoga mat out of my bag and lay my bag in the corner of the room with everyone else's.

Spreading out the thin pink mat beside Miranda's yellow one—blasted yellow—I sit down to begin the deep breathing exercises.

Most of time I do yoga at home now, but it's still fun to join a class when we both have time.

The class lasts an hour. When it's over, we say our goodbyes and I head home. I make a sandwich, scarfing it down in seconds because I'm starving—positively withering away by the second.

Abel's not home, so I decide to tackle cleaning the place while he's out of the way. Trying to clean with someone else hanging around is a headache waiting to happen.

Before I start, I grab my Jonas Brother's vinyl record and place it on my Crosley player I bought from Urban Outfitters like the aesthetic obsessed twenty-one-year-old I am. Except, most women my age *probably* wouldn't have hunted down and paid more than two-hundred dollars for a Jo Bros record. I'm not most people though.

I also realize now, I have no room to judge Miranda and her Hannah Montana obsession.

Clearly, we're trying to relive our youth.

I let the music play as I pick up things, wipe down the counters and coffee table, and vacuum the floors.

When one of my favorite songs comes on, I use the handle of the vacuum as a microphone, shaking my ass to the music. I give it my all, dancing like my life depends on it.

A chuckle behind me has a shriek emitting from my throat and I let go of the vacuum like it's burned me. In my haste, I lose control of my feet and fall backward onto the couch, all the air being knocked out of my lungs.

Abel crosses the room and turns the volume down on the record player.

"Nice dance moves." He towers above me where I still lay splattered on the couch, shocked by his sudden appearance.

Though, I guess it wouldn't seem so sudden if I had

been paying attention to the time. He told me he'd be home from work around this hour, and his t-shirt is covered in grease stains, those same dark stains dotting his hands and arms, with the distinct scent of motor oil clinging to his skin.

It should be illegal for him to look so hot while dirty.

"Um ... thanks."

He holds out a hand to me and I take it, letting him pull me up.

I stand in front of him, unsure of what to do or say. I mean, he just caught me singing and dancing to the Jonas Brothers. There's no possible way I'll ever live this down.

"So," he tilts his head and grins, "you're a Jonas Brother's fan?"

"Obviously." I add on an eye roll for good measure to make sure my sarcasm bleeds across my face. "I'm shocked you're admitting you know who they are."

"Blondie, I'm pretty sure anyone growing up at any point in the two-thousands knows who they are. There's no sense in trying to deny it."

"True."

His grin widens. "So who'd you like most?"

"W-What?" I stutter, confused.

"Well, everybody had a favorite brother, right?" He muses, crossing his arms over his chest. His amused smile tips the corner of his lips. "So, were you a Nick or Joe girl?"

"There was another brother you know." My hands fly to my hips defensively.

He waves away my words like he's swatting a fly. "Nobody cared about him. Should I guess or are you going to tell me?"

I hang my head and mutter, "Nick. I was—I *am*—a Nick girl. I'd let him break my vagina anytime."

Abel stifles a snort, shaking his head in amusement. "Have fun babysitting?" I guess he decides it's better to change the subject before I go into detail on all my Nick Jonas sexual fantasies.

"Yeah, always." I tuck a piece of hair behind my ear. "That might sound like a lie, but it's true. I love it. I went to yoga after and then came back here to get some chores done. I need to do laundry and a grocery run."

Abel groans, running his fingers through his hair.

"I need to do that too. How about we grocery shop today and do laundry tomorrow?"

I hesitate. "Like ... together?"

He chuckles. "Well, why not? I need to go, and so do you. At least if we're together the time should pass faster."

"Okay."

It's not like I can really argue with that, because he's right. Grocery shopping and laundry are about the two most boring things you can do in the world, but I can't wrap my head around him wanting to spend time with me. Don't get me wrong, I know I'm awesome, but the popular kids growing up always steered clear of my weirdness, or as I call it *uniqueness*. Abel, on the other hand, seems to be drawn to it.

"I need to shower first," he warns, lifting his shirt up.

Holy hell abs.

If there was an abs god, I would be saying a prayer right now.

"Y-Yeah, me too." My tongue gets twist-tied in my mouth as he removes the shirt completely. Then, because I'm the most awkward human being on the planet, I lift my arms and smell my pits. "Yep, definitely showering before we go."

"You can go first." He hesitates, his steps toward the bathroom faltering.

"No, no, go ahead," I urge. "I need to finish cleaning."

"You sure?" He raises one brow.

"Yep." I nod my head up and down rapidly. It's a miracle it doesn't fall off and roll under the couch.

He gives a small chuckle, walking backward toward the bathroom.

"Last chance," he warns.

"To what?" I blurt. "Join you?" My eyes widen when I realize what I've said and his grin ticks up a notch.

"I wouldn't complain."

Oh my God.

I think I might spontaneously combust on the spot.

Before I can find my voice, he turns and shuts himself in the bathroom.

I collapse on the couch.

"What the hell is happening?" I whisper to myself, feeling hot all of a sudden and *not* from the temperature in the room.

CHAPTER THIRTEEN

Abel

I push the cart through Food Mart with Lou walking alongside me, her eyes scanning the aisles hungrily. Her hair is damp, pulled up into a knot on top of her head. Her face is clear of any trace of makeup and she's wearing sweatpants and shoes that I'm pretty sure are actually slippers. She sips on that pink colored drink from Starbucks, because she insisted I stop there before we came here.

"We should get those." She points, smiling around her straw, at a bag of Cheetos.

"Or not." I keep moving past the chips.

"Ugh, fun sucker." She stomps behind me, but quickly catches up. "All your green stuff and chicken needs some junk food to round out the food groups."

"Mhmm," I hum, looking down at the list in my hand and turning right at the end of the aisle.

She does some sort of skip-hop-twirl thing into the next aisle, bumping the cart in the process. I try to hide my amused smile. I'm sure I fail when she grins back.

"How about this?" She grabs a bag of marshmallows and waves it around.

"You don't even like marshmallows."

She scoffs, plopping the bag back on the shelf she got it from. "How could you possibly know that?"

I turn from what I'm looking at to meet her gaze. "I read minds."

"Ooh." She dances on her toes, her drink sloshing. "What am I thinking about right now?"

"Starbursts."

"Wrong!" she cries, shoving an arm into the air and then lowering it to point at me. "I was wondering how big your dick is."

I choke on my own saliva and she bursts out laughing. "Gotcha." She dances ahead of me and I push the cart behind her, acknowledging my list as I go so I don't forget anything.

Stopping, I grab a box of protein bars and put them in the cart.

Lou hops onto the end, holding onto the cart with one hand and her drink in the other.

"Onward, Mr. Popular."

I shake my head at her ridiculous nickname for me. I might seem like the guy who has it all to anyone watching on campus, but none of that stuff is what matters. This part of our lives is fleeting. College is a blip of time, gone in a millisecond. Like high school, who you are here doesn't matter. It's who you become.

"You know," she muses as I turn down the next aisle, "you should really try living up to your reputation more."

I raise a brow in question. "What part of my reputation would that be, exactly?"

"The jerk part. I mean, I've heard you're a womanizer too, but the idea of having a bunch of strange girls coming in and out of the apartment isn't appealing. I'm not a Madam, and this ain't no brothel."

She hops off the cart, ice sloshing in her cup.

I stifle my laughter, reaching for a box of cereal. She grabs a box of Froot Loops from one of the lower shelves and cradles it to her chest.

"I'm getting these and don't you dare try to sneak them out of the cart. I know where you sleep."

Dropping my box of cereal in the cart, she does the same with hers all while staring me down.

"Back to this jerk thing, how exactly should I go about it?"

"I don't know." She pretends to think. "Stop being as nice as you actually are?"

I throw my head back, laughing. Lowering my head down to her height, I graze my lips against her ear. "Get used to it, Lou. I'm a nice guy."

She shivers, backing a step away.

Clearing my throat, I move back behind the cart and carry on my way. I don't know why I love pushing her so much. Maybe it's my own limits I'm testing.

Reaching the freezer section, she runs ahead and grabs a box of frozen pizza, carrying it back to the cart.

"Frozen pizza is a staple in any student's freezer. Actually, screw that, *anyone's* freezer."

"You're really not helping me with my whole healthy eating thing."

She wraps her lips around the green straw and shrugs. "I like healthy food too, but I have to balance it out with some sugar and carbs."

"I think the last thing you need is more sugar." I flick her plastic cup, pushing by her. "You're hyper enough without it."

"Are we done?" She eyes the cart and everything I've piled inside.

"Almost, I need to hit the produce section first."

"You know," she muses, biting her lip, "I've never seen anyone start at the back of the store and work forward before."

My brows furrow. "Makes the most sense to me. Checkout is at the front. Start at the back and then make it to the end zone."

"Such a football player." She rolls her eyes playfully and bumps her arm against mine. I'm not sure if it's accidental or on purpose, but it doesn't matter. Just from that brief contact with her I feel my body tighten all over.

I wish I could stop wondering how soft her breasts would feel in my hands and how her body would writhe against mine as I brought her pleasure.

My celibacy pact with myself is fucking with my head—actually, it's just Lou fucking with me. No one else elicits this response from my sex-deprived body. Not even Danika practically begging for it in front of me did.

I'm not ashamed of my playboy past or fucking anyone who came onto me. I got what I wanted and they did too, but something changed in the last year. It seems immature to me now. I blame my sister. Seeing her happy with her husband and kids has clearly shifted my priorities. I want a life filled with meaning, not one of emptiness and selfish thoughts.

Lou finishes her drink and sticks the empty cup in

the cart. Doing a little skip-hop-jump thing she makes her way down the aisle and twirls.

When she faces me, she smiles and it's the blinding kind that radiates pure happiness.

Reaching the produce section, I grab what I need and head toward the checkout.

"No, no, nope." Lou pushes the cart to the side and points. "Self-checkout is the way to go."

"What's wrong with the regular checkout?"

"Um ... people. Duh."

Shaking my head, I follow her to the self-checkout and she starts dividing our items.

"Don't do that." I put my hand on hers to stop her movements. Her eyes flick up to mine in surprise. Today the blue hue is light like a cloudless sky, and up this close I can see the freckles peppered across her nose. "I've got this."

"No." Her nose scrunches. "You're not buying my food."

"You got, like, three things."

"Yeah," she says in a *duh* tone, "because you kept saying with everything you got there was enough for me too. You don't need to buy all that extra food *plus* the things I want."

"Lou." I draw out her name. "It's not a big deal. *Lou—*"

She swipes her Froot Loops, challenge shining in her eyes.

"Lou." I pinch the bridge of my nose.

She slides the cookies 'n cream ice cream across the scanner, still staring at me as she does it.

Grabbing her pack of Capri-Sun she goes to scan it next.

I snatch it from her hands. "I told you, I've got it."

"Ugh, Abel!" She jumps up, trying to take the box from me, but I hold it higher than she can reach. Considering I'm probably a foot taller than her, there's no chance she's getting it. "Give it back! I can get my own stuff."

My voice lowers, as does the box in my hands. "I know you can. I don't think you're incapable of doing anything."

"Then let me buy my own damn groceries." She lifts her chin defiantly.

I pretend to think. "No."

"Abel!" She shouts, drawing attention our way.

When I look toward the curious onlookers she uses the distraction to her advantage.

I grunt when she jumps onto me, her legs wrapping around my waist. In my surprise to catch her, I drop the box and she grabs it into her all too eager hands.

My hands, however, land on her ass. Her breath leaves in a startled gasp and her wide eyes meet mine.

The moment seems to stretch out, neither of us moving or saying a word.

Then, she rolls her hips into mine and lets out the softest moan only my ears can hear.

Still watching her I notice the hard swallow she takes, her breath catching.

She feels it too.

I know I should set her down, but I make no move to, and she doesn't unwrap her legs from my waist.

We're eye fucking in the middle of Food Mart and it's the hottest form of foreplay I think I've ever been a part of, because there's nothing I can do about it. Stripping her bare in the grocery store would most definitely lead to an arrest on both our ends.

Her pink tongue peeks out and I don't know whether she's licking her lips or thinking of licking me.

Fuck.

Picturing her mouth wrapped around my cock sends blood rushing to my groin.

Her eyes fall to my lips and her lower lip trembles like she's holding herself back from kissing me.

It takes every ounce of self-control I have not to lean in and kiss her.

"Y-You should put me down." Her voice is shaky and her eyes drop from mine.

"Right." Reluctantly, I let go and her feet fall to the

floor. I miss the heat of her body pressing into mine, and my cock *definitely* misses it.

Not meeting my eyes, she scans her Capri-Sun box, pays for her items and sets them in the cart before she starts swiping my items since I can't seem to function or move.

I couldn't have been holding her longer than thirty seconds, but it felt like minutes.

A woman passes by and smiles at me. "You and your girlfriend are so cute."

I'm too surprised to correct her, blurting out a *thanks* before she heads to her own self-checkout stall.

When I look back over I find Lou bagging my stuff, so I grab my card out of my wallet and pay.

She won't look at me and I feel like I should apologize, but I won't.

Apologies shouldn't be handed out freely, that's a lesson my dad taught me. Only apologize when you mean it, otherwise it's empty and meaningless.

Taking the receipt, I push the cart out of the store and through the lot, loading everything into my truck. Lou helps, not saying a word.

Following her lead, I don't say anything either.

She takes the cart and returns it and I hop in the truck, rolling down my window.

I hate the awkward silence filling the cab as I drive back across town to our apartment, but I don't know what I can do or say. Nothing can erase the moment we shared in the middle of Food Mart. It's imprinted in my mind. I'm not sure I'll ever forget it.

Her phone buzzes and she looks down at the screen in her lap.

Blonde hair swirls around her face from my open window but she makes no move to redo her bun. My eyes follow the soft curve of her cheeks and—*fuck, eyes on the road, man.*

"It's Jamie," she finally breaks the silence, "he says he's dropping by the apartment so you can sign the new lease contract."

"Okay."

I wince at my pathetic answer.

Everyone thinks I have my shit together, that I'm so smooth with the ladies and can have any pussy I want. While that might be true to an extent, there have never been any feelings involved before, just lust, and day by day I find myself growing to like Lou more and more. Most of the women I've been with I barely knew. It was one night and then we went separate ways.

I've never been surrounded by the object of my desire day in and day out and it's wearing on me.

I park my truck in the lot beside the building and we each grab a few bags, managing to get it all in one load.

Lou sets her stuff down by the door and pulls out her key to unlock it.

It swings open, revealing Jamie sitting at the breakfast bar, his hand buried in a box of Cheez-Its, snacking away with his legs propped on top of the bar.

"What the fuck?"

Lou looks at me over her shoulder. "It's Jamie." Her tone of voice tells me this is just how he is.

I step past Lou, dropping my bags on the floor and stomp toward our thirty-something landlord. Even if he was standing I'd be a few inches taller. With him sitting I dwarf him.

"You have no right coming in here when we're not home."

He sets the box down, which I'm pretty sure he brought with him since I've never stumbled across Cheez-Its in any of the cabinets. Dropping his feet to the floor he clasps his hands together and looks up at me.

"Actually, I'm the landlord. That means I can." He grabs something from his pocket—keys—and dangles it in front of me. "I have a key."

My fists clench at my sides. This guy is asking to be punched in the face. I think he gets off on being an asshole.

"You should only be allowed to let yourself in if there's a problem or—"

"Well, you see," he grins as he stands up so we're chest to chest, "there is a problem. The little fact that *your* name isn't on the lease. Only little Ms. Louise's. I could have your ass out of here in a heartbeat considering you haven't signed anything yet, so if I were you, I'd watch myself."

There's a challenge in his eyes, one I want to match, but Lou's small hand wraps around my elbow and she tries to pull me away. I let her, taking two steps away from Jamie before I punch him in his smug ass face.

"Where are the papers?" I want to get them signed and escort him out of here.

He pulls a rolled-up sheet of papers from his pocket and slaps them down on the bar, along with a pen.

"Feel free to read it." He crosses his arms over his chest, fighting a grin. "Though, I promise it's on the up and up. I might be an asshole but I don't have time for legal battles because of shitty paperwork."

I grab the pen and bend over, reading each and every word carefully for anything he might've slipped in.

Everything looks legitimate but I read it one more time to be sure, while Jamie huffs out an impatient breath. If he has some place to be, I'll drag this out as long as possible.

Finally, I sign my name and add the date, then hand Lou the pen so she can sign the amended contract. As she leans past me to sign, I get a whiff of her perfume. It smells of amber, pineapple, and something else that's uniquely her.

Grabbing the pen and papers, she shoves them

against Jamie's chest where he grapples to hang onto them.

"You got your papers, now get out." She points to the door.

"Is that any way to talk to your favorite landlord?"

She glares at him. "Go, Jamie."

"Fine." He grabs his box of Cheez-Its and starts to pass by her, but stops. Wetting his lips he says, "Tell that hot brunette friend of yours to give me a call sometime. You have my number."

He sweeps out the door, closing it with a bang behind him, which echoes through the apartment.

"God, he's annoying."

"He's a creep," I amend.

She sighs and bends down to pick up some of the bags. Placing them on the counter, she starts unpacking stuff.

"He's ... Jamie," she finally says. "He enjoys pushing everyone's buttons."

"I don't like the way he looks at you." I start putting away the items she pulls out, working in unison.

Un-bag. Put away.

Wash, rinse, repeat.

"It's not like he's that old."

I pause in the middle of the kitchen, not liking that she's defending him.

"What?" She stops too, blinking innocently up at me.

"I've had eighty-year-olds hit on me. Jamie isn't half-bad compared to that. At least he's hot." I snort at her comment. "I mean, he is." She gives a small laugh. "I would never go near him, so don't worry. Cocky playboys aren't my type."

She starts to turn back to one of the bags on the counter, but I touch her arm, halting her progress.

Her wide blue eyes blink up at me, a question lingering in their depths.

"Is that what you think I am?"

She expels a disbelieving grunt. "I think you're my roommate."

"That's all?"

I try to ignore how suddenly aware I am of my beating heart.

She lowers her eyes and tugs away from my hold.

"It's all we can be."

CHAPTER FOURTEEN

Lou

Striding across campus, my backpack digs into my shoulder.

I adjust it and keep going, heading toward the cafeteria. There's only a short window between my classes when I can eat and if I miss it, then I turn into a hangry bitch no one wants to deal with.

"Lou!" A voice calls behind me. "Lou, wait up!"

I glance over my shoulder to find Tanner running to catch up to me. He nearly trips in his designer shoes.

He slows as he nears me and we fall into step together.

"Where are you headed?" He inquires, holding his messenger bag steady so it'll stop swaying from his jog.

"Dining hall. I only have thirty minutes before my next class, so I'm trying to grab something quick. I really need an IV coffee drip right about now, but since that isn't a feasible option, food and a caffeinated soda it is." The words spew from my mouth in rapid succession and I momentarily wonder if maybe that rap career I considered when I was twelve might have actually had potential.

"Good, because I'm starving too."

We cross the path, nearing the building.

My stomach rumbles embarrassingly loud and Tanner gives a chuckle, holding the door open for me.

He follows behind me as I grab what I want, which ends up being a refrigerated Starbucks drink—not as good as the real thing, but it'll do—and a container of fries and chicken tenders. I take a bottle of water too, because cold coffee with chicken tenders doesn't sound appetizing.

Tanner goes the healthier route with some kind of chicken wrap and water.

We both swipe our student cards and head to a table in the back near the windows.

"What have you been up to?" Tanner twists off the cap of his water bottle and takes a drink.

"Babysitting, homework, the usual."

Oh, and jumping on my hot roommate in the middle of Food Mart while almost kissing him and simultaneously nearly dry humping him.

"Sounds boring."

"It's not too bad." I open a packet of honey mustard and break one of my chicken tenders in half, dipping it in the yellow sauce. "I like staying busy."

I'm the kind of person who likes to stay home, cozy up in my pajamas, and watch a movie or two, but I'm okay staying on the go as well.

"Uh-oh," Tanner blurts, his eyes widening on something over my shoulders.

"Wha—?" I start to ask, glancing behind me, but I don't finish my question because I get my answer.

Abel stands from the table he's sitting at with a bunch of his jock friends, grabs his stuff, and crosses the room toward us.

"Why does he look like he wants to murder me?" Tanner looks at me with wide, panicked eyes, and appears like he's a second from making a run for it.

"Ignore him—he's a gentle giant. He might look big and scary, but he's not."

"Is that a euphemism for having a giant penis and being a gentle lover?"

I snort at Tanner's hissed question, but I don't have time to answer as Abel pulls out the chair beside me and plops down.

"Blondie." He looks me up and down, heat in his gaze.

I try to act like him checking me out doesn't get to me, but my body responds anyway. My skin tingles, and I'm all too aware of him and his presence.

Dipping a fry into the honey mustard I try to ignore him, but I feel him staring at me.

"What?" I turn to look at him. "What do you want?"

"Just having lunch with my roommate and her boyfriend. No big deal."

I snort, but don't correct him because jealous Abel is amusing. Across from me Tanner's lips twitch with the threat of laughter, but he doesn't tell Abel he's gay either.

"Well, I have less than twenty minutes to eat and get to my class, so I apologize for the way I'm about to inhale my food, but I've never claimed to be a lady." I break off another chicken tender.

"So, how'd you two meet?" Abel's eyes flick between Tanner and I.

Tanner stifles a snort and I glare at him. "You should tell this one, *baby*."

I finish chewing and swallow. "He tried to steal my

table at Griffin's, I wasn't having it. We ended up sharing, I acted like a bitch and the rest is, as they say, history."

Tanner's cheeks are puffed up and his face is red as he holds in laughter. If Abel would look at him, he would know something is up, but his eyes never stray from me.

"That so?"

"Yep, it's the truth. It'll be quite the tale to tell our children one day. They already have names you know. We thought long and hard on them."

He grunts something and turns to glare at his food.

I don't know why I'm messing with him. All I know is pushing his buttons is way too fun.

The chair on my other side is yanked out, as well as a few more around the table. Looking around, I realize in surprise that Abel's friends have joined us.

"Bro, you just got up and left. Not cool."

The voice beside me grates on my nerves, but I force myself to ignore him and not look in his direction.

"Wanted to check in with Lou." His reply is grumbled and he picks his fries apart, apparently not as hungry as I am.

"Lou, huh?" The voice beside me goads. "I know a Lou."

I whip my head around and narrow my gaze on him. "Yeah, it's me you ass face."

Kit Jacobson, a linebacker on the football team and

one of my questionable hookups, leans back in the chair with a cocky grin smothered across his face.

"Miss me?" He makes a kissy face at me and I want to punch him in his smug face. I'm smarter than that, though.

"That would require you being memorable."

The guys around the table give out a collective, *'ooh!'*

I don't pay them any attention, but I feel Abel staring and wondering what's going on.

Kit leans forward, getting into my personal space. "I would think a girl like you would remember a night with a guy like me." He motions to himself like he's some prize stud.

I smile, nodding my head. "You're so right. Except a girl like me doesn't care about status. I just wanted to be fucked, and good, but your three-inch penis was like fucking a limp dishrag. Dirty, flaccid, and useless way too soon."

Anger flashes across his face and before he can retort I stand up, tossing my water in his face, and storm out of the lunchroom.

I reach the doors and push them open roughly, blasting outside into the warm early fall air. The doors slam closed behind me, but I hear the telltale clank of them being opened again.

"Blondie!" Abel calls after me, but I keep plowing on,

running as fast as I can because I don't want to deal with him right now.

I'm sure he'll have questions and frankly, I don't think it's anyone's fucking business who I've slept with. Kit was one of those bad decisions I made and one of the many reasons I won't sleep around anymore. I deserve better than any guy like him.

"Lou! Come on, wait up! *Lou!*"

I hear Abel's thundering steps behind me, but I don't stop. He's in a lot better shape than I am, with much longer legs. He'll catch up.

Reaching the pavilion I crash into the fence surrounding the water feature and grab onto it. A second later the warm, all-encompassing presence of Abel fills the space behind me.

"What was that about?" he presses, and I hear something fall to the ground by my feet. Looking down I spot my backpack. In my haste to leave the cafeteria, I hadn't even thought about it.

I flip around, facing him.

We're chest to chest. Every breath I take has my breasts brushing against his chest. I want to push him a step back, but I know it would be both useless and only prove how I'm affected by his nearness.

"I could say the same to you, marching over to where I sat and acting like a jealous ex-lover."

"Well, I'm so sorry if my presence dampened your time with your boyfriend."

I flick his chest—pathetic, I know, but in the moment it's the only thing I can think to do. "Tanner is gay, you idiot."

"Gay?"

"It's a pretty self-explanatory word. He likes dick, not pussy."

Shaking his head he blurts, "What was all that with Kit?"

I let out an undignified and very unlady-like snort. "Guys like him think they're on top, that because they're popular, they're a celebrity or something. It means they can treat people like dirt. We had sex, he was lousy, and after it was over he made some dickish comments about my weight. And you know what?" The words tumble out of me and he just stands there listening as they fire out, hitting him like bullets. "I'm sick and tired of people thinking their *opinion* on my weight, or how I dress, or what I say is somehow important. What is important is how *I* see myself." I slam a finger into my chest. "And I *love* me. I'm beautiful, I'm hot, I'm sexy. I didn't defend myself to him last year, but I sure as hell will now. I'm fucking awesome and my worth isn't determined by him or anyone else. People like him are a dime a dozen, but me? I'm rare. I'm—"

My words are cut off as his large hands frame my

face. Heat flares in his eyes and before I can blink, his mouth crashes into mine. I can barely suck in a breath before his tongue slides against mine, my body melting into him as my fingers curl in the fabric of his cotton shirt.

My body leans back as he kisses me deeper.

I'm pretty sure if this were a movie this is moment the cheesy music would start playing and doves would fly out of somebody's ass.

But this is real life, and a college campus, so all I hear is clapping and catcalls.

Abel ignores our audience and kisses me like he's starved for my lips. I shouldn't kiss him back but I do. Ever since the moment we met there's been an attraction pulsing between us. It's unexplainable. Undeniable. But it's real.

His lips part from mine and move to my ear. My head swims with surprise at the kiss and the lack of oxygen.

"Perfect," he whispers, "you're perfect."

He stares into my eyes as he takes several steps backward, finally turning and heading toward his class while I stand underneath the pavilion in shock.

A full minute, maybe two, passes before I realize he finished my sentence.

I'm rare. I'm perfect. I'm flawless.

CHAPTER FIFTEEN

Abel

It's late and Lou isn't home yet. Maybe it's pathetic for me to be worried, but I am. I haven't seen her since this afternoon when we kissed, and I can't shake the feeling she's avoiding me.

Sure, there have been times she's stayed out late working on an assignment for the school paper, but never *this* late on a school night. It's nearing eleven and I'm wondering if I should call someone or go in search of her myself. I've called her phone an unhealthy amount of times and it goes straight to voicemail, which means she's either redirecting my calls there or her phone's dead.

I keep pacing the floors like a maniac. I want to believe this is only avoidance but with each passing second, my gut shouts at me that it's more.

Finally, unable to stand it, I grab my truck keys and rush out the door.

If I had any of her friends' numbers I'd call them first to see if she's with them, or if they have any idea where she might be, but I don't. It leaves me in a guessing game of where she is.

I decide to check Griffin's and the nearest Starbucks to campus first. Lou is a coffee fiend, drinking the stuff like it's the elixir of life. I'm pretty sure if she could hook up to an IV tap, she would.

Both places turn out to be a dud, her purple Dodge Neon nowhere in sight.

"Campus," I mutter to myself, feeling like it's the next logical place to look.

If she's not there then ... I have to hope she's with a friend and hunt them down systematically tomorrow at school to make sure she's okay. If that proves to be a bust, then I guess I'll be filing a police report.

"Fuck." I slap my hand against my steering wheel.

I don't worry, not like this, very often. The last time I

was this worried was after my mom died and I saw my dad slipping away day by day.

Pulling onto campus, I drive around, searching for her car. Most of the spaces are empty in this section at this hour, and only full around the dorms, but I search there anyway.

Reaching the other side of one of the many buildings, my headlights shine across a small car and I slam on my brakes. Pulling forward slowly I breathe out a sigh of relief as I confirm it's Lou's.

I park beside it and kill the engine, running to the door. Yanking it open, I burst inside and a cleaning crew member looks up from the tile floor he's mopping, giving me a speculative look.

"Have you seen a girl around here? Blonde hair? About this tall?" I hold out my hand to demonstrate.

"Second floor, third door on your left."

"Thanks, man."

I race for the stairs, taking them two at a time.

Bursting through the door he directed me to, I find Lou fast asleep with her arms on the table and her head lying within their cradle. The headphones she had on are now skewed to the side, and the computer monitor in front of her flashes some kind of early 2000s looking screensaver.

I bend down beside her and shake her shoulder slightly. She stirs, making a little humming sound in her sleep. "Lou," I whisper, not wanting to scare her, "wake up."

She exhales a breath, her eyes moving behind closed lids.

"Lou." I brush stray hairs off her forehead. Finally, her eyes open.

"Am I dreaming?" She stifles a yawn, sounding groggy.

"No, not dreaming, Blondie." I skim fingers along the curve of her cheek and she shivers.

"Why are you touching me?" The question is soft, not accusatory.

"Because I want to."

Her lips tip up into a smile. "You kissed me."

I grin back. "I did."

"It was a hella-good kiss."

My smile grows bigger. "You're welcome."

"Asshole." She pushes my shoulder and sits up fully, stretching her arms above her head. The fabric of her shirt stretches across her full breasts and I stare, because why the hell wouldn't I? She has great tits. Pressing a hand over her mouth as she yawns she blinks at me. "What time is it?"

I look down at my phone. "Eleven-forty-five."

"Jeez." She rubs a hand over her face "I was finishing my article and I guess ... well, I got sleepy."

She wiggles the mouse as I stand up and the screen comes to life.

"At least it's not midnight," she mutters to herself as she reads over what she's written, and then clicks submit. "Arnold would kill me if I sent it after twelve."

"Who's Arnold?"

What kind of name is that anyway?

"The editor." She clicks some more buttons on the screen, logging out and shutting down the computer.

She pushes the chair back and stands up, grabbing her backpack from the floor. I take it from her before she can sling it across her shoulders.

"Why are you here anyway?" She follows me out of the room and closes the door softly behind us.

I pause in the hallway, raising a brow. "I was worried about you."

She gives a small laugh and then her eyes widen when she looks at me. "Oh, you're being serious."

"Of course I'm being serious."

We walk side by side down the wide stairwell.

"This happens a lot. There's no need to worry about me."

"That's like saying rain isn't wet," I scoff in disbelief.

"What does that mean?"

"It means I worry."

"Oh," she cajoles, nodding rapidly, "you're one of *those* people. Seriously, it isn't a big deal for me to be working on an article and fall asleep. One time I didn't wake up until morning. Now that sucked. I had to go around all day in the same clothes without brushing my teeth. No one should be subjected to my dirty breath all day. It's a miracle anyone was left standing on campus."

I open the exit door and she passes through first.

"You're riding with me," I command, and she halts her steps stopping right in front of me.

Whipping around, she plants her hands on her hips and tips her chin defiantly. "I can drive back to the apartment just fine, Mr. Popular. You're not the boss of me."

"Are you five?" Sparring with Lou is becoming one of my favorite pastimes.

"Ugh, you're impossible."

"I'm the impossible one?" I cover my mouth with my hand to hide my threatening laugh.

"Yes. Yes, you are." She shoves a finger against my chest.

Lowering my head I hear her breath catch on an intake. I brush my lips against her neck before skimming them up to her ear. "You didn't think I was so impossible when I was kissing you. In fact, if I remember correctly there was this small pleading moan you made. That was your body begging me for more. You might say one thing with your mouth, but your body sings an entirely different tune."

Before I pull away from her completely, I skim my

lips over hers. It's not a kiss, barely even a meeting of flesh, but she mewls and I smile in victory.

"Get in the truck, Blondie."

"No." She glares back at me, her eyes shining from the lights in the parking lot.

"Don't make me break your Jonas Brothers record in half."

She gasps—not a pretend one either. Oh no, this is a full on shocked, *I can't believe he said such a thing*, gasp.

"Do *not* threaten my Jo Bros." Stomping her foot she shoves a single finger in the air. "I declare on this moment, that Karma is going to bite you in the ass for threatening such an outrageous crime."

"Then get in the truck."

"How am I supposed to get back to campus tomorrow?"

I grin back at her, eating this up. "With me."

"Of course," she sighs. "But you're taking me to get crepes and fancy cookies again before class."

"You mean macarons?"

"Like I said, fancy cookies."

"Whatever you want, Blondie."

When she smiles up at me I know it's only a matter of time before I'm a goner.

Maybe I already am.

CHAPTER SIXTEEN

Lou

"If heaven has a taste, I'm certain it tastes like this." I suppress a moan as I sit in the passenger seat of Abel's truck, parked along the curb of Oh, Crepe as we devour our breakfast.

This makes giving in and riding home with Abel last night completely worth it.

Neither one of us has said a word about the kiss,

though I did leave an interesting note in the bathroom for him to find this morning.

Kisses are addictive. You can't have just one.

P.S. I'm referring to the chocolate.

He made no comment on the note, but he did leave the bathroom with a smirk and glint in his eye. I feel certain he's planning something.

"I have to agree with you there." He chases a blueberry around the container as it rolls away from him.

"Hey." I pout, pretending to be offended. "You're supposed to say, 'I've tasted heaven and it tastes like you, Lou.'" I swore to myself I wouldn't say anything about the kiss, but here we are. I haven't lasted even twenty-four hours. The only way I'll ever win anything is if they start handing out trophies to the first loser.

"I don't know," he hedges, spearing a bite of crepe, "crepes are pretty fucking hard to top. Then there are *fancy cookies*," he throws my words back at me, "so maybe you're third."

I'm tempted to grab him and show him how good I am at third place.

I don't, of course, I'm not a complete fiend.

I save that shit for Tuesdays. It's the least talked about day of the week and deserves some love.

Instead, I say to him, "Yeah, I bet you like fancy cookies even better than the idea of your cock in my mouth."

Game. Set. Match.

He chokes on his food, his face turning red as he sputters and coughs. He grabs a bottle of water and chugs it down, trying to clear whatever is lodged in his throat.

"You are the Devil." He wipes his mouth on the back of his hand and re-caps his water.

"Nah," I shake my head like I'm giving this serious thought, "the Devil eats lemon Starbursts, therefore that makes you him, or at least his kin."

"You are without a doubt the oddest person I have ever met."

"I'm taking that as a compliment." I smile around a bite of my breakfast.

Shaking his head, he laughs lightly under his breath. "It is. It definitely is."

A moment of silence passes between us.

"There's a game tomorrow night."

"And?" I raise a brow, my lips twitching with a smile. "Are you going to remind me of this every time you have a game? I have more important things to do, like work on cross-stitching my mom's birthday present or go play Bingo. Blythe won last time, and I won't stand for that blasphemy."

"Bingo?" Shock registers on his face.

"It's a very competitive sport." I cross my arms over my chest defensively.

"It's a game, not a sport."

"Need I remind you that you just referred to football as a *game?*"

He tosses his head back against the headrest. "I can't win with you."

I look at my nails, pretending to scrutinize them. I truly do need to get them painted. The soft blue polish has grown out, leaving my naked nail showing. No nails shall be naked on my hands.

"I don't know why you even try."

He chuckles, scrubbing a hand over his jaw. "I want you to come."

I feel something catch in my throat.

Oh my God, I think it's *feelings*. Why isn't there a Plan B for this shit? Pop a pill and boom feelings gone.

"Just because you kissed me doesn't mean I'm obligated to be your cheerleader. I don't shake pom poms but I might shake my ass for the right price."

"What price is that?" He rests one arm on top of the steering wheel and leans toward me smirking, his brown eyes dancing with amusement.

"Don't worry, you couldn't afford it."

His smirk turns into a full-blown grin and I feel my stomach dip.

Damn him for being so attractive. It's entirely unfair.

"But I also have an advantage." He leans closer to me, brushing his nose along my cheek and I feel my treacherous breath catch in my throat.

"W-What's that?" The words stutter from me and I mentally curse myself for not keeping my cool.

I feel his breath against my skin and there's a slight hum emanating from him. My whole body seems to be tuned into whatever frequency he's on and my nipples pebble, pushing against my bra, and I'm sure if he looks down he'll see them straining against the confines of my shirt.

Stupid, no good, nipples! Always giving us ladies away! Lady boners are an unfortunate, very real, thing!

He pulls away from me suddenly and his smile is dangerous. So are his chocolate brown eyes.

Right here, right now, I've decided brown eyes are the bane of my existence. Those warm brown eyes are something I could get lost in, like my favorite fluffy blanket. They see too much, know too much, and I like the way they make me feel when he looks at me. They're kind, comforting, and soulful. Kind of like a dog. Maybe I should get a dog and then I'll grow an immunity against brown eyes—

"A good player never reveals his advantage this early in the game."

For a moment I forget what he's responding to, but as it clicks into place my mouth falls open.

Fucking hell.

I didn't know we were playing a game, but apparently Abel just won round one.

He won't be so lucky from now on.

He doesn't know it yet, but I'm highly competitive and I *always* win.

Sobering, I smile back at him in challenge, even as my body yearns to be closer to him. "Game on, Mr. Popular."

Tossing our trash in the back he starts the truck back up and pulls out. Glancing at me as he comes to the stoplight at the end of the street his eyes scour my body, slowly, tantalizingly, before settling so he stares straight at my soul.

I'm sure it must look like a pink starburst.

"Good luck, Blondie."

CHAPTER SEVENTEEN

Lou

I stick the Post-It to the mirror and step back, admiring my doodle. I decided today a drawing was necessary, not words.

In it, I've drawn a stick figure of myself making a touchdown and Abel off to the side as a cheerleader, shaking his pom-poms. The message is clear.

I'm winning this game.

He's out for the moment, on one of his daily runs.

He's such a show-off. No normal person runs five miles every day on top of playing football and whatever workouts he does for that. It's insane and I'm not sure he's entirely human.

The team won their game last night and the next one is out of town. I won't know what to do without having a roommate for nearly a whole day.

Finishing up in the bathroom, I throw on some clothes and head out the door to my babysitting job. Giulia has already sent a text message confirming I'm coming and I had a small laugh to myself, because her desperation for a break was palpable even through an electronic screen.

Once in my car I call her and she answers with a frazzled, "Hello? MATTEO DO NOT PULL YOUR SISTER'S HAIR! ONE DAY SHE'LL LEARN WHERE YOUR BALLS ARE AND YOU'LL REGRET THIS!" She exhales a breath. "Sorry about that. Yes?"

I suppress a laugh. "I was wondering if I should bring a treat for the kids, like donuts or something, but maybe I shouldn't. It sounds like they're plenty hyped up."

"You can if you want. I'll pay you back. Their uncle is picking them up today to go to the zoo so you'll only have Cristian and you can leave the hyped up heathens to him."

I bust out laughing. "That's cruel, Giulia."

"That's what sisters are for. MATTY I SWEAR TO GOD IF YOU SHOOT YOUR SISTER ONE MORE TIME WITH YOUR NERF GUN IT'S GOING IN THE TRASH AND SO ARE YOU! Ugh," she sighs heavily, "I'll see you in a bit, Lou. I have to make sure my children don't kill each other."

With a click, the line goes dead and I smile in amusement.

I swing by Dunkin Donuts and get a dozen of the donuts with icing and sprinkles. They're my favorite and I don't know any kid who doesn't like them either.

I pull into the driveway of the Wilson's house and hurry inside into the middle of chaos.

Matteo runs past me in only his underwear with Buzz Lightyear on them.

A second later, Giulia runs after him around the corner. "Give them back you little gremlin."

"I have donuts!" I call out and Matteo makes a complete U-turn in my direction, stopping in front of me like an eager puppy waiting for a treat. I tilt my head down at him, giving him my best glare. "What did you steal from your mom?"

He drops his head forlornly and behind him Giulia tries not to smile. Opening his palm he shows me two diamond earrings clasped in his hand. "Bad kids don't get donuts," I warn him. "You'll have to give them back to your mom and apologize first."

"Do I get donuts? I'm a good girl." I turn to find Bella crawling out from her hiding place behind the couch.

"Of course you do, angel." I ruffle her dark hair.

Turning around to his mom, Matteo apologizes and hands over her earrings.

"Why do they listen to you?" She fixes her earrings in place.

"Because, I'm not their mom. I'm pretty sure it's ingrained in kids DNA to ignore anything their parents say."

"I think they just like you more."

"You look beautiful." I take in for the first time the fitted white dress she wears and how her glossy dark hair is curled to perfection. She's even done her makeup and her red lipstick pops against her darker skin color.

"Thank you." She beams, smoothing her hands over the dress. She looks amazing considering she only had a baby a little over a month ago. "Leo is taking me to a winery, so I'll be pumping and dumping. My brother offered to watch the kids tonight." In a conspiratorial tone she adds, "I'm so getting laid tonight."

"I heard that." Her husband comes around the corner and smacks her butt. "I whole-heartedly agree with this. How are you, Lou?"

"I'm doing good." I still stand in the entry holding the box of donuts like the awkward unicorn I am. Leo nods, tucking his hands into his pants pockets, looking at his wife like she's the most gorgeous creature he's ever laid eyes on. I want my future husband to look at me like that, and if he doesn't ... well, then he's clearly not the one.

"Glad to hear that." His response is for me, but he's still checking out Giulia like it's the first time he's ever laid on eyes on her and not like they have three kids together. Honestly, they're a gorgeous couple. Giulia is stunning and exotic and Leo reminds me of that guy on Game of Thrones who fucks his sister. Okay, that sounds majorly gross and awkward and I want to wash the vision of this straight out of my head.

I move past them, leaving them to their lovey-dovey staring contest, and set the donuts down on the kitchen island.

Within seconds I'm rushed by two eager, sugar-addict, children.

"Donut," Matteo demands, holding out his hands eagerly.

Beside him, Bella mimics his grabbing gesture, looking up at me with round brown eyes.

"Excuse me?" I raise one brow. "That isn't how we ask for something, now is it?" I use my best mom voice and it has its intended effect.

"Please?" Matteo responds hopefully.

"That's the one." I reach out and ruffle his hair with a smile. "Bella?"

"Pwease?" She clasps her hands under her chin and her bottom lip juts out.

I grab a donut and break it in half. "You're going to *share* and you can each have another half later if you're good for your uncle and he allows it."

Matteo pouts as he takes the donut and gives me a reluctant, "Fine." At my look, he tacks on a thank you before walking off in search of his iPad.

"Tank you."

I smile at Bella's sweet toddler voice and bend down so we're eye level.

"You're welcome, sweetie."

Once they're occupied with their treats, Giulia pulls me aside and asks me to make sure Bella and Matteo are dressed and ready to go to the zoo in the next hour. She also lets me know Cristian should be waking up from his first morning nap in about thirty minutes before going over in detail where everything is and what I need to do.

"Giulia," I grab her arm, quieting her next tirade, "I know where things are and what to do."

"I know," she exhales. "I'm nervous leaving them overnight. I'm not sure my brother can handle this. It's *three* kids. Cristian's just a baby. Oh, God." She clutches her chest. "Leo, that's it, we're staying home. I can't do this."

Leo looks over from where he's pouring a sippy cup of milk for Bella and eyes his wife skeptically. "G, it'll be fine. You're stressing for nothing. We wouldn't be going overnight if I didn't have full confidence in your brother."

"I still don't know." She looks down at her pretty dress and I sense her turmoil. It has to be hard being a mom and wanting to have your own life while not wanting to be separated from your children.

"Babe." Leo crosses the room and wraps his arms around her. "It's your birthday. This is a special day and we should celebrate. We're not going far and can be home in forty minutes if something happens."

"But—"

He silences her protest with his lips.

I look away, feeling weird for watching them.

I hear Giulia exhale and agree to go. "But if I get any weird feelings we're coming straight home. Promise?"

"Promise." He grins at her and I feel like my heart is going to burst from their sweetness.

Within the next ten minutes Matteo, Bella, and I stand on the front porch and wave goodbye as the silver Mercedes backs out of the driveway.

As soon as the vehicle is out of sight, Matteo screams and runs back inside, still only his underwear, screaming, "We're free! The house is ours!"

I laugh, shaking my head as I pick up Bella and carry her in. Matteo is one funny kid.

Coaxing the kids upstairs, I manage to bribe them into getting dressed by promising to read them a book before they go. When Cristian starts crying, I send the two off to pick out the book they want, while I cross the hall to the master bedroom where Cristian sleeps in a small bassinet.

"Shh, shh," I coo, as I gently cradle his squirming body. "I've got you." I lay him against my chest, bouncing him as I walk across the hall to the nursery so I can change his rank diaper. "If I smelled that bad I'd cry too." I kiss the top of his downy soft baby hair.

Laying him down on the changing table I clean him up and put on a fresh diaper. His cries stop once he's no longer dirty, turning instead to small whimpers as he sucks on his closed fist. Swiping a binky I press it to his lips and his mouth opens greedily. I stifle a laugh as his siblings come flying into the room. Matteo holds the book protectively against his chest.

"We picked one," he announces, skidding to a halt before he slams into me.

"Alrightie, then." I take the book from him and sit down in the rocker, allowing Cristian to lie on my chest.

Bella and Matteo sit down cross-legged on the floor in front of me, but before I can even open the page the doorbell rings.

"He's here! He's here!"

Matteo and Bella take off out of the room, barreling down the stairs like their cute little butts are on fire.

"Don't you dare open that door!" I yell after them as I

get up with the baby and follow them at a much slower, less dangerous, pace.

They stand in front of the door, dancing on their toes while they wait for me to open it.

I unlock it, letting it swing open and—

"What are you doing here?" The words tumble out of my mouth in astonishment.

In front of me, Abel grins like he's won some fucking prize. "Blondie."

"Mr. Popular," I retort. "You didn't answer the question."

"Uncle Abie!" Matteo bounds at Abel and somehow —super human speed and strength, I guess—he's able to catch him.

"Uncle *Abe-e*?" I raise a brow and he shrugs, grunting as Bella launches like a missile at him too.

He steps inside with the two kids clinging to him like little baby monkeys.

"Matteo couldn't say Abel and Abie stuck." His eyes rake up and down my body and it feels like he's undressing me with each sweep. I've never had a look do that to me before and I hold back my shiver, because I don't want him to know what he does to me. "How's my littlest nephew?" He reaches out and his large hand swallows the infant's head whole.

"Ready for a bottle," I answer, but I'm positive it was a

rhetorical question so I immediately want to facepalm myself.

He moves toward the kitchen and somehow I'm the one following him. I don't think my brain has started computing since opening the door and finding him standing on the threshold. The last thing I expected was for Giulia's brother, the kids' *uncle*, to be Abel. I was expecting someone much older.

"Wait." I stop in my tracks and Abel does too, setting down the kids before looking at me over his shoulder. "You mean to tell me, you're staying the night here and watching three kids by yourself?"

He turns around fully. "Um, yeah." He crosses his arms over his chest and while it looks defensive, his smirk tells me this is entirely in challenge. He *likes* me underestimating him. I think the jerk gets complete enjoyment out of surprising me at every turn.

First, he's not *actually* a jerk. He's a decent guy.

Then there's the fact he's not the womanizer I thought he was.

Now, he's fucking Uncle Abie—actually make that Fuckable Uncle Abie. It's clear in only these few minutes he loves these kids and they love him, which means *dammit he's great with kids.*

He's the whole fucking package and for some reason, it makes me both want to hit him and fall dramatically into his arms like a damsel in distress—a damsel who promptly rips off her bodice.

I always did like sneak reading those bodice ripper novels my mom hid from me. Clearly, they've left an impression all these years later.

"Are you guys ready for the zoo?" His eyes are focused down below on the two eager children ready to soak in attention from him. Meanwhile, he opens a cabinet, blindly grabbing a cooler and pulling it down.

"Yes!" Matteo jumps up and down, barely able to contain his energy.

"Oh, yes," Bella responds, clutching her hands under her chin. It's her go-to gesture and I'm a sucker for it every time.

"You guys want peanut butter and jelly sandwiches for lunch?"

They nod eagerly and he gathers everything he needs while I grab breast milk from the freezer to prepare a bottle for Cristian.

Watching Abel, I remember the conversation we had about him living with his sister and her family. I just never imagined it would be one of the families I babysit for. What are the odds?

Fate, my mind whispers in my ear in quiet reminder.

"You should come."

It takes me a moment to realize Abel is talking to me.

"Huh?" I swivel around to look at him, sure I didn't hear him right.

"The plan was for me to only take these two," he tosses a thumb over his shoulder where Matteo and Bella pillage through the pantry for snacks, "while Cris stayed home with the sitter for the day, but since that sitter is you..." He trails off, shrugging his shoulders as he smears peanut butter across a slice of bread. When I don't say anything he stops, his eyes meeting mine. "You should come," he repeats.

Me, Abel, and three kids in a zoo. This sounds like the start of a really bad idea.

"Cristian and I will be fine here." My reply is hesitant, because frankly I'm not sure my ovaries can handle an entire day watching Abel interact with the kids.

He lays his hands flat on the marble counters. I stare at his hands. His tan, muscular hands, with thick, corded veins running up into his arms—

"What if I want you to go?"

"I ... I..." Words flee my brain. Up, up, and away they go too far out of my short reach to grab.

"It'll be fun," he says, and begins making a *fourth* sandwich. I guess it's decided then.

Abel, Matteo, Bella, Cristian, and I are all going to the zoo—as if this whole thing isn't enough of a zoo already.

Abel is driving a mini-van.

A mother-fucking *mini-van*.

And here I am riding beside him in the passenger seat with three kids in the back.

Just call us Mom and Dad.

Glancing behind me I peek in the mirror attached to the headrest so the driver can see the baby in the rearview mirror and find that Cristian has fallen sound asleep. Matteo and Bella are currently distracted by *Lilo and Stitch*, which immediately started playing when the car started.

My gaze drifts to Abel and I'm still stunned that he's here.

My brain seems to refute the fact that he's their uncle and now we're on a road trip of sorts—the drive to the National Zoo will probably take us at least two hours, especially with the weekend traffic.

Abel's lips turn up but he doesn't take his eyes off the road. "Like what you see, Blondie?"

My cheeks redden at being caught, but I stick my chin haughtily into the air unwilling to cower at being called out. "Maybe there's a bug on your face."

That smile of his widens. "There's not."

"So confident," I mutter, crossing my arms over my chest and staring out the windshield.

"Why wouldn't I be? You kissed me."

"I kissed you *back*, big difference." I kick my flip-flops off and rest my bare feet on the dashboard.

"Kissing back is still kissing."

"Ugh," I toss my hands up, "you're impossible."

"Impossibly handsome? Charming? Irresistible? All three? Definitely all three." He answers his own question.

"Abie? Are we dare yet? I wanna see the snakes. Sssssss. Snakes are my fave. Specially da yellow one. It looks like a banana. I wike bananas. Did you bwing bananas?"

I look over my shoulder at Bella and find that despite her question her eyes are glued firmly to the movie.

"Not yet, Princess. I'll make sure you see the snakes. And no, I didn't bring bananas but I'm sure I can get you one if you really want."

Princess? He calls her Princess? Be still my heart.

"Otay."

"How many times are they going to ask if we're there yet?" Humor laces my words, because we only left ten minutes ago and haven't even gotten on the interstate.

"Um..." He pretends to think. "Approximately a million more times. It's a blessing Cris can't talk yet."

"But he can cry."

"Don't remind me." He gives a small laugh and I know he's not at all bothered.

As he glances in the rearview mirror at the three kids something in my heart stirs. A longing, not for him, but for *this*—a family of my own with a husband who loves me and adores our children more than anything.

When Abel peeks at me, catching my eyes, something inside me jolts. I know it's my heart. I might think it's not him I'm longing for but my heart disagrees. That treacherous, emotional bitch is waking up and saying *him, I choose him.*

And that thought terrifies me because when something is *real* that's when your heart doesn't just hurt it *breaks.*

———

The trunk slowly lifts up and Abel and I stand behind it like we're waiting with bated breath for the villain in a movie to appear. Except, it's empty.

Abel curses under his breath and I smack his chest.

"Language." I narrow my eyes on him. "The kids can hear you."

Actually, they're watching *Toy Story* now and don't have a care in the world for us. In fact, I think they've entirely forgotten about the zoo.

"We forgot the stroller." He runs his fingers through his hair roughly and exhales a breath.

"*We* didn't forget anything, buddy." I waggle my finger at him. "I wasn't supposed to be going on this little outing of yours."

He glares at me. "Not helping, Lou."

"I was just stating facts, there's no reason to get snappy."

"Mhmm." He stands with his hands on his hips, staring at the empty trunk like he can magically will a stroller to appear.

"Maybe they have those stroller rental things," I propose.

He cocks his head in my direction. "I really fu—flipping hope so."

We unload the kids and I strap Cristian to my chest in one of those baby wrap things I find strewn on the floor. Abel grabs Bella into his arms and Matteo hops out, content to walk beside us. I'm sure Bella would walk too, but since she's small and the parking lot is busy it's safer to keep a hold of her.

A stroller is still necessary, though, because there's no way Bella's legs won't get tired.

After entering the zoo, we ask someone about strollers and are directed to the kiosk across from the Visitor Center to rent one.

Abel decides to splurge and spend twelve dollars for the double stroller in case Matteo gets tired of walking.

With the zebra decorated stroller in hand, he places Bella in it and we finally start through the zoo.

"Have you ever been here?" I pose the question as I

adjust the wrap so Cristian's head is protected from the sun.

"No. You?"

I shake my head, trying not to smile at how hot he looks pushing a stroller down the lane. Matteo stands between us, his hand clasped to the stroller. His head swivels around, taking in all the sights even though there are no animals to see yet.

"Snaaaakes." Bella makes a hissing noise. "I wanna seeeeee the snaaaakes."

Abel chuckles, leaning down to peer at her in the stroller. "I know, Bells. We're going to see the snakes."

"But when?"

"Yeah, when, Uncle Abie?"

Matteo looks up at Abel and I fight a grin. The kids' nickname for Abel is actually pretty adorable.

"Whenever we get to them." He laughs at the eager kids, not at all bothered with their pestering.

Glancing down at Cristian, I find him fast asleep, using my boobs as a pillow. At least those things come in handy for something other than being a major pain in my ass.

Walking around the zoo with Abel and the kids proves to be not only an adventure, but fun. I'm glad now he insisted I go, because this is an experience I wouldn't want to miss out on. Not the zoo itself, per se, but seeing Abel with his niece and nephews. He lifts Bella up onto his shoulders so she can see better and she covers his eyes with her chubby hands.

"I'm covering your eyes, Abie. You can't seeee," she sing-songs to him and his laughter fills the air. "Don't dwop me."

"I would never drop you, Princess."

Hey, Lou? It's your ovaries—we want that man to get you pregnant.

Abel takes her hands, peeling them off his eyes and turns to smile at me.

Heart stops. Skin dampens. Tummy drops. Butterflies explode.

"Having fun?"

If you were shirtless it would be even better.

I force the attacking butterflies away and nod. "So much fun."

We check out the lions, giraffes, zebras, and even tigers before we finally make it to the snake exhibit Bella has been begging to see. Even Matteo has now joined in on asking about them.

"It's time to see the snakes, Princess." Abel takes Bella out of the stroller and into his arms, using one hand to keep pushing it forward even though I step forward to take it. He shakes his head, urging me not to.

"I have two hands." I wiggle my fingers in a mockery of jazz hands. "Let me push it."

"No." He shakes his head adamantly.

"Men." I roll my eyes good-naturedly and he chuckles.

"What a beautiful family." At the words I turn and find one of the zoo workers smiling at us. "Would you like me to take a photo of you guys?"

I open my mouth to protest, to explain we're not a family, but Abel beats me to it.

"That would be great, ma'am. Thank you so much."

He unlocks his phone, opening the camera app, and hands it to her.

"Up you go, Bells." He lifts Bella back onto his shoulders. "Come here, Matteo." I stand there awkwardly, not sure what to do. Do I run away? Pretend I don't notice what's going on? "Lou?" He raises a brow. "Get over here."

The worker smiles at me. "Stand beside your husband."

My husband. Jesus, fuck.

I'm sorry for adding fuck after your name Jesus. I'm not very ladylike and I should definitely go to church more, so yeah, sorry. I'd say it won't happen again, but I know I'd be lying.

I skedaddle over to Abel and he holds onto Bella with one hand, wrapping his other around me. He pulls me in against his hard, muscular body and I try not to squeak.

He's hot, Lou. That's all. Stop acting like his touch means something to you.

But it does, it so does. It brings me to life in a way I've never felt before. My cells zing any time I'm near him and it's entirely unfair.

I'm allowed to be attracted to him. It doesn't mean love. It doesn't mean marriage. It doesn't even mean we'll have sex. This feeling can simply exist without anything happening.

Somehow, I don't believe myself.

"Smile," the worker coaxes.

I smile and at the last second I look up at Abel and find him looking down at me.

I glance away hastily, but it's not soon enough. It doesn't rid me of what I felt when I looked into his eyes.

The employee hands Abel his phone back and he smiles before tucking it into his pocket and letting Bella down.

"Thanks," he calls after her as she returns to her post.

Turning around, she smiles. "You're welcome. Enjoy the zoo."

Finally, we head into the snake exhibit and Bella screams so shrilly I'm certain my eardrum is going to burst.

"Snaaaakes! Snakes! Snakes Snakes!"

I glance at Abel, raising a brow. "She sounds like me when I want snacks. Do you know that little kid *snaaacks* GIF? That's me. I've never felt more connected to anything in the world than that GIF. I feel it on a spiritual level."

He busts out laughing, bending down to pick up Bella so she can peer into the glass at one of the snakes. Matteo stands on his tiptoes so he can see better and I feel my heart warm as Abel reads off the placard information about the snake.

Inspired by our previous photo, I take out my phone and snap one of Abel with his niece and nephew.

Cristian still snoozes peacefully against me, but I know soon he'll be ready for a bottle and diaper change. My stomach is also demanding lunch.

Abel carries Bella to the next window and Matteo tags along.

"Oh, hey. Look at this, Princess." Abel points inside. "It's your yellow snake you wanted to see."

"Oooh, pretty."

"It's actually called a yellow ball python," he explains.

She turns her big eyes up at him. "Dat's a long name. I want to call him Lemon."

"Lemon?" He chuckles, looking at me over his shoulder. "Lou hates lemon."

"Lemon *Starbursts*." I stick my chin in the air defiantly. "Lemon Starbursts are a cruelty against humanity."

"Is that so?" Challenge sparkles in his eyes.

From my purse I pull out a pink starburst and pop it

into my mouth—not before I stick out my tongue with the candy sitting proudly on the end.

"Can I have one?" Matteo holds out his hand eagerly and I grab another starburst and give it to him, taking the wrapper back when he unwraps it so he doesn't just toss it on the ground all willy-nilly. We're not litterers.

Before we can leave the snake exhibit another employee exits a side door with a snake wrapped around his shoulders.

"Can I pet it?" Bella shrieks from Abel's arms, reaching her chubby hands out for the snake like she wants to cuddle it.

"I don't know, we can ask."

My feet stay firmly rooted to the ground as Abel takes the kids over to the snake.

The snake that's not behind a glass enclosure.

The snake that's looking at me like I'd be a tasty morsel.

Dear Mr. Snake, I taste like Starbursts—not the good pink kind, but the yellow kind. They're the worst. You don't want to eat me.

The next thing I know, Bella is petting the snake and Abel is calling me over.

I shake my head adamantly. I'm not moving until that thing is *gone*.

"Lou!" Abel waves more frantically.

I shake my head again, wrapping my arms around the

baby strapped to my chest. "He's getting fussy. I'll just wait for you guys."

Abel eyes me. We both know the baby is still sound asleep and not fussing at all.

I sit on a throne of lies and I'm okay with it.

"Louise," he says sternly, "Hank here isn't going to bite you."

"Is Hank the man or the snake, because the snake definitely wants to bite me?"

The zoo employee stifles a laugh.

"Be brave." Abel stares at me, willing me to take a step and then another.

Fuck, why am I such a sucker for a challenge?

Somehow, in the next ten minutes Cristian ends up in Abel's arms and I have a snake wrapped around my shoulders.

"When my mom calls the pink phone hotline tonight and you have to tell her you caused my death, I hope she curses your very existence and you get some kind of rare rash on your balls that leads to your dick falling off."

Abel's lips quirk, fighting a smile while I internally freak out because *oh my fucking God there's a snake touching me.*

"Smile." Abel holds up his phone and snaps a photo. Hopefully the kids are too young to understand what the one finger salute I give the camera means.

"You're the Devil wrapped in a nice package," I grumble as the employee takes the snake back.

Abel grabs my waist and pulls me into his body. My palms land on his chest, but I tip my body back, not wanting to touch him because I'm *pissed* he convinced me to do that.

"My actual package is even nicer." He whispers the words seductively in my ear, and my treacherous eyes, *curse them*, drift down to the zipper of his jeans. He chuckles and releases me. "Come on, kids. Let's have lunch and then we'll see more."

"I hate you." If looks could kill the glare I'm smiting him with would have turned him to ash.

The jerk simply smiles even bigger. "No, you don't."

I don't.

After a potty break and a diaper change for Cristian, we find a picnic table in a shaded area near a café and sit down to eat the lunch Abel prepared.

He passes me a peanut butter and jelly sandwich. "I made it with extra love. That should earn me back points for the snake thing."

My eyes narrow. "You wish, bud."

He unwraps Bella's sandwich and hands it to her, fighting back a smile.

I try my best to feed Cristian his bottle while I eat, which leads me to balancing his bottle with my chin and feeding myself with my hand.

Whatever works, amiright?

Despite the whole snake incident, I'm glad I came with Abel and the kids. Watching him with them, this whole day really, makes a longing bloom in my chest.

After my past treatment with guys, I'd written the notion off for the time being, but the feelings he stirs in me makes me ache once more for love. Not lust, fleeting and insubstantial, but real true exhaustively beautiful and achingly painful kind of love.

One day, I'll have that, but for today I'm just going to enjoy this—a friendship I never thought I'd have, with a guy who's so much more than I believed him to be.

CHAPTER EIGHTEEN

Abel

When we arrive back at my sister's house, Lou and I unload the very sleepy kids, who immediately come to life when they smell the Happy Meals I picked up before getting here. Except Cris, of course, he keeps snoozing away.

"Lou, can you stay and tell us a story? You didn't get to do it before." Matteo watches her over the kitchen table, dipping his fry in honey mustard, just like Blondie beside me.

"Yeah, I can do that if Uncle Abie is okay with it?" She turns those impossibly blue eyes up at me, blinking her long dark lashes.

In an ideal world I'd lean forward, kiss her, and then defile her on the kitchen table, but with my niece and nephews in the house that won't be happening.

"I don't mind."

"Yay!" Matteo throws his hands up in the air and starts dancing on the chair.

"Sit down and eat your food." I point for him to park his butt and he does as he's told with a reluctant grimace.

Beside him, Bells smiles up at me showing her half-chewed chicken nugget in her mouth. Her yellow stuffed animal snake I bought her at the zoo is wrapped around her tiny body. It's aptly named Lemon despite Lou's protests against lemon anything.

Cristian begins to cry and Lou starts to get up to grab him, but I gesture for her to sit down. If she'd been any other sitter she would've been gone when we got back. Instead she's stuck around and, selfishly, I don't want her to go.

I cradle my squirming baby nephew in my arms and make him a bottle before I sit down again to finish my dinner.

I don't make a habit of eating fast food, but after the long day, I knew it was the easiest route to take with the kids. My sister might kill me for feeding her kids junk but when the cat's away the mice will play or something like that.

As soon as everyone's fed, Lou leaves me with the baby and goes to give the other two a bath. I protest, since I'm the one who volunteered to stay the night with them so my sister could have a night out for her birthday, but the kids tug her away saying they want Lou and not me. Frankly, neither one of us wants to argue with them.

I change Cristian into some footy PJs and rock him to sleep in my arms, humming like I've heard my sister do, and soon enough he's out. Carefully, I slip him from my arms into the bassinet beside the bed and turn on the camera so I can keep an eye on him. No way in hell am I sleeping in my sister's bed. That's fucking weird.

Tiptoeing out of the room—which is not easy for a guy my size—I ease the door closed and head down the hall where I detect voices coming from Bella's room.

"Make the voices." I hear Matteo plead. "You do the best ones."

The next second I hear Lou making voices for the characters in the story she reads. I stand outside the door, out of sight, smiling to myself.

When I peek around the door I find her sitting in the chair in Bella's room, with both kids seated eagerly at her feet. She's captured their attention and nothing else exists in their little world.

I'm not sure anything else exists in mine either, not for the moment at least. It's only her.

I venture into the room and Lou looks up, taking in my presence, before she returns to reading and acts like I'm not there.

Leaning against the wall with my arms crossed over my chest, I wonder how she can be so unaffected by my presence, because whenever I'm in a room with her she's all I feel and see anymore. I wasn't prepared for someone like her. Beautiful, smart, uniquely herself. Too many people try to be something they're not. Not Lou, she's who she is through and through and I not only admire that in her but I'm insanely attracted to it as well.

There are so many reasons I should stay away from her.

She's my roommate.

My promise to myself of no sleeping around this year.

I'm not good enough for her.

But all of those reasons fall on deaf ears.

She finishes reading the storybook and the kids plead with her for another.

She shakes her head, a smile dancing on her lips. "Nice try, guys. It's almost past your bedtime already and it's been a long day. We can read more stories next time."

"Come on, Matteo," I call out, and he turns around

from his cross-legged position on the floor. "I'll tuck you in."

"But I want, Lou." He pouts his lips, accentuating his whiney tone.

I shake my head adamantly and snap my fingers. "Lou's not even supposed to be here still. Bed, now. March those little legs." I urge him out the door, hands on his shoulders.

He looks up at me. "One day I'm going to have bigger legs than yours and I'll be telling *you* to march."

"Mhmm, *bed*."

Over my shoulder Lou laughs. "I'll get Bella to bed. Have fun with Matteo." Her eyes sparkle with laughter.

I leave her with Bells and get Matteo to brush his teeth before he climbs into bed. I draw the blankets up over him and tuck him in the way I've seen my sister do.

"Sweet dreams." I turn off the lights and push the button for his nightlight.

"The sweetest," Matteo echoes, and I smile. I love that my sister has carried over our mom's nighttime tradition with her kids.

I ease the door closed and head downstairs, making sure to keep my normally heavy footsteps quiet.

Lou stands in the kitchen, gathering up her stuff. She turns to face me and the way her fingers dance along the side of her leg I know she's nervous.

"Thank you for coming today."

"I like spending time with the kids."

I reach out and grasp a piece of her hair, watching the way her throat bobs and her eyes watch me steadily. "I like spending time with you."

In a normal circumstance, I'd bend down and capture her lips with mine. True, I've already kissed her, but I feel like we're both scared, dancing around our feelings and I don't want to constantly be making a move on her. The last thing I want is for her to think I'm just another one of those guys who took advantage of her and hurt her.

"Why?"

It takes my brain a moment to compute what she's asking.

"Because, you're smart, funny, sassy, kind, gorgeous —everything. You're everything."

"I-I should go." She backs away from me, her steps jerky as her eyes land anywhere around the room except on me.

I find myself desperate to keep her here. I don't know why. It doesn't make any logical sense, but suddenly the idea of watching her go while I stay behind isn't appealing.

"Stay." I let the word I know I should keep caged fall loose from my lips.

Her hands hang listlessly at her sides and when her eyes reluctantly meet mine I see the same question swimming in her eyes.

Why?

Mine answer, *I don't know.*

There's no logical explanation for what I feel for her, how quickly I was drawn to her, but I know I don't mind feeling this way.

She's one of the most genuine people I've ever met.

The silence stretches between us and finally she replies, "Fine, I'll stay. But *only*," she wags a finger at me, "if you get me Starbursts."

I grin, shoving my hands into my pockets. "Are you going to share?"

Her eyes sparkle back at me. "Only the yellow ones."

I drop the Walgreens bag onto the kitchen counter. "Your Starbursts, milady." I bow dramatically.

She shakes her head at me, fighting a smile as she grabs the bag and opens them. Dumping out the contents she sorts the pink ones to her side, yellow to mine, and puts the rest back in the bag.

I watch as she carefully unwraps one of the pink candies and pops it onto her tongue.

With a challenging grin, I reach out for the Starbursts. Not yellow, but pink—and not one, but the whole pile.

Her eyes narrow. "Don't you dare."

I lay my large hand over the pink candy and all the squares nearly disappear beneath.

"Abel," she says my name slowly, in warning.

In the blink of an eye, I swipe up the pink candies and make a run for it.

"Abel," she whisper-yells since the kids are sleeping, "I'm going to kill you."

I hear her feet padding behind me, but I'm taken off guard when the sound vanishes.

I grunt as she lands on my back, wrapping her body around mine and holding on like some kind of sloth or monkey.

"Give me my Starbursts back if you want your dick to ever feel the touch of a woman again." She reaches one short arm around me, trying to grab them from me, but I easily hold them out of her reach. "Abel," she growls, her hold tightening. "I will crush you like that Goddamn boa constrictor you made me hold."

"Is that a threat or a promise?" I glance at her over my shoulder and find her blue eyes barely peeking over.

She narrows them as I grab one pink Starburst.

"Don't do it." Her threat is clear, and I revel in the promise of it.

I unwrap it.

"Abel."

In my mouth it goes.

"I hope you choke."

I grin at her threat, showing the pink Starburst in my mouth.

I don't know what she does, or how she does it seeing as her entire body is clinging to mine, but suddenly I'm falling with her still attached to my back like some freakish ninja.

She doesn't let go as we fall.

I groan as I hit the hardwood floor and do, much to her satisfaction, choke on the Starburst as it gets lodged in the back of my throat. With a cough, it dislodges from my airway.

Rolling over I clasp my hands around her so she can't leave.

"That wasn't nice."

She stares down at me, her blonde hair every-which-way. "I told you not to touch my Starbursts."

I'd like to touch other things.

"You should learn to share."

She smiles in challenge. "I'm an only child. Sharing isn't in my vocabulary."

My fingers, of their own volition, skim the soft skin of her cheek. "You're beautiful," I murmur, and they flush.

"You're okay, I guess." She rolls her eyes playfully with a small shrug. For some reason, we haven't moved, but I find I'm okay with that.

My eyes flick to her lips and once again the urge to

kiss her sits in the pit of my stomach. Her eyes widen a fraction, waiting, maybe even hoping I'll do it.

But I took our first kiss, she owes me the next.

Somehow I find the will to stand us both upright.

She looks crestfallen that I didn't capitalize on the moment. Perhaps it's stupid of me, wanting her to come to me this time, but I want to know she feels something for me too.

"We should get ready for bed."

Her head nods jerkily and she tucks a piece of hair behind her ear. "Y-Yeah, we should."

I'm surprised she's not insisting on actually leaving considering what just went down, but maybe she's too stunned.

Grabbing my overnight bag I start to head to the bathroom to change when Lou speaks up from the kitchen.

"Abel?"

I pop my head around the corner. "Yeah?"

"I don't have anything to wear, considering, ya know, I was supposed to be home hours ago."

I should feel bad for asking her to stay. She probably had plans, or homework, or something far better to do than hang with me and three kids. But I don't. I'm glad she's here.

Unzipping my bag I pull out my favorite t-shirt for the football team and toss it to her.

She holds it up. "What exactly is this going to cover?"

I grin. "I'm curious to see."

"Ugh," she groans, the shirt flopping dramatically in her hands. "You're impossible."

She storms off in the direction of one of the bathrooms and I head to the other.

Since she took my shirt I end up only having a pair of my gym shorts to sleep in.

She's not back by the time I finish brushing my teeth and changing, so I fix the couch into a bed for myself, planning to give her the guestroom.

"I hate you." At her voice, I flip around and my throat goes dry.

Nothing could possibly prepare me for the sight of her in my shirt. It hugs every curve and barely skims the tops of her thighs. I can see a hint of pink panties peeking out from under the gray cotton tee. I should look away, staring is rude, but I can't help keeping my eyes latched onto her.

She's the most magnificent woman I've ever seen.

"This doesn't fit." She tugs on the bottom, trying to cover her legs more.

"Stop," I plead. My voice cracks and it's a higher pitch than normal. Her eyes flick up to meet mine.

"Oh, for fucks sake, now you're shirtless? Don't you guys know those shorts make women's brains go in all kinds of directions and *without* a shirt it's even worse." She waves her hand dramatically at me and then her eyes drop, her lips parting, and I know she's seen the bulge I can't hide. As soon as I laid eyes on her my dick came to life. "Oh," she whispers.

I flop my body onto the couch and grab a pillow, using it to cover my erection that's growing by the second and her staring isn't helping.

"Sit down," I beg, instead of command, looking at her over the back of the couch. "Let's put *Psych* on and then you can head up to the guestroom."

She moves around the couch, standing in front of me. Still she tugs on the bottom of my blasted shirt.

I've never wanted to be a piece of fabric so badly in my life.

"I'm not sure that's a good idea." Her eyes drop to the pillow in my lap before darting back up to me.

"If you go up to bed now all I'm going to be able to think about is what I want to do to you. I need a distraction."

Her eyes flash with something—interest, desire maybe—but it's gone too quickly for me to be sure what exactly it is.

"Okay." She grabs the remote and turns the TV on.

I let her take care of everything, hoping the show will distract me, but instead all I can focus on is the two feet separating us. I want to scoot closer to her, but I know it's a bad idea.

Staying away feels like an impossibility, but I know it's what I have to do.

The sound of Cristian crying from the monitor wakes me from a deep sleep. I'm not comfortable and as I blink my eyes open I see why.

Lou and I are tangled together with half of her body between my legs and the other lying across my stomach. She's on her stomach too, with her head twisted to the side. She's fast asleep and I don't want to wake her, I'm certain I could stay like this forever, but the screaming baby demands attention.

"Lou?" I give her a gentle shake. She doesn't stir. "Lou?" A little more insistent this time and she stirs, groaning in her sleep.

"Hmm?" she hums, blinking sleepy eyes at me. "Oh my God." She reels back and falls off the couch in her haste to get away from.

"Are you okay?" I sit up and offer her a hand.

"I *mauled* you in my sleep." She clutches a hand to the collar of her shirt—well, *my* shirt—and I'm pretty sure if there was a pair of pearls there she'd be clutching them instead.

"You didn't *maul* me. We fell asleep watching TV."

"My face was practically on your dick."

"I mean, as long as you don't bite I'm quite okay with that."

"Oh my God," she cries again, jumping up. I can't help but stare as her breasts jiggle with her hasty motions. "I should've gone home." She tugs on her hair, looking anywhere but at me.

"You do realize I'm your roommate now, correct? That means we *live* together. You can't exactly escape me."

Cristian's cries sound through the monitor.

"The baby." All thoughts of me flee from her mind as she runs for the stairs. "Why are we arguing when he's crying?"

It's been a minute, maybe less, since we started arguing, but I don't tell her that as I run behind her up the stairs.

She pushes open the partially closed door into the master and picks up Cris gently cradling him into her arms. He instantly quiets.

"Can you make a bottle for him?" She rocks him in her arms, looking at me over her shoulder.

"Yeah."

I should take him from her, tell her to go and I'm sorry for asking her to stay, but I don't. Instead, I do as she asks and go downstairs to make a bottle for the little guy.

When I carry it back upstairs I find the master empty.

Down the hall I find her in the nursery, rocking him in the chair and singing a lullaby softly. She has a nice voice. It's raspy, not at all what I would've expected.

I could stand there all day and watch her, but instead I force my feet one in front of the other and hold the bottle out to her.

"Thanks." She takes it and presses it to his eager mouth. "I'll get him settled back down."

It's code for *go away I don't need you*, but I don't budge. I sit down on the floor by her legs and she exhales a breath.

"What are we doing, Abel?"

"I don't know."

It's hardly an answer, but it's the only one I have.

CHAPTER NINETEEN

Lou

"Boys suck." I wrap my lips around my Starbucks pink drink, making an awful sucking noise in the process that earns me a few glares from other guests in the coffee shop, but I hardly care.

"You're not telling me anything new," Miranda huffs, adding sugar to her already sugary latte. I take another sip, savoring the strawberry flavor on my tongue.

Anything strawberry I'm a sucker for—clearly. "So, what's pretty boy done now?"

She stirs her drink, waiting for my reply.

"I haven't seen him much this week. It's like he's avoiding me."

"You did fall asleep on his dick." She places the lid back on her cup and lifts it in a toast. "That's unacceptable during a blowjob."

"I wasn't giving him a blowjob." She knows this. "And *he* asked me to stay." I exhale a heavy breath before continuing my rant. "Guys think girls are so complicated, like we're the ones who send mixed signals. I call bullshit. They're way worse than us."

"I mean ... you could finger his asshole and probably get all kinds of answers. Some guys love that shit."

"Miranda," I whine, nearly spitting out my drink, "I didn't bring you here for this."

"You didn't even bring me. *I* picked you up."

"Semantics. Besides, I bought the coffee."

"You're not even drinking coffee."

"Semantics."

"God, you're moody today. Are you on your period?"

"No," I snap. When she narrows her eyes I add, "I'm supposed to start tomorrow, okay?"

"Mhmm." She hums as she takes a sip of her extra sugar latte. "Where's Slim Shady today?"

"He said something about going to the mall."

She grins wickedly and I know something terrible is about to go down.

"Then so are we."

"This is ridiculous."

"You didn't say *over*."

"This is ridiculous. *Over*." I speak into the walkie-talkie Miranda gave me.

I don't even want to know why the fuck she has walkie-talkies and *disguises* in her car as if this is an every day occurrence.

"It's not ridiculous. And don't forget to use my code name. Over."

I press the button, speaking into the tiny device I'm pretty sure she bought at a kid's store. "I'm wearing a fucking mustache and bucket hat speaking into a walkie-talkie. People are staring."

She doesn't respond.

"Miranda?"

Nothing.

"Do you see him?"

Oh My Fucking God, she's really going to make me do this.

"MacDaddy-Spank-My-Titties, are you there? Over."

"Why, yes, I am, Louis-Vuitton's-Dirty-Ball-Sack. No,

I don't see him, and let people stare. They're just jealous they don't have a fake mustache and a walkie-talkie. This is very important spy business. Over."

"We look like we're twelve."

Nothing.

"MacDaddy-Spank-My-Titties, we look twelve. We need shorter code names. These ones are ridiculous. Over."

"LVDBS, you vetoed the My Little Pony ones I came up with. Over."

"MDS—oh fuck this shit, it's stupid. Where'd you even go? Over."

"Fine, forget the code names. Just look around the corner. Over."

I lean around the potted plant I'm hiding behind, not very well I might add, and find Miranda waving at me from behind a column that's in plain sight of everything, wearing a large hat with yellow feathers.

She looks like fucking Big Bird.

"These disguises suck. Over."

"Stop dissing my idea. We need to keep our eyes open for the subject. I'll check out another part of the mall. Over."

"Ditch the hat first, Big Bird. Over."

"You suck. Over."

I watch as she grabs the hat and dramatically tosses it

in a trashcan, leaving behind a trail of evidence in the form of yellow feathers.

The two of us head in different directions of the mall, searching the stores for Mr. Popular, but never see him. I feel stupid, even once I toss the bucket hat and fake handlebar mustache in a trashcan. This is borderline stalkerish ... okay, *actually* stalkerish, and I don't know why Miranda thought this was a good idea.

Yes, it's been a week since Abel and I have actually talked other than a quick *how are you* or *see you later*, but this is insane. I don't know why I let Miranda talk me into this.

I'm on the far end of the mall, inside the Belk store I'm ninety-nine point nine percent positive Abel would never set foot in when Miranda screeches across the walkie-talkie earning me glares from the old ladies shopping.

"The subject has not been spotted. I repeat, has not been spotted. He's nowhere to be found. Over."

"Well, I'm hungry. Over."

"Me too. Over."

"Food court? Over."

"Yeeeees," she drawls. "Over." She tacks it on at the end in a stern tone.

Turning off the walkie-talkie I stuff it in the back of my jeans pocket and head across the mall to the food court.

Spotting Miranda I direct her to the line for Chinese food. "You get lunch, I'll get dessert."

"I like the way you think." She salutes me, her brown locks swishing as she twirls dramatically and heads for the end of the line.

I stand in line at the donut stand, a new addition to our mall and perhaps the best thing here.

My mind strays to Abel, even though I've tried to keep those thoughts on a careful leash, but I'm completely baffled by the kiss beneath the pavilion and then last weekend with the kids ... it seemed like things were headed in a certain direction and now he's been radio silent.

Maybe it's presumptuous of me to assume it has anything to do with me. He could be stressed about classes, or football, or any number of things in his life that I have no idea about.

Finally it's my turn to order, and I get a dozen for good measure. I don't want to know any psycho who only gets what they *need*. You always *need* more donuts.

Grabbing the box, I head in Miranda's direction, finding her struggling with a tray of food and our drinks. I grab the drink holder from her and we pick a table near the windows, overlooking the parking lot and movie theater attached to the mall.

"I've never been so hungry." She plops down with her declaration, opening her Styrofoam takeout box.

Setting everything down, I grab my food box and a fork.

As soon as I open the lid, I'm hit with the delicious tangy smell of sesame chicken.

"Mmm." I spear a bite of chicken and hum as I chew it.

"Do we have any idea what pretty boy could actually be up to?" She wipes her mouth on a napkin, giving me a serious look as she does, and I know without a doubt she's already brewing her next spy mission.

"No, no, no." I wave my arms frantically like I'm trying to land a plane. "It's a waste of time trying to figure him, or any guy, out. I've been down this path before and mixed signals are a hard pass for me. If a guy likes you, he'll let you know, and right now, he's ignoring me, so I take that to mean he's not interested and doesn't know how to tell me."

"Lou." Her face falls.

"I've been with his type before. It never ends well."

For a girl like me.

I feel anger at myself the second the thought comes to me.

What *is* a girl like me, exactly? I'm beautiful, confident, happy, smart, and fucking *thriving*. I'm just like everyone else. My past mistakes with guys have nothing to do with me, and everything to do with the wrong kind of guy.

"He seems different."

"Seemed," I correct. "He *seemed* different."

I still think Abel is different, I have to give him credit there, but I also have to accept the fact that something between us scared him away. Our chemistry is intense, and it's one thing that can't be faked. It's enough to scare anyone, including myself.

Definitely myself.

"Does he know you *like* him? Maybe he thought he was being too pushy? Guys don't like to do *all* the chasing, you know."

"I honestly don't know, and I'm not going to waste my time trying to figure it out."

I close the lid on my takeout and reach for the box of donuts.

Donuts won't do you dirty like men will.

"Well, if you're sending him mixed signals…" She trails off, giving a small shrug and a look that says *then it's your fault.*

I give her my best withering death stare and grab a donut.

I bite into it and suppress a moan at the delicious, doughy, flavor.

"What did the world do before donuts?" I wonder out loud.

"No idea." She grabs a chocolate-covered sprinkle one for herself.

Taking another bite I get to the best part, the cream filling. "You know," I swipe a bit of the white filling and lick my finger clean, "cum is such a nasty, dirty word. Crème de la penis is much more enticing."

Miranda's eyes widen, and I think it's at my crudeness, but she's not looking at me.

"Crème de la penis, huh, Blondie?"

I spit bits of donut across the table, some even landing on poor Miranda as my head whips around to find Abel standing *right* behind me.

He grins, tilting his head as his eyes take in the mess I've made. "So you're a spitter, not a swallower? Good to know."

I don't embarrass easily. I'm *always* doing something stupid, but this ... yeah, this is really freaking embarrassing.

"Um..." I flounder searching for words.

What are werds?

His smile grows. "What are you guys doing?"

Before Miranda can fill him in on our spying I blurt, "We really wanted donuts."

"Donuts *or* ... crème de la penis?" His eyes sparkle with amusement and I want to crawl under the table and die.

"Lou definitely needs anything involving a penis."

I kick my best friend beneath the table and she groans.

"Well," Abel tosses a thumb over his shoulder, "I have some things to do, but I'll see you later. It's been a busy week. Coach has been running us through the ringer, so I'm sorry I haven't been around."

Miranda gives me a shit-eating grin that says *see, he wasn't avoiding you*.

"Yeah, see you later."

I need him to go, far away, preferably to a whole other state, while I recover from my mortification.

I watch him walk away, and when I turn around to find Miranda laughing her ass off at me, I toss it at her and mutter, "I hate you."

She picks it up and pops it in her mouth. "You might hate me, but you want a taste of Abel's donut."

She punctuates it with a wink.

I can't even argue, because she's right.

CHAPTER TWENTY

Lou

Walking into the empty apartment, I drop my stuff in my bedroom, change into comfy clothes, and then proceed to clean the apartment from top to bottom like a madwoman.

If I clean like crazy, then I can't possibly think about Abel and the fiasco at the mall.

Crème de la penis. I'm an idiot. Why doesn't someone

ever tell me to shut up? Like come on Miranda, you could've given me a warning that he was right there.

Blasting a playlist full of songs from the Backstreet Boys, N*SYNC, Spice Girls, One Direction, and my beloved Jonas Brothers, I dance along to the music as I dust off shelves. It helps empty my mind for the most part.

Dancing my way over to the jar of Starbursts I reach for a pink one, popping it into my mouth as I sing along to the Jo Bros song *Lovebug*.

"Oh my God!" I scream spitting out the Starburst.

It lands on my already mopped tiled kitchen floor. Only instead of being pink like it should be, it's fucking yellow.

"Bleh, nasty!" I dash to the refrigerator and grab a Capri-Sun to get rid of the disgusting lemon taste clinging to every one of my taste buds.

Slurping down the Capri-Sun, a thought occurs to me and I tiptoe across the floor to the container. I get my hand around another pink one and pull it out, unwrapping it carefully.

Yellow.

Once, I could see it possibly being a manufacturing error and a stray yellow Starburst ended up in a pink wrapper, but *twice*? That's too much of a coincidence for me.

Picking another I remove the wrapper, again, it's yellow.

Before I know it I've opened more than ten Starbursts that should be pink and delicious strawberry, but they're all yellow and stupid, no good, disgusting lemon.

"Abel!" Grabbing the Starbursts I carry them and the wrappers, tossing them on his perfectly made bed.

As I storm out of his room, the front door opens and he appears in the flesh.

"You suck," I cry, and pounce on him.

His eyes widen in startled surprise, but his arms wind around my body anyway, keeping us upright as the door closes behind him.

"What'd I do?"

So fucking innocent.

"You covered all the yellow Starbursts with pink wrappers! You tricked me!"

"Still don't like lemon?" That cocky grin of his surfaces, and with him holding me—his hands cupping my ass—we're eye level.

"No! No one in their right mind *likes* lemon."

"I do." His voice lowers and he reaches up tentatively to capture a lock of hair that decided to go rogue and hightail itself out of my messy bun. "And I like you."

His words freeze me in place.

I've barely seen him this week and in that time my

brain went on a tailspin, telling me lies about why he wasn't around, and it's hard to reconcile what it deluded me into believing wasn't the truth.

And the truth is, for whatever reason, we like each other.

Fate, my mind taunts me.

Fate has been my guiding force in life. I've relied on it to steer me in the right direction, to show me reason when things don't make sense.

Abel and I ... we don't make sense, but somehow we do.

The words *I like you too* are on the tip of my tongue, but I don't release them.

Instead, I show him.

Our lips collide and my fingers delve into his silky dark locks, pulling him closer.

With him holding me like this, my pussy presses against his groin and an ache fills my belly.

There are so many reasons why I shouldn't be going down this path.

He's my roommate.

We're kind of sort of friends now.

I swore off guys.

But I throw all those worries out of my brain.

Fate keeps pushing me toward Abel, and I've always trusted that bitch, so why should now be any different?

His back knocks into the door from the force with which I kiss him. We're both frantic, gasping, absolutely needy with desire for each other. I feel like a spark has been lit and now we're combusting.

"You're making me break all my rules." He murmurs the words in a low growl, his brown eyes darker than normal. Before I can ask what he means, we're kissing again and all rational thought goes out of my mind.

His hold tightens around me and I clasp his face between my hands, the stubble there rubbing roughly against my palms. He carries me away from the door, and with what feels like only a few steps thanks to his long legs, we're in my room with the softness of my mattress suddenly pressing against my back.

My legs fall open and his body fits between them like he was always meant to rest there.

A low growl hums in his throat as we kiss, and I gasp when he grabs my hands, forcing them above my head.

He trails kisses down the curve of my neck, and I really wish I was wearing something much cuter than the sweatpants and sweater I tossed on when I got home. My clothes scream frumpy homebody, not *dear roomie, fuck me.*

Thankfully, Abel doesn't seem to notice, or if he does he clearly doesn't mind because his erection pressing into me tells me he's all for it.

This day has gone from 0 to 100 faster than seems possible. It's all too easy to misinterpret something and have your mind spin it into something it's not.

"I don't know what it is," his breath is husky as his fingers glide under my sweatshirt, "but I'm fucking crazy for you. You're all I can think about."

The feeling is mutual, but my brain isn't working properly to give him any sort of response.

His lips find mine once more as he removes one hand from mine, but is still careful to keep a tight hold so I can't move, and cups my face with it. Tilting my head back he kisses me with fervor, a desperation to devour me.

I've never been kissed like this before.

It's not sloppy, or possessive.

It's worshipful, like I'm some goddess lying beneath him and he's desperate to win my favor.

He grinds his hips against me and mine rise to meet his.

My fingers push against his hand, wanting to break free, to touch and feel him.

"Not yet, Blondie." His voice is a croon as he rubs his lips against the shell of my ear.

I let out a small whimper, unable to stop the sound from leaving my lips.

He gives a small chuckle, his chest vibrating against mine and my whimper turns to a moan.

His kisses grow more urgent and need builds low in my belly, ready to combust, even though he hasn't really touched me. I'm going to explode when he finally does.

He releases my hands and I cry out in relief. Before I can touch him, he's pulling away and shoving my sweater up and over my body revealing my jog bra. Girls with big boobs like mine don't get to wear cute bralettes, this is the best we can do. The way his eyes take in my breasts makes me think he doesn't care that it's not some lacy scrap of nothing.

He wants *me*, not what I'm wearing, and fuck if that doesn't make my pussy pulse with need. There's an ache I need filled and he's the only one who can.

I sit up and reach for the bottom of his shirt. I lift it slowly, but he grabs the hem and rips it off, tossing it to a far corner of my room.

Grasping my chin he lowers his head, devouring my lips once more. I just want to get to the good part, but he's determined to drag this out and savor every moment.

I reach out as he kisses me, finding the button and zipper of his jeans.

"Lou," he rasps as I rub my hand over his length.

My eyes flick up to his. He still holds my face in his hands, but he's frozen, his breath the only indicator he's still alive.

I'm not inexperienced in the sex department, even if most of those encounters weren't the best time, and it's safe to say *none* of those guys ever looked at me like Abel is. It's the kind of look some people spend ages searching for, only never to discover it.

My brain screams at me to not let this go, that this is the guy I've been hoping for all along, but I'm still afraid of getting hurt. Not scared enough to stop this, however.

"C-Can I touch you?" My question doesn't sound nearly as confident as I meant it to, but his look has stripped me bare of all my pretenses and walls. There's something about my vulnerability that seems to make this moment mean infinitely more. What's about to happen between us, it isn't going to just be sex.

It's more. So much more.

He gives a small nod, so insubstantial that at first I don't realize he has until he whispers, "God, yes."

I stand up, which forces him to take a step back.

His eyes are on me as I lower to my knees in front of him.

"I've never done this before," I admit, and his eyes widen a fraction.

"Sex?" The words leave him in astonishment.

I laugh a little, tugging his shorts down past his perfect ass. "A *blowjob*," I emphasize. "I've never met someone worth kneeling for."

"Fuck." His head drops back. "I think that's the hottest thing I've ever heard."

I tug his jeans off the rest of the way and he steps out of them.

He's left in nothing but his black boxer-briefs. His erection presses against the confines of fabric and I glide my hand along his length, air hissing between his teeth as I do. I rise up a little higher, licking a trail from his navel down and stopping at the band of his briefs.

His hands reach for my hair, fisting it in his large hand.

"Don't tease me," he begs, his eyes pleading.

"Me?" I blink innocently. "Never."

I might not have ever given a blowjob, because like hell was I ever kneeling for any of my douchebag hookups, but it seems easy enough to figure out.

Or maybe all the porn I've watched has just made it seem that way.

Regardless, here goes nothing.

I hook my fingers into his boxer-briefs, looking up at him as I do, and tug them down.

His giant dick smacks me in the face and I grab my cheek in surprise. "Oh my God."

I eye the monster cock in front of me.

"What the hell am I supposed to do with that?" I blurt.

He chuckles huskily, entirely amused, but I'm not kidding. This thing is *huge*. Like porno huge.

God, what is with me and porn tonight? I have the real deal right here.

"It's a good thing I like a challenge."

I grip him in my hand and he lets out a low moan. My tongue slides out and I lick the tip of his cock, rubbing my tongue back and forth over the sensitive skin.

When I take him in my mouth, well as much as I can, his knees start to shake.

If he falls, I'm pretty sure my throat will be impaled by his cock and if that isn't one hell of a way to go then I don't know what is.

Here lies Lou. Death by cock decapitation.

My mother would be so proud of that.

Stop thinking about your mother, Lou! She does not belong anywhere near this situation!

"Lou." He growls my name in a husky moan as I guide my mouth up and down his length.

I never thought I'd like this, and maybe if I'd done it with those other guys I wouldn't have, but I like knowing what I do to him is making him weak.

His quiet begging, pleading, and my name as a prayer on his lips is something I could get used to.

"Never done this before? I call bullshit," he gasps, his fingers flexing in my hair as he holds it back.

I let him go with a *pop* and his cock sways tauntingly in front of me.

"It's true. I think I just like your cock."

"Fuck, woman," he growls. "Bed. Now."

My eyes widen at his command, but I obey, crawling on the bed.

He yanks my sweatpants off within seconds and I giggle as they fly across my room and knock over a lamp. Abel doesn't even notice.

"You're wearing too many clothes." His tone is frustrated even though I'm only in my bra and panties now.

I sit up and pull my bra off and I swear my boobs sigh out loud in relief at no longer being trapped. My boobs are big, with stretch marks, and are far from perky but Abel's eyes lap them up like he's ready to devour a tasty morsel.

Sometimes, I can't help but think about my thick thighs or pudgy belly when getting naked in front of a guy. I'm confident, but that doesn't mean I don't have my insecure moments, and usually they arise in these situations when I'm bare and exposed to another human being.

But Abel doesn't look at me like he wishes I was someone else, or that my body was different. He just sees me, as I am, and he loves it.

"You're beautiful. So fucking beautiful."

He kisses me, sucking the air from my lungs. I feel him grasp my panties and I wiggle my ass to help him get rid of them.

He breaks the kiss, gazing at me beneath him.

We're both stark naked, but there is no embarrassment, only longing and a feeling of *need* I never knew could exist.

He's become the oxygen in the room, my way to another breath, and if he doesn't touch me I'm going to suffocate.

He lowers his body and I gasp when his tongue swipes along my center. My fingers grip the sheets and my hips move of their own accord, trying to get closer to his mouth.

He swirls his tongue around my clit and I moan, slapping a hand over my mouth in the process to quiet my sounds.

His mouth leaves me for a moment and he grabs my hand, jerking it away.

"I want to hear you, to see you. I want everything. Don't deny me this."

His words elicit a whimper from between my lips. I'm used to hard, fast, over-before-you-know-it, sex. Not *this*.

I don't think I've ever experienced this amount of pleasure before.

"Abel," I moan his name, my fingers tugging at his hair. "Oh my God."

My hips roll against his mouth of their own accord.

He sucks on my clit and my back bows off the bed as an orgasm shatters through my body.

Holy fucking shit.

"It should be illegal to have an orgasm that good."

Abel chuckles as he makes his way up my body, placing kisses strategically on my skin as he goes.

One kiss is pressed to the top of my pubic bone.

My belly button.

My breasts.

Until he reaches my lips, pressing a long lingering kiss there. I taste myself on his tongue and I find I don't mind it. His erection brushes against the inside of my legs and I shiver, anticipating the feel of it in my body.

"Condom!" I cry suddenly, my arms careening where I whack him across the face. "We need a condom!"

"Hell, Blondie." He rolls off of me and grabs his face. "I think I'm going to get a black eye."

"Well, at least then we'll be even—considering your massive dick punched me in the face."

He gives a soft chuckle as I turn onto my stomach and reach over to my bedside table and grab a condom out of the little trinket box there. I'm pretty sure my mother intended for me to put jewelry there, or something else equally as respectful, but it's an excellent place to store condoms.

I feel Abel's hand palm my ass and I turn my head slightly, looking at him behind me. His body looks like it's carved from stone, all hard planes, and angular slopes. My body, by comparison, is fluffy and dimpled but both of us are equally perfect in our own unique ways.

"Love your ass," he murmurs. I don't think he even knows he's said the words out loud.

"You can fuck my ass some other time. Pussy first." I slap the condom down on the bed covers and his long fingers reach out to grab it.

His eyes heat at my words and my heart dips.

We're doing this.

We're actually going to do this.

I'm going to fuck my roomie.

Deep down I know this will be more than just a fuck. It both scares and exhilarates me.

He rips open the foil square and rolls the condom on. It barely fits and he smirks when he notices where I'm looking.

He has every right to be cocky packing a weapon like that. My vagina might break.

Not going to let that stop me, though.

His body hovers over mine and his dark hair brushes my forehead as he looks down at me.

"Ready?"

My eyes rise to his instead of staring below where his cock rests at my entrance.

I nod, even though I'm not.

It's not that my body isn't ready, or that I'm having doubts. It's my heart I'm worried about. I'm not sure I'm ready for how this will change things.

I guess the fact of the matter is things changed a long time ago.

He wraps his hand around his cock and I tense when it pushes against my entrance.

"It's just me," he whispers huskily in my ear. "Look at me." I do. "It's me and you, Lou."

"Me and you." I mirror his words as he pushes into me, slowly. "Oh my God," I shudder out a moan as he fills me to the hilt. I can't even begin to fathom where I end and he begins. As cheesy as it sounds, we've become one.

"Fuck, you feel so good. Better than I imagined." His words are a raw, guttural sound, entirely manly and sexy all at once.

"You imagined this?" The words blurt from me in surprise.

"More times than I want to admit," he rasps, pumping in and out of me. My body stretches to accommodate his length and girth. "Your fucking shower has witnessed me rub more than one out."

I grasp his stubbled cheeks in my hands and kiss him. I'm beyond turned on by the knowledge that he's fantasized about me. It makes this mean even more than it did before. This isn't spontaneous. This is something we've been heading toward for a while and it finally just ... exploded.

"Fuck, you feel so good."

He grasps my left leg, pushing it toward my chest. The new angle sends him deeper inside me and I gasp out a raw, *"Yes."*

My hands slide up the hard planes of his chest, settling at his shoulders as he pumps in and out of me. He's not using my body as a means to an end, he's taking his time, and making sure I'm enjoying this.

His hand moves between our bodies and when it makes contact with my clit, a startled breath puffs out of my lips.

"Oh my God. Don't stop," I bite out, my head tipping back from the pleasure.

He uses the opportunity to his advantage, sucking on the skin of my exposed neck. Normally, I'm ticklish in that spot, but for once I don't mind my neck being touched.

"I'm gonna cum, don't stop." I keep begging, and with a strangled gasp my orgasm shatters through my body. I swear I lose consciousness for a few seconds.

He pumps into me a few more times before he reaches his climax. I watch his face in awe as he growls through the shudders wracking his body. He pulls out of me and I lay there, feeling entirely broken in, as he gets rid of the condom in the wastebasket.

My mattress dips as his body joins mine on the bed.

I know I should get up and go pee, but I just need another moment to let my world turn right side up again.

His arm wraps around me, pulling me against him until we're rolled over on our sides facing each other.

"That was…" He begins, searching for words.

Incredible.

Life-changing.

Earth shattering.

"I know."

CHAPTER TWENTY-ONE

Abel

An alarm blares and I blindly slam my hand to shut it up, except my hand smacks against solid wood.

Opening my eyes, I slowly blink into awareness, taking in my surroundings.

A pink hue cascades over my body and I look up, finding Lou's neon sign above the bed.

Turning my head I find her spread out beside me on

her stomach, the sheet barely covering her ass. She begins to stir as the alarm penetrates her sleep like it did mine.

Consciousness hits me fully and I realize it's not an alarm clock we're hearing.

"Shit, Lou, wake up." Even though she's nearly there I shake her roughly, jolting the last recesses of sleep from her. "There's a fire."

"Fire!" Her limbs flail and I nearly take a knee to the face as she rolls out of bed and falls on the floor.

Since we're still both stark naked, we scramble to yank clothes on and rush outside, where other tenants are gathering. In the distance, I hear the sounds of sirens.

I don't see any smoke, so I'm hoping it's a false alarm.

I glance down at Lou and see she's wearing my shirt, my shorts, and a pair of bunny slippers with a robe haphazardly hanging over top of her shoulders.

It's only when she looks at me that I realize I'm only wearing my underwear because *she's* in my clothes. She snickers as she looks me up and down.

"Here, take this." She shrugs off the robe and holds it out to me.

"It's not that cold." I wave the outstretched unicorn robe away.

She rolls her eyes. "You're practically naked. Put it on."

I grin. "Only because you took my clothes off."

She stifles a laugh and shakes the robe. "You're going to freeze."

"So concerned about my health." I finally take the garment and force my arms into the sleeves. It's stretched around my muscles and I swear I hear a stitch or two tear.

"I need you well and whole if you're going to fuck me like that again." She smirks up at me, crossing her arms beneath her breasts.

"Again, huh?" I try to hide my grin behind my hand, but then I *do* hear stitches in the sleeves rip, so I let my hand drop to my side.

Lou tilts her head, appraising the building as the sirens grow closer.

"Maybe Jamie was blowing out a candle and his hair caught on fire from all that hairspray he uses. You know, a big *whoosh*." She gestures with her hands, trying to show an explosion.

I snort at the visual. "I didn't think Jamie lived here?"

"He doesn't, but sometimes he hooks up with one of the girls who lives upstairs," she points her out in the crowd, "and she always lights this obnoxious candle that smells up the whole fucking building, I swear. I call it her sex candle."

"That so?" I raise a brow. "Do you have a sex candle?"

She shakes her head. "No, Starbursts are my kind of aphrodisiac."

"Does that mean you can get turned on by *lemon?*"

"I still can't believe you switched all my pink Starbursts with yellow ones."

"I also threw the pink ones away instead of rewrapping them."

The fire truck turns the corner, coming to a screeching halt in front of the building.

Lou is oblivious to the men in yellow filing into the building, where I now can see smoke slipping from a window upstairs. Her eyes are focused on me, her jaw dropped open.

"That's just ... no. First and last blowjob for you."

I chuckle, pressing a hand to her back and she squeaks as she collides with my body. My growing erection presses into her and her blue eyes jump to mine. "We both know that's a lie."

I'm not sure if her shiver is from my words or the cool air. I know giving her the robe back would be pointless. She's tenacious.

I ghost my fingers over her cheek and her eyes drift closed as if she's remembering exactly how and where I was touching her earlier.

My vow of celibacy sure as hell didn't last long. But I wasn't expecting this girl when I made it.

"Do you ever feel like you've spent your whole life waiting for something and when you finally have it, nothing changes, it just feels impossibly and unexpectedly right?"

I don't answer her with words. I kiss her.

Yeah, Lou. I know exactly what you mean.

It feels like forever before we're finally let back into the apartment. One of the upstairs apartments left their oven on and … well, thank God for alarms and the fire department. Luckily, the damage is minimal and contained so everyone except that tenant is allowed to return to their homes.

Lou stomps inside tiredly and collapses onto the couch, tossing an arm dramatically over her eyes.

"I can't go on. Is life canceled yet?"

I hover over her. "Sorry, Blondie, life goes on even when we don't want it to."

She lowers her arms and pouts. "I never want to see cute firemen again unless it's because I'm at the station playing Bingo."

"You really do play Bingo?" I fight to hide my smile, but it's kind of hard to and she tosses a pillow at me that I let bounce off my chest. I'm pretty sure if I moved my arms to deflect it, her robe would rip to shreds. I shrug out of it and toss it on the chair before I damage it further.

"Of course I play Bingo. It's *fun*. That bitch Blythe is a cheat, though." She wags a finger at me. "I don't know how she does it, but she is. I'm going to figure it out one of these days."

"I want to go."

She looks at me in stunned surprise. "You, Mr. Popular, want to go with *me* to Bingo? Are you feeling okay? Do you have a fever?" She sits up to press the back of her hand to my forehead which she can't even reach.

I laugh, sitting my ass down on the coffee table so I don't have to keep straining my neck to look at her.

"You make it sound fun."

She narrows her eyes. "I'm still never going to a football game."

I grab her outstretched hand and playfully nip her fingers. "Never, Blondie? You know what they say about that word?"

"What?" She blinks at me, her eyes growing heavy with lust.

I bend and press a kiss to her cheek before I slide my lips to her ear.

"Never say never."

CHAPTER TWENTY-TWO

Abel

"What did he just say?" I lean over, trying to peer at Lou's Bingo board and what block she stamped but she covers her board with her hands. "It's not like I can cheat!" I cry in irritation. "We have completely different boards."

"Go buddy up with Blythe then. If you don't hear it, it's not my fault."

I'm beginning to regret my decision to join Lou for

Bingo night. She's right, this isn't a game, it's a goddamn sport—a fight to the death based on the way all these old people and Blondie are going at it.

The older gentleman that calls out letters and numbers does it so quickly I'm convinced he must actually be an auctioneer.

By the time I give up he's already called out three more numbers and I stare helplessly at my board.

"Gotta learn to keep up." Lou bumps my arm with her elbow, punctuating her joking banter.

"There is no keeping up. This is insanity."

"I'm doing just fine." She places a dot over whatever has been called this time. How she can have a conversation with me and still listen to this dude is beyond me.

"That one's crazy." Blythe, the lady Lou can't stand, sits on my other side.

She's ninety, been married seven times, and has already grabbed my ass.

Spitfire, that one. I feel like I'm looking at the future version of Lou—hopefully sans the seven husbands part.

"She's crazy," I agree with Blythe and Lou's jaw drops, "but I like her."

Her open mouth quickly turns into a smile. A small amount of color flushes her cheeks.

It's only been a week since we slept together, and it's happened repeatedly since. We haven't put a label on what we are, but I know what I want, and it's her as my girlfriend.

"I like you, too."

"Cheesy fucks, either play the game or find a closet. There's one that way and to your right. I've used it with Henrietta," Chuck, the old guy sitting across from us speaks up. I start to laugh, but when he glares at me, it turns into a cough.

"Shut up, Chuck." Lou sticks her tongue out at him and he laughs.

Her camaraderie with these people is endearing. It's obvious she's been coming here for a while and gotten to know these people. When we first arrived she walked around greeting people, asking about their families, all the while introducing me as her roommate.

That part grated on my nerves, because I want to be her boyfriend. I haven't had a serious girlfriend, but it feels right for us. For now, I'm not saying anything since I'm trying to feel her out and see if that's what she wants. It's possible this is a casual hookup for her and I don't want to be the pathetic idiot begging for more.

Across the room someone calls out, *"Bingo,"* loudly and Lou groans beside me.

"Can't say I cheated this time, girly." Blythe leans around me, wagging her finger at Lou.

"Suck my dick, Betty Boop."

Instead of looking offended Blythe starts laughing.

"Keep a tight hold on that one, I tell ya. Don't let her get away."

I look over at Lou and find her smacking out some orange Tic-Tacs into her hand and popping them into her mouth.

"I won't."

After Bingo I drive the two of us home, but as I kill the engine I know I'm not ready for the night to end.

"Walk with me?"

Her brows furrow in confusion. "Where? Why?"

"It's a beautiful night." The sun has completely gone down, but the stars are bright, not hidden by clouds. In the downtown area the trees are wrapped with twinkling lights and the old streetlights glow with an orange hue.

Where I grew up, it didn't look like this—like some idyllic small town you'd only find in the movies.

"Okay." She nods and hops out, her feet smacking against the ground. "Are you coming?"

I shake my head, realizing I stare at her like an idiot way too much.

I've never been like this before, and I'm only beginning to realize what it means.

I climb out of my truck and lock it, joining her on the passenger side.

"This was your idea. I'll follow you."

I reach for her hand, entwining our fingers together. Her eyes widen in surprise as she looks from our joined hands to me.

"Is this okay?"

She nods, her lips parted, and I think for once Lou doesn't know what to say.

I like knowing I've rendered her speechless. She's always got a quip for almost anything.

We walk side by side down the street and the rightness of this, of her, settles inside me.

My mom told me before she died that I'd know when I found *the one* and she was right, because I feel it deep in my gut. This girl, she's it for me. That elusive *one* you spend your whole life searching for, questioning whether it exists at all. I knew she was different the first time I talked to her and she spoke of fate. I understand what she meant now. Fate is everywhere, in everything, and it was guiding us to each other the entire time.

"Want to get some ice cream?" I point across the way to Red Fox Creamery.

She lets out a small laugh, spinning in front of me but not letting go of my hand. "Are my habits rubbing off on you? Developing a taste for sweets?" She pokes my hard stomach.

I have a taste for her, but I know that isn't what she means.

"Sweets are always a good idea. It doesn't mean some chicken and greens aren't a good idea too."

She pouts. "If only I could eat all the pizza, ice cream, donuts, and crepes without gaining an ounce. That'd be perfect."

I grab her hips and tug her against me. Her palms land flat against my chest and she has to tilt her head back to look at me.

"You're perfect, exactly as you are." She shivers when I glide my fingers over the soft curve of her cheek. It's ridiculous the amount of satisfaction I get from touching her.

Lowering my head her eyes widen.

"The people—"

"Fuck them."

I don't care who sees me kiss this beautiful girl. She deserves to be kissed right now and the people strolling by can enjoy the show.

The moment my lips press against hers she melts beneath me. Her mouth moves against mine, our tongues entwining.

When I step back her blue eyes shine and I take a mental picture of what she looks like in that moment. Her hair ruffled by my hands and the wind, eyes glittering with desire, and lips swollen from mine.

"Ice cream?" I ask again.

She grins and nods. "I'll never say no to ice cream."

This time she reaches for my hand and we walk across to the shop.

There are a few people in line ahead of us, making the small shop crowded. I use it as an excuse to pull Lou closer to my side.

She twists, wrapping her arms around my middle and resting her chin on my chest. "You *like* me."

It's a statement, not a question, but I answer anyway as I curl a stray piece of hair around my finger. "Yes."

"I like you, too."

"Good." I kiss the top of her head.

Even though there are no labels on what we are, the feelings can't be denied. Some people fit perfectly into your life while others always seem abrasive and out of place. I'm convinced now I've been missing a Lou-shaped piece, and now that she's here, things finally feel complete. With her, I find myself envisioning a future filled with silliness, love, incredible sex, and a family.

Lou orders first when it's our turn. I'm not surprised when she gets the strawberry flavor and asks for sprinkles. The girl working there passes her the cone and I place my order for blueberry ice cream.

Taking my cone from her, I pass my credit card over before tucking my wallet into my back pocket.

Outside, Lou and I find a spot to sit beneath one of the many trees lining the walking mall. She licks her ice cream greedily, but thankfully it's not hot enough anymore to melt it in seconds.

"Look at us with our berry ice creams." She beams at me, completely oblivious to the ice cream clinging to her lip. I close the distance and kiss her, licking the ice cream from her lip as I do. Giggling, she pushes me away. "Abel," she scolds, "let me enjoy my treat."

"I was enjoying *my* treat."

"Such a player, Mr. Popular."

Her playfulness disappears as she looks over my shoulder, her eyes narrowing.

I turn around and find her glaring at Kit as he walks out of a bike shop.

"I hate that guy."

He might be on my team, but we've never been what I'd call friends. I merely tolerate his presence. "He's an asshole."

The shit he spews in the locker room about girls is disgusting and it makes me sick now realizing at some point one of those girls he was talking about was probably Lou.

Kit spots us and an angry look overtakes his face. I don't know what he has to be pissed about. It's doubtful what Lou said to him in the cafeteria is the worst he's ever heard. He looks like he wants to say something, but thinks better of it and walks away instead.

She gives a small laugh and I raise my brow in inquiry.

"I find it hilarious he's afraid of me," she answers my unspoken question.

"You're a force to be reckoned with."

"As I should be." She licks her cone.

I tap her nose with my ice cream and her jaw drops. "You *didn't*."

"I did."

She sticks her finger in her ice cream and swipes it down my cheek.

Grinning evilly, she sits back and waits.

"Are you challenging me, Blondie?"

Her teeth rest against her bottom lip as she tries to hide her smile. "Maybe."

Before I know it, we're both smearing ice cream on the other, making a complete mess of ourselves in front of various townspeople.

I can hear mutters from some of the people about us being ridiculous and unruly, an absolute fucking mess, but I don't stop. Lou's teaching me how important it is to live in the moment, and I know this is one of those things I'll never forget.

We stumble inside the apartment, ice cream drying on our skin, hair, and clothes. Lou's giggles filter into the air and it's music to my ears.

"You need a shower." I reach for the bottom of her shirt, yanking it over her head.

"You do too." Her eyes are bright as she works the button of my jeans.

It's a slow progression to the bathroom as we strip each other of our clothes.

We bump into the sink and she laughs as I pick her up, perching her ass near the edge. Behind her head, sticking to the mirror is a pink sticky note.

Life's purpose isn't what you do. It's who you do.

The note made me chuckle when I found it this morning, and now it's all the more fitting.

I let her go for a moment and turn the shower on. Fitting myself back in between her open thighs she wraps her arms around my shoulders.

Her breasts heave with each breath she takes and her hair is a wild, chaotic mess just like her.

"Are you going to fuck me, Abel?"

I wet my lips, lowering my head to the crook of her neck. I kiss her jaw and murmur, "No, I'm going to make you mine."

She shudders in my arms as I pick her up, carrying her into the shower where the water quickly drenches us.

She kisses me passionately, making these sweet little

mewling sounds. I don't think she evens knows she's doing it.

As the dried ice cream washes from our bodies, the heat builds between us.

She reaches down, wrapping her hand around my cock and air hisses between my teeth when she begins to pump it.

Leaning my head against the tiled wall I bite out, "I need to be inside you."

Her eyes jump from my cock to my face. "Then do it."

"I don't have a condom."

She licks her lips, and I can tell she's thinking. "I'm on birth control and you can pull out. You're clean, right? I am."

I nod, not trusting my voice right now with the way she's touching me.

She kisses my left peck, then the right. "Then I'm yours."

Fucking hell, she's going to make me cum on the spot.

"Turn around." My tone is a low command and her blue eyes deepen to the color of the ocean.

She does as I say and I squeeze her ass, my fingers finding her pussy as I do. She's already wet and she moans, wiggling her ass.

"You ready for me, Blondie?" There's a small hint of amusement in my voice.

"Yes," she gasps breathlessly.

I grab the base of my cock and enter her slowly, relishing in every delicious sound she makes.

I lower my body over hers, kissing the back of her shoulder.

My hands grip her hips as I thrust in and out of her.

"God, you feel so good," she moans as I reach between us to rub her clit.

Her soft little sounds are nearly my undoing. "Fucking beautiful." I nip at her skin, leaving behind marks from my teeth.

I'm lost in her. Nothing else exists outside of the two of us.

The heat of the water pours over us, our wet bodies gliding together.

She reaches her arm back, wrapping it around my neck. My hand flexes against her hip and I rub her clit faster. Her noises increase in volume.

I get off on making her feel good. Her pleasure is mine. I can feel her orgasm building as her pussy pulses around my cock and when it finally hits her I hold her body as she bows over. Pumping into her a few more times I pull out, gripping my cock in one hand I watch my cum cover her delectable ass, my groans filling the bathroom.

When I'm finished, she turns around so we're pressed chest to chest. Her blonde hair is plastered to her head from the water and her skin is flushed.

"I wasn't expecting you, I wasn't even looking for you, but here you are."

"Back at you, Blondie."

I kiss her again, and once more we're lost in each other.

CHAPTER TWENTY-THREE

Lou

"Hey, I'm here!" I call out, entering the Wilson residence. I still can't believe Giulia is Abel's sister.

What are the odds?

"Lou, we're in the den." I follow the sound of her voice and find Matteo and Bella playing together at her dollhouse. Apparently dinosaurs live there now. There's even one taking a shit on the too small toilet.

Cristian is asleep on Giulia's chest and she's dressed in workout clothes—she told me she planned to go to Pilates while I'm watching the kids.

"I feel like I haven't seen you in forever."

She gives a soft laugh. "The flu hit us out of nowhere. I blame Matty's stink-face kindergarten class." I snort in amusement. "You know," she grins as she stands, holding the baby carefully so she doesn't jostle him awake, "since I haven't seen you I haven't had a chance to talk about something I found on the security cameras."

My heart drops. I know I haven't stolen anything or done something I shouldn't have, but I freak out anyway wondering what it could possibly be.

"Uh … you found something on the security system?"

"Oh, yeah."

There's something I don't quite understand in her eyes. She crooks her finger, encouraging me to follow.

She grabs an iPad from where it's hooked up charging in the kitchen and opens an app.

A moment later she's thrusting it into my hands. There I am, fast asleep on her *brother*.

My panicked eyes dart up and she tries to hide her smile. "Interesting, isn't it?"

"I … I."

I have no words. No explanation.

I mean, thank God we're only sleeping, and very clothed—unlike how we've been lately. But it still looks suspicious considering my body is sprawled on top of his, our legs entwined together, and his arms wrapped in a bear hug around my torso.

"You and my brother?" she probes, almost excitedly.

"H-He's my roommate," I stutter, feeling heat rush to my cheeks because he's definitely more than my roommate now.

"Your roommate, huh?" Her tone implies there's clearly more to the story, which obviously there is.

"Yeah, we're roomies. We braid each other's hair, spill secrets, and freeze each other's bras."

She laughs. "You're adorable, Lou." She takes the iPad back from me and sets it on the counter, rocking the baby back and forth in her arms. "That right there ... well, your roommate excuse is feeble. Are you and my brother together?"

"We are actually roommates." I don't know why I feel so nervous and defensive. She's clearly kind of excited by the idea of Abel and me. "When your brother showed up that day to take the kids I wasn't expecting to see *him*." My hands flounder as the words pour out of me. I'm sure I look like a psychotic pigeon. "He asked me to go to the zoo and when we got back he..." *fuck,* "...asked me to stay."

Her smile grows brighter. "Are you guys together?" She poses the question again.

I shrug, itching to grab something to keep my hands

busy. Standing here with them dangling at my sides feels silly. "I don't know."

Her smile falls. "Oh. It's just sex then?"

From anyone else I might be offended by the probing, but I've gotten to know Giulia pretty well since I started watching her kids and she *is* Abel's sister.

Before I can answer her she exhales a sigh and rests her hip against the side of the kitchen island. "It's just ... I love my brother, and I've watched him chase after meaningless flings for too long. You're an amazing girl, Lou, and after I saw that I realized how perfect you two would be together."

"Giulia," I stop her, "I honestly don't know what Abel and I are to each other. I just know it is different."

"Really?" Hope floods her.

"I can't explain it, but it is."

"He's a great guy."

"He is." There's no denying it. Abel Russo is one of the best men I've ever met.

"This makes me so happy." Tears fill her eyes and she fans her face with one hand. "Damn hormones."

Finally she passes me the baby and after drying her tears with a tissue she says her goodbyes and leaves.

Once I have Cristian placed in his rocker I sit down to play with Matty and Bella.

Fear clenches my chest as I look at them, and I know

it's because my brain is accepting that if I lose Abel I could lose them too, and I love them as much as I—

Oh, hell.

As much as I love Abel.

CHAPTER TWENTY-FOUR

Lou

"You and Hotty-Pants, huh?" Miranda quirks a brow, sipping on her drink. "Can I just say *I knew it?*"

"Don't gloat."

She sticks her tongue out at me.

"I think you guys are cute together." Tanner picks up his iced coffee, wrapping his lips in dramatic fashion around the straw.

Over my shoulder I watch Abel grab our order. Since we all decided to meet up at Griffin's, I forced him to get whatever magical drink it was he gave me the first time we met. I haven't had it since, and I'd be lying if I said I hadn't thought about it ... possibly even dreamed of it.

Abel smiles cockily when he catches me staring and saunters over with our drinks. He pulls out the chair beside me and sits down across from Tanner.

Clearing his throat, he says, "I feel like I need to apologize for how I acted toward you initially. I was—"

"Jealous," the three of us echo simultaneously and I laugh when Abel hangs his head in shame.

"Just remember what I told you." Miranda stares him down, popping the lid off her hot chocolate and counting the mini marshmallows floating on top.

"What did she tell you?" I twist in my face toward Abel.

He clears his throat, scooting awkwardly in his chair. "It was just a casual conversation."

"Yes, very casual," Miranda repeats with an evil grin.

Why do I have a feeling Miranda has Abel's murder planned out if he does something wrong?

"Are you guys ... like ... a couple now?" Tanner probes, his eyes shifting between the two of us.

We look at each other, neither seeming to know what to say.

It was just yesterday when I admitted to myself I've

fallen in love with him, but technically we're not even together.

Abel quirks his head, fighting a smile. "What do you say, Blondie? Want to be my girlfriend?"

Because I'm me I can't give him a straight answer. Instead, a very undignified and not at all ladylike snort leaves me. "I've already blown you, so we might as well make it official."

Across the table Tanner chokes on his drink, coffee spraying everywhere.

"I don't know why I'd ever expect a normal answer from you." Abel's hand twines around the back of my neck and he pulls me in for a kiss.

"Bleh, okay, enough of that Mom and Dad." Miranda pretends to gag as we break apart.

I toss a balled up napkin at her. "No need to be jealous."

The door into Griffin's chimes and Miranda's face goes pale—which is quite a feat with her darker complexion. I watch as she slowly sinks down into her chair, like she wants to disappear.

Over my shoulder, I find Jamie stepping into line. He hasn't spotted us, thank God, since he's busy perusing the menu.

My eyes slowly slide back to Miranda and even Tanner now watches her in confusion. Abel hasn't seemed to notice yet.

"Miranda?" There's hesitancy in my voice, because frankly I don't know if I want an answer. "Why do you look like you want to disappear since Jamie walked in?"

"No reason," she squeaks, her gaze darts around the room.

"Oh, my God." I slap a hand on the table, more forcefully than I mean to and she jumps while I curse because *fuck that burns*. "You totally slept with my landlord."

She looks like she wants to disappear.

"Wait ... what?" Abel's head swivels between us as he finally takes note of what's going on.

"It only happened..." She pauses, counting on her fingers. "Three times."

I choke on my own saliva. "You slept with Jamie three times?"

She bites her lip, looking like she wants to curl in on herself. "What can I say? Homeboy is hung like a stallion and fucks like it's his job. If this whole landlord thing doesn't work out for him he should totally go into porn."

"Oh, my God." It seems to be the only phrase I can come up with at the moment. I'd kind of like to bang my head against the counter while I'm at it. "But he's ... *old*."

Miranda's posture straightens as she grows defensive. "He's only thirty-three."

"That's twelve years older than you!" I cry out incredulously. "He was practically a teenager when you were *born*. He was already jacking his knob when you were shitting yourself."

She covers her face with her hands, her shoulders shaking with laughter. "Knob? Really, Lou? Are you British now?"

"You know Angry Lou is far more creative with wording than I am. When did this happen? I'm so confused, how do I not know about this?"

"Only recently," she admits, as we continue our back and forth and the guys stay silent. "And then it happened again ... and again ... not going to lie, I'd be down for it to happen another time."

Kill me now.

"I can never look my landlord in the eye again. He's seen you naked! Oh, shit, that means you've seen *him* naked."

"And it's a glorious sight to behold." She licks her lips, eyeing him as he finally reaches the counter to order. "I have pictures. Do you want to see?"

She reaches eagerly for her phone as Abel and I both shout, "No!"

Tanner on the other hand shrugs and leans over. "I'm game."

She must show him because his jaw drops. "Damn, girl. You weren't kidding. Do you need a crane to lift it?"

"I make it work." She winks.

Silence descends upon the table as an ominous shadow falls over us.

"Louise." *Fucking Jamie. Except, can I call him that now since he's actually fucking my best friend?* I try not to shudder at my thoughts. *"Miranda,"* he purrs her name, the sound of it curling around his tongue like a fine wine.

If wine could curdle, I'd will it to happen right now. Maybe have it solidify and choke him to death.

Too morbid?

"James." Miranda rests her elbow on the table, chin in her hand. All the while eye-fucking him.

"James?" I bite out the name, my tongue smacking my lips like I taste something sour.

Jamie—oh, I mean *James*—raises his cup in goodbye. "I'll be seeing you soon to collect rent." He gives me a dirty look like he expects me not to have his money. Right now I'd love to have one of the shitty diapers I change to make money so I could throw it at his head for being an asshole.

Once he walks away Tanner laughs and gives Miranda a high-five. "If he was gay, I would so do him. Good for you."

My head drops to the table. "Wake me from this nightmare."

Miranda taps the table in front of me and I sit up. "This is all reality, baby girl. Deal with it."

"But ... first Charlie and now *Jamie?* We hate Jamie."

"Yeah, Jamie's the fucking worst," Abel pipes in, and I give him a grateful nod for having my back.

"I can hate Jamie and still fuck him. It's called just that, Lou—a hate fuck, and it's amazing. Best. Sex. Ever." She mouths the last three words.

"I'm surrounded by crazy people."

Abel laughs at my complaining. "You're the craziest of them all."

He has a valid point.

Miranda checks her phone and stands up. "I better get going." She grabs her jacket from the back of the chair and shrugs it on, shaking her hair out from under it.

My eyes narrow to slits. "You're meeting up with Jamie, right?"

She picks up her drink and sticks her tongue out as she winks. "Maybe."

She totally is.

She sways her hips as she heads out the door.

"Well," Tanner leans back in his chair, "I think that's my cue to leave. Third-wheeling isn't my thing."

"Aw, Tanner, don't go."

"You'll be fine without me." He stands and begins gathering his stuff up. "See you guys later."

"Bye," I say weakly, watching him go.

Abel drapes his arm over the back of my chair. "Want to head out?"

I sigh, taking a sip of whatever this delicious secret drink of his is. "Yeah, I guess. Can we go somewhere else?"

"Sure. Where do you want to go?" His brows dip as he waits for my answer and I itch to reach out and touch the stubble that's growing thicker along his angular jaw.

"Surprise me."

"First the sunrise, now the sunset." I kick my legs back and forth, the two of us sitting side by side in the bed of his truck in Jim Barnett Park.

"Hey, you told me to surprise you." He grins, leaning back on his elbows.

"I like it here. I hadn't set foot in this place before you."

"If only we had some crepes."

"And fancy cookies." I snap my fingers. "Love me some fancy cookies."

"Do you think you'll stay here after college, or move back to where your mom is?"

I'm taken aback by his question, but I realize that we *are* together now and inevitably these kinds of questions will come up.

"I like it here." Exhaling a sigh, I watch the blazing sky for a moment. "I think I'd stay, but move closer to

D.C. if I could afford it. I want to work for a bigger publication and there are more journalistic opportunities there. What about you?"

I know his sister is here, but I assume his father is still in New Jersey. He told me he's going to be a physical therapist, and that's a job he could do anywhere.

"I love it here. I came here to be closer to my sister and her family, but I didn't plan to stay long term. But ... it's home now."

"It is." Wetting my lips, I clear my throat. Serious talks are not my jam, but I feel like in this case, it's necessary. "Abel?"

"Yeah?" He sits up at my serious tone, his hand brushing my pinky finger in the process.

"Things are moving fast between us."

"They are." His tone implies he's waiting for the punch line.

"I'm scared." I hate admitting such a weakness, especially to a guy I like—*love*—but I've been burned time and again in the past. I don't trust my feelings when it comes to guys anymore. Maybe I'm thinking things are better than they actually are? "I wasn't planning on you."

"Can you plan on anybody? Sometimes things just happen and even if the timing or situation seems rushed or wrong, it might be exactly right. In time you'll see the why."

"Fate," I whisper my beloved word.

"Exactly."

"Are you a believer now, Mr. Popular?"

He chuckles and his warm hand grasps the back of my neck, pulling me in close to kiss my forehead. "I believe in you, and that's the only kind of fate I need."

CHAPTER TWENTY-FIVE

Abel

"And done!" Lou announces, snapping her laptop lid closed and placing it on the coffee table. "No homework for the next oh..." She pretends to look at a watch even though she doesn't wear one. "Twelve hours or so."

"You have a whole other year of this. I only have a few months."

"Don't rub it in." She stretches her legs into my lap,

lying back. "You know what would make tonight really great?"

"If we were naked?"

"No." She crinkles her nose. "If there was pizza. Pizza makes everything better."

"Basically, you're telling me to order pizza?" I raise a brow in challenge.

"Yep. We can watch some more *Psych* while we're at it."

"Naked?" I try to keep the excitement out of my tone.

She groans and her feet drop from my lap to the floor as she sits up. "No, not naked. I'm on my period."

"You're not in the mood then?"

Her lips thin. "Actually, I always get really horny on my period for some reason, but that's just nasty so let's go with I'm not in the mood."

I chuckle, sliding my hand up her thigh. "I wouldn't mind."

She gags and shoves my hand away. "Nice try, but I'm not cool with my sheets—or yours," she adds when she sees I'm going to protest, "looking like a murder scene. That's just nasty. Besides, what if I forget to take my tampon out and your giant schlong rams it inside my uterus. Toxic Shock Syndrome is a real thing."

"Okay, okay." I raise my hands in defeat. "Sex is off the table. Honestly, I'm cool with pizza and *Psych*."

That's one of the best things about Lou—yeah, I love having sex with her, but I also like being with her.

"All right." She hops up and claps her hands together. "You order the pizza while I take a shower. I smell like Zac Efron's sweaty ball sack."

"Um..." I don't know how to respond.

"He might have the face of a god, but you know that boy's peen has seen way too much pussycat action to ever be clean."

Before I can retort, she flips around dramatically and saunters into the bathroom.

Lou is a hard person to keep up with, but damn if I don't like trying.

I place a call to Woody's for a delivery and then grab the cash from my wallet, setting it near the door so it's ready when the pizza arrives. I tuck it under the landline phone and nearly shit a brick when the phone rings shrilly.

"Jesus, fuck." I flounder, my arms reeling back like I'm trying to dodge a bullet Matrix style.

The landline rarely rings, and only seems to be telemarketers or Lou's mother. Since this is usually the time her mom calls I'm voting on the latter.

I reach for the obnoxious pink phone and answer. "Hello?"

"You're not Lou."

"No, ma'am, I'm not." I try not to laugh. Lou's mom sounds so much like her it's scary.

"Either you're breaking and entering or you're the roommate."

This time I do laugh. "Definitely not a burglar, ma'am."

"Well, nice to meet you then, roommate."

"It's Abel. Lou's in the shower. I can tell her to call you back or—"

"Are you having sex with my daughter?"

Her question catches me off guard and I sputter then begin to choke. I swipe my blue Gatorade from the counter and take a sip, trying to clear my throat.

"What? No. Of course not. Definitely not."

"Mhmm," she hums. "My Lou might act like a toughy, but she has a soft heart. Be gentle with her."

"Um..."

This is awkward as hell.

"And if you're not having sex with my daughter, she's a great girl. Wonderful, really. Doesn't get out enough and really needs to stop going to Bingo and hang out with more people her age, but she's a great catch, I swear."

"Uh..."

"I really want grandbabies some day."

Fuck, this escalated extraordinarily fast.

"I'm sure grandchildren are definitely in your future."

And I'd love to be the father of your daughter's kids

way, way, way *down the road.*

"I want six."

I choke again and gulp down some more Gatorade. At the rate I'm going, this conversation is going to empty the entire bottle. Too bad it's not alcoholic.

"Wow, six is ... a lot. My sister has three kids."

"I always wanted more, but I'm thankful I was blessed with Louise. She was such a funny child."

"I bet she was."

She must've been a little spitfire.

"Oh, she was hilarious. She kidnapped the neighbor's cat once."

"The neighbor's cat?"

"Yeah, ruined her brand new Easter dress while doing it. Crawled under a hole in the fence, snatched the cat, and hid the thing in her bedroom for two hours until I found it."

I laugh. "Yeah, I can see her doing that."

"Want to hear some more stories?"

I grin. "Absolutely."

Two stories later, Lou exits the bathroom with damp blonde hair and steam billowing around her. She pauses, looking at the pink phone clasped in my hand. Slowly, her mouth widens in horror.

"What is she telling you?" She runs at me, the towel she's wearing barely able to hang on with all the movement.

I hold the phone out of her reach. "She's just getting to the good part about the time you mooned the mailman when you were six. *Oomph*." She slams into me, tackling me to the ground.

Fuck, she might be useful on the team.

The phone drops from my hand and dangles off the counter from the cord. I can hear her mom asking if anyone's still there.

"If you don't want me to cut your body into teeny-tiny pieces and trick Jamie into eating it you'll never listen to my mom's stories ever again."

"But I like her stories. You were a funny kid."

"*Funny kid*," she scoffs. "I'm goddamn hilarious. Always have been, always will be." I hear the phone disconnect and start to bleep but she ignores it. "What else did she tell you?" Her eyes narrow and her small hands are dangerously close to my throat.

I wet my lips—kind of afraid of her, but a whole lot turned on. "You kidnapped a cat, and one time you decided to take a bath in macaroni when you were three."

"I really liked macaroni and cheese—specifically the Kraft Spongebob shapes."

"Who didn't?"

Shaking her head back and forth she exhales a breath. "My mom *lives* to tell people embarrassing stories about me. Trust me, those aren't even the tip of the iceberg."

"Oh, I know. She's sending pictures too."

"Oh, my God I'm going to kill her!" She stands up hastily and in the process her towel melts from her body. She grabs at the towel and then shrieks in a way I know something is seriously wrong.

"Wha—"

"THE PIZZA GUY SAW MY PEPPERONI SLICES!" She points wildly to the window.

"Huh?" I gather my legs under me and stand.

"MY AREOLA AND NIPPLES, ABEL! HE SAW MY BOOBS!" Hanging her head in her hands, her body once more encased in a bath towel she all but whispers, "I can never eat pizza again. This is the greatest tragedy of my life. No pizza ... that's no life at all."

There's a knock on the door and she screams again, running for her bedroom and slamming the door closed behind her.

Hanging the phone back up, I grab the money from under it and open the door. The teenager on the other side stands there with a smirk.

"What are you leering at?" Already I want to punch the guy in the face, and the kid probably isn't older than sixteen.

His eyes widen when he sees me, taking in my size. "N-Nothing."

"Mhmm, that's what I thought." I hand him the money and take the pizza. Now I regret having the money set out already, because the kid definitely wouldn't be getting a tip after the conceited smile I opened the door to.

Locking the door, I set the pizza on the counter, grab paper plates, a fresh Gatorade for me, and a Capri-Sun for Lou before I move everything to the coffee table so we can watch the show.

Lou's bedroom door opens and she exits wearing a pair of sweatpants and a sweatshirt, like she's trying to make sure no part of her body is exposed after the incident.

She shudders as she walks toward me. "I don't embarrass easily, but the pizza guy seeing me naked tops the list. I'm really rethinking my whole love of pizza thing. It's always treated me so well until now." She flops onto the couch. "Screw it, I can't say no to pizza."

I open the box and slap two slices on a plate, handing it to her with a Capri-Sun.

"You're too good to me."

She takes both gratefully and I fix myself a plate before sitting down beside her, kicking my feet up on the coffee table. She eyes their position but doesn't say anything.

Reaching for the remote, she starts the show, and scoots closer to me in the process. I'm pretty sure if we hadn't given in to the chemistry between us my balls might've exploded by now. I might not have kept my vow, but maybe it was never about being celibate for a period of time and actually about finding a woman I want to be with for more than just my body's needs.

After a couple hours of binge-watching, Lou goes slack against me. I tilt my head, finding her fast asleep against my shoulder.

Grabbing the remote from the blanket, I turn the TV off and gather her in my arms.

She stirs as I carry her and mumbles, "Too heavy, put me down."

"Never. Not when I have you right where I want you."

She gives a small sleepy laugh.

I transfer her onto my mattress and she makes a sexy little sound, burrowing against the pillows. Yanking at the sheets to pull them over her, I join her in bed.

She wiggles her body against mine, expelling a sigh when she rests her head on my chest.

"Why do you like me?" Her question surprises me. "I'm quirky and weird, I like to play Bingo with old people, I live off of pizza and coffee, and can't stand football. I'm all wrong for you."

"No, Lou. That's exactly why you're right for me."

I press my lips against the soft skin of her forehead and the short baby hairs there. I wait a moment for her response but when I angle my head to look at her I find she's sound asleep.

CHAPTER TWENTY-SIX

Abel

"Do we need so many snacks?"

Lou spreads out a bag of pretzels, Starbursts, some kind of sour cream and onion popcorn that actually looks good, and even some Tic-Tacs.

Her head pops up, and she makes an indignant noise under her breath. "You can't study without snacks, even in the library."

I look around at the other full tables.

None of them have snacks, but I don't point it out.

Instead, I pull out a chair across the table from her, because I know studying won't be happening at all if I sit beside her.

"Afraid I'll bite?" She grins evilly as she opens her laptop.

"No, I'm afraid I will."

A small squeak leaves her and her eyes focus on the screen. "Now be quiet, I have to concentrate."

"Yes, ma'am." Already her fingers clack against the keyboard, typing at a pace I could never keep up with. "I can feel you staring." She doesn't look away from her screen.

"Noted." I pull books out of my backpack and spread them around because I *do* need to study, which is why I agreed to stay at school after my classes had ended. Normally, I can't wait to get as far from here as possible once class and practice are over, but when Lou said she was staying, this sounded more appealing than being in an empty apartment by myself.

My senior year has been kicking my ass. It's crunch time and I want to come out on top, and hopefully, if I'm lucky, be able to get a job quickly. It's fucking scary going into debt to get an education and not being able to get a job doing what I want right away. I've wanted to be a physical therapist for years. It was something I knew by the time I was a junior in high school. I don't want to fail myself, not when I'm so close to what I've been working toward.

Thirty minutes into our study session, Lou opens the bag of popcorn and Starbursts. "Want any?"

Her eyes on her computer screen, and headphones on, she holds the popcorn bag out to me and I grab a handful. Shoving them into my mouth I chew, impressed with the taste. "Those are good."

There's no point to my words since she can't hear me.

Tearing out a piece of paper I scribble a note on it, ball it up, and throw it at her. It smacks the side of her face and falls onto the keyboard.

Her mouth pops open and she gives me an incredulous look, reaching for the note and unraveling it.

Grabbing a pen, she writes something beneath my note and tosses it back.

I wrote, *Hey, Blondie, want to know a secret?*

Her reply, *If it's that lemon Starbursts are actually good, that's a lie, not a secret.*

I can't study. I'm too distracted by you, I add to our ongoing written conversation. Reaching over the top of her laptop I drop the note onto the keyboard.

She sighs, glaring at me before she picks up the note and unfurls it.

Scrawling a hasty note she throws it back to me.

That's what other tables are for. But I'm secretly glad to know you're hot for me, Mr. Popular.

I grin. *But if I move to another table I'll still only be thinking about you.* I can see her glaring at me as I write, so I finish with, *I'll stop now because I do need to study too.*

I pass the note back to her and she reads it. "You better," she mouths.

I refocus on my textbooks, grabbing my own laptop to write up a paper that's due way too soon.

Like, tomorrow.

It's a good fucking thing I work best under pressure.

Another hour or so passes and a shadow falls across the table.

I look up and find Danika leaning against the edge. I haven't encountered her since she showed up with her *house-warming present* and that's partly because I've been avoiding her. If I spot her, I'm hauling ass in the other direction. She needs to keep her panther claws firmly away from me. Last I heard, she hooked up with Kit at my birthday party. As far as I see it, those two are made for each other.

"Can I help you?" There's a bite to my tone I don't normally have. Even if I don't like someone I'm usually nice. My parents taught me not to spread around hate, because it only breeds more. It's words I've learned to live by.

Her tongue slides out, wetting her too pink lips, and her denim mini-skirt slides up her thighs as she presses further against the table, lowering her torso so her breasts are practically in my face. The warmth of summer is still hanging on, but barely, not nearly enough to merit her skimpy outfit.

This kind of getup on a woman used to drive me wild. Not anymore. I've found a person who sparks those things in me. I don't need a sexy outfit to do it for me.

Across the table I sense Lou paying attention, and even though she leaves her headphones on, I'd bet anything she's not listening to music right now.

"Haven't seen you in a while." She skims the nail of her index finger over the top of my right hand. I jerk it away, dropping my hand under the table and out of her reach.

"No, you haven't." It's all I'll give her.

"It's a shame. We have fun together." Her eyes slide toward Lou, whose eyes have narrowed and pink stains her cheeks.

"What fun?" I've never been able to tolerate her presence, and her acting like it's the opposite in front of Lou is pissing me off. It's like she wants to mark her territory, only I'm not hers.

Her fake smile falls a little. "Abe, don't be silly."

It grates on my nerves how she wants to call me Abe. *Nobody* calls me Abe. Ever. I don't fucking like it.

"Danika," I echo her tone, "don't be silly."

Her mouth screws into a pout, which looks ridiculous and childish. "Have fun with your overweight frumster." She eyes Lou's sweatshirt and jeans combo. "When you're done with whatever this phase is, let me know."

I grab her wrist before she can take two steps away and she stops, a winning smile on her face.

"Don't you *ever* say anything like that about my girlfriend again."

With an irritated sigh, she rips her arm from my hand and storms away, her hair swishing behind her shoulders like an inky dark curtain.

Lou stands up and begins gathering her stuff. "I want to go," she announces, and the dejection visible in the slouch of her shoulders and the softness of her voice breaks my fucking heart.

"Okay." Packing up my stuff, I take her hand and we leave.

"When I said I wanted to go, I meant *home*, not here."

"Come on, you can't say no to crepes. It's our thing, Lou."

Her bottom lip pops out a little, and unlike Danika's ridiculous pout I know Lou is considering what I've said.

"Fine, but my fat ass still wants some fancy cookies."

I grin in response, glad to see some of her humor returning even if her blue eyes are a little sadder than normal.

"Stay here." I jump out of my truck and run inside Oh, Crepe, ordering our food as quickly as possible. I wait off to the side for our order and as soon as it's ready I take the plastic bag of to-go boxes from Ines, waving to Michel in the back.

Lou has the window rolled down, her feet sticking out of it with her white Converse hanging loosely on her feet since she undid the laces as soon as we got in the car.

I slide back inside the truck and she rights herself, rolling up the window.

"Gimme those thin pancakes. Never thought I'd like them, but they're almost as good as fancy cookies and Starbursts."

I chuckle, handing her the bag to hold as I buckle up. "Fancy cookies, thin pancakes, what's next?"

"No idea." She rifles through the bag. "But I'm sure I'll think of something."

"I figured we could go home and eat."

"That sounds nice." She wraps her arms around the bag, like she's trying to protect it.

I pull out onto the street and near the stoplight when she says in an eerily calm voice, "What. Is. That?"

"Huh?" I look out the windshield, finding nothing.

Since I can make a right on red and nothing's coming, I do, still not sure what caused her question.

"There's something crawling in your truck and I don't know what it is. I have a feeling we're both going to die, though."

I look over at her and find nothing. "What?"

"Right there." She points and my eyes land on a giant ass wasp crawling over the dashboard.

Suddenly it takes flight, landing on the steering wheel as I slam on the brakes.

Lou screams, or maybe that shrill sound is coming from me, and then the wasp takes flight again and I can't see it.

"Put your window down!"

Both of us frantically crank the windows down.

"Where'd it go?"

"I don't know," Lou whispers, moving her eyes and not her head to search for the bug.

"I have to drive. Don't let it kill me."

"No promises. If it flies out of nowhere I'm ducking and rolling out of here."

She's not even kidding, and I know it.

I ease to a stop at another stoplight. We're only a few blocks from the apartment, nearly in the clear.

"I think it's gone." Lou breathes an audible sigh of relief.

My eyes scan the truck. "I don't see it either."

We both look at each other. "Should we put our windows back up?"

"I don't know," she nibbles on her lip, "what if it's still in here, waiting for us to do just that?"

"True."

"*But* it could be gone, and then something else could get in."

Both of us hasten to roll the windows up.

Reaching the apartment, I park the truck and exhale a breath I didn't know I was holding.

Bugs don't generally freak me out, but I got stung by a bee when I was six and it was a traumatizing experience. I've hated all of those flying fuckers since.

Lou reaches for her door and—

"Fuck!" I scream as the wasp races out of one of the air vents, flying straight for my face.

"Hi-yah!"

I wince when her hand collides with my face—and the wasp—bug guts getting all over my face and her hand.

"Oops," she says in a small voice. I blink my eyes open, which had closed in reflex, and find she looks apologetic but also like she's tempted to bust out laughing. "That happened a little more aggressive than I intended ... but at least it's dead, right?"

"There are bug guts on my face."

"But I saved you." The words sound like a song and she does a little dance for good measure.

I press my lips together, trying not to laugh.

This ranks pretty high on the list of funniest things to ever happen to me.

I'm not one bit surprised Lou is involved.

"Grab your thin pancakes and fancy cookies. I need to wash my face before I stuff it."

Cradling the bag to her chest as she climbs out of my truck, I follow her around the side of the building to the front, giving chase so she runs, her laughter trailing behind her.

I think the wasp, while annoying, did the job of getting her to forget Danika. I'm grateful for that. I don't want her worrying about some insignificant woman like Danika.

Lou is incomparable to any other woman.

She's the person I've been searching years for, when I didn't even know I was looking.

I grab her ass when she has to stop outside the door to unlock it.

"So handsy." She swats me away, nearly dropping the food in the process.

The door swings open and I lock it behind us. She drops the bag on the counter and grabs a paper towel, dampening it and coming over to me to wipe my face free of bug intestines.

"There, all better." She's standing on her tiptoes, her sapphire hues staring into the deepest parts of me. It's on the tip of my tongue, the urge to tell her I'm in love with her, but I'm scared.

Terrified.

Goddamn petrified.

I've never been in love, and I never believed it could happen so fast.

Two months ago I met her and nothing's been the same since.

I find I'm perfectly okay with that, even if it scares me.

Lowering my head, I take her lips in a soft kiss.

It's not as good as telling her how I feel, but fear?

Well, fear's a bitch, robbing us all of time, happiness, and sometimes even our lives.

Tonight, fear wins.

And I fear my loss might be bigger than I expect.

CHAPTER TWENTY-SEVEN

Lou

I've grown so used to Abel's presence that whenever he's gone the apartment feels empty without him. It's such a stark contrast to the irritation I felt at the idea of having a roommate.

I pull out my cross-stitching supplies and curl my legs under me on the couch so I can get started on my side project. It's going to be a cute little llama with *Ain't No*

Time for a Drama Llama stitched beneath it. The one I'm making for my mom's birthday is my main project, but I need a break from staring at it.

My record player is going in the corner and I hum along to the Zella Day song.

Halloween is coming up and for the past two years Miranda and I have dressed up in matching costumes. The first year I chose, last year was her turn, so that means this year it's up to me again. I really want to go dressed as Starbursts, but I know what I envision is never going to be purchasable, which means I either need to learn how to sew, and quick, or scratch my idea and come up with something new.

After about thirty minutes, I set the cross-stitching aside to give my wrist a break. My stomach rumbles and when I look at the time, I realize I need to be eating dinner. The last thing I feel like doing is making a meal, but I know I can't live off pizza forever, as much as I'd like to.

Raiding the refrigerator, I pull out some chicken, asparagus, and a few other ingredients. Yes, it's food Abel has bought, but any time he cooks, he insists I eat it too. Since I'm actually his girlfriend now, it shouldn't matter and I'm sure he'll enjoy coming home to a meal already prepared. I'm not the best cook, or a cook at all, but surely I can't fuck something basic up too much?

Lou, you are beyond overthinking this.

Focusing on the task at hand, I somehow manage to put together a decent looking meal and pop it in the oven.

As I'm washing my hands there's a knock on the door, but it doesn't surprise me since Miranda said she might drop by. She wants to borrow one of my dresses for a date. I didn't ask if this *date* is with my landlord because I don't want to know.

Drying my hands on a dishtowel, I head to the door and swing it open.

"Oh." I rear back in astonishment.

Danika stands on the other side of the door, her long glossy brown locks draped over one shoulder. She's dressed in a tight black bodysuit that shows off her cleavage with high-waisted jeans. It might actually be a cute look, if she wasn't the one wearing it.

I haven't seen her in three days, not since the library, and I'm definitely not happy about seeing her now.

"Hi." She gives me a smile that's anything but friendly. I feel uncomfortable standing in front of her in only a pair of sleep shorts with cherries on them and a loose top sans bra. Normally, that kind of thing wouldn't bother me, but I've dealt with her type in the past and I can see the judgment in her eyes.

"Can I help you with something?" My tone implies I wish I could make her disappear.

She stands on her tiptoes, pretending to peek around me. "Is Abe home?"

"*No*, he's working." I draw out the one word, encouraging her to get to the point, and quickly. I'm tired of her wasting my time. Crossing my arms over my chest, I stick out my hip, silently blocking her entrance, because her body language makes it very clear she expects to be invited inside for some odd reason. "If that's all," I continue when she stands there blinking at me like some plastic Barbie toy, "you can go."

I start to ease the door shut and her hand lashes out, stopping it from closing.

"Wait!" Her tone is desperate, and even though I want to force the door closed I don't. "I-I came to pick up something from Abe's room." She blurts the words quickly, looking almost unsure of herself, which confuses me.

"Abel's room?" My mind jumps from thought to thought, wondering why she'd need to get anything from Abel's room.

"Y-Yeah, I left something there the other night."

"The other night?" I realize I'm repeating everything she says and sound absolutely ridiculous, but my brain refuses to process what I think she's implying. "When?"

"I don't know." She waves a dismissive hand.

"When?" I demand, desperate to pinpoint when she would've been here, in *my* apartment, with *my* boyfriend.

"Uh ... Saturday."

My stress eases. She's lying. I was here all day with Abel. We watched *Psych*, a few movies, and did a lot of creative things with our clothes off.

"You're lying. We were both here all today. *Together.*"

Her eyes widen in surprise, but then she straightens her shoulders and lifts her chin haughtily. "Sunday. It was Sunday. I told you I couldn't remember exactly when."

Sunday. What was I doing Sunday?

My mouth parts with realization.

Babysitting. I was babysitting. Abel said he was going to the gym, but since I babysat all day there's no way he was in the gym all that time, which means...

"Get whatever you need." My voice is laced with venom and I snap the door wide open.

She gives me an evil grin and saunters past me, purposely bumping into me as she does. Danika might think she's the bee's knees, but in reality she's just like every other mean girl in the world. There's nothing unique or memorable about her. One day she'll realize there's nothing real about her. Not her nails and certainly not her personality.

I wait by the door for her to grab whatever it is she needed to get. After a minute or two she emerges from his room and strolls past me.

"Thanks, Laura."

"It's Lou."

"Right, Lou. Sorry." She waves goodbye and that's when I see what's clasped in her hand.

A lacy black thong.

I see red and slam the door, but not before I miss the satisfied, catty smile on her face.

Leaning my back against the door I feel the tears well up.

I promised myself no tears over a guy this year, and I here I am already losing my shit.

Without feelings, life would be pretty dull, but damn when they hurt it feels like you're dying.

My phone buzzes incessantly, and I know it has to be Miranda waiting to be let it in. I'm content to stay buried beneath my covers, crying my eyes out, for the next month. Where I will then emerge from my cocoon of blankets magically turned into a beautiful butterfly.

Since I know that isn't a feasible option, I force myself from beneath the blankets, wrap my robe around me, and open the door.

Miranda takes one look at me and blurts, "Okay, who do I need to kill? I have black trash bags in the trunk and sterile gloves."

Her words have the intended effect and I give a small laugh as I let her in.

She sniffs the air and her face sours. "Is something burning or is it you I'm smelling?"

"Shit!" I run over the oven, grab a mitt, and quickly pull out the meal, throwing the pan on top of the stove burners. The meal isn't ruined, maybe a little dry, but I don't care. I'm not hungry anymore. I hope Abel enjoys his overcooked chicken and that it scrapes his throat raw like his actions have my heart.

I leave the meal there and shuck off the mitt, tossing it on the counter.

"What happened?" Miranda grabs my arms, forcing me to stay still.

My bottom lip begins to quiver. I feel pathetic crying over this, over him. I should've known this would happen—that I was only temporary. It's all I've ever been to guys. I thought he was different, but I was wrong.

Why ask me to be his girlfriend and do this? He could've been honest about wanting to see other people, that we weren't exclusive. Sure, I would've said I wasn't interested but he owed *me that.*

Miranda's hands move my face and in a motherly tone she pleads, "Come on, Lou. You can tell me anything."

Dropping my head to her shoulder I sob, telling her everything.

When I finish, she steps back. "I'm going to mur—muppet him."

"Muppet him?"

"It's code. You can't be an accomplice." I laugh and she grins. "Just remember, you're worth more. Our value isn't determined by what others think of us, but what we think of ourselves. He doesn't deserve you, but somewhere, out there, is a man who does. When you find him, it'll be magic."

"This felt like magic," I admit, biting my lip to hold back more tears. I'm sure I look ridiculous with puffy eyes and a stuffy red nose.

Her lips thin. "We can fool ourselves into believing something is magic just because we want it to exist. Let it come to you."

"I didn't go looking for him. It just ... happened."

Her frown deepens. "Are you sure she got panties from his room?"

"Yes!" I cry, throwing my hands in the air. I storm around her and head to my room, where she follows. It looks like a darkened dungeon and I know Abel should be coming home any minute. I don't want to see him, because I'm scared when I do I'm going to beg him to tell me I'm wrong. But I'm terrified that even if he lies straight to my face about nothing happening I'll believe him because I care for him that much.

Flopping dramatically onto my bed I cuddle a pillow

to my chest, tilting my head so I see Miranda as she sits on the end of my bed.

"I'm sorry." She reaches out, brushing my hair off my forehead. It's something my mother did when I was little and I feel a pang of homesickness hit me square in the chest. "Guys suck. It's in their DNA or something. They can't help it."

"I'll be okay. I always am."

"Love you, girl. I have to go." She bends down and hugs me awkwardly since I'm sprawled on my bed.

"Love you, too."

I watch her leave, hearing the door shut behind her. I should get up and lock it, but I don't want to move.

It isn't long before the door opens again.

I hear Abel's duffel bag drop to the floor and then the sound of the door clicking shut and locked.

"Lou?"

My body stiffens and I squeeze the pillow tighter.

A moment later the door to my room squeaks open.

"Lou? Are you okay?"

No, I'm not.

"I think I'm sick," I mumble, turning my head away from him.

"Oh. Can I get you anything?"

"No."

He continues to stand there.

I feel the need to yell at him rise inside me, to rant and rage, but I refuse to give voice to any of it.

"Well, if you need anything let me know."

Blessedly, he leaves and I'm alone once more with thoughts I wish I could silence and a breaking heart that even the strongest glue can't keep together.

CHAPTER TWENTY-EIGHT

Abel

Lou emerges from her room the next morning with her hair a mess, her eyes red and tired looking, with a slouch to her shoulders. She wouldn't eat anything last night, even when I offered to pick up some soup. I ended up sleeping in my room, which was weird by myself. We've been sleeping together in one of our beds and I missed her presence, but since she's sick, I respected her need to be on her own.

"Hey, how are you feeling?" I turn from the stove where I'm making scrambled eggs to see her grab a blanket and roll into a burrito on the couch.

"Just smashing."

"All right, Nigel Thornberry." I wait for a small chuckle or a snort of amusement, but I get nothing in return. "Do you want some eggs? Toast? Starbursts?" I tack on the last thing, once again hoping for some spark of life.

"No."

"Should I take you to the doctor?" I'm getting worried now.

I slide the eggs onto my plate alongside the spinach I already prepared and carry it over to the chair by the couch.

She draws the blankets over her face and gives me another mumbled, "No."

"Lou, shit, tell me something I can do. You're worrying me."

"I don't need your help."

There's a bite to her words and I feel like I've been slapped. "Fuck, what'd I do? I'm trying to help."

"And I said I don't need your help."

"Fine." I stand up with my plate. "If you change your mind you can holler for me."

I swear I hear a sniffle like she's crying, but I can't be sure. I carry my breakfast into my room and shovel it down even though it tastes rubbery. I know something more is going on with her than she's just sick.

She's being fucking *weird*.

A thought hits me like a freight train and the plate drops from my hand, the remains of my breakfast splattering on the floor.

I fly out of my room and Lou's head pops up from her bundle of blankets at the sound of my quickly approaching footsteps.

"Are you pregnant?"

It doesn't seem plausible, but shit happens, and it would definitely explain her behavior.

She sits straight up. "Are you crazy? I just had my period. I'm not pregnant you ignorant dick-bearer." *Not sure exactly what that's supposed to mean.* "Now leave me alone."

She lies back down, covering up with the blankets.

Well, then.

Taking her dismissal for what it is, I get dressed and head out for school. I know when I'm not wanted, and I won't force my presence on her.

She knows how to get ahold of me if she wants to talk or needs me for something.

If I don't hear from her ... I'll think about what that means later.

The whole day passes without a single text or phone call from Lou. I have no clue whether she stays home or comes to school. I send a few texts after the last of my classes but they all go unanswered. It leads to me being extremely frustrated during practice and more aggressive than normal.

Stomping into the locker room, I tear off my uniform as quickly as possible, which isn't quick at all. Every piece wants to stick to my sweaty body and I slam my fist against my metal locker in agitation.

"Whoa," Kit calls out from a few lockers down, "a little frustrated over there? Is your potato puff not giving it to you good enough? There's a cure for that, you know. *Hotter girls.*"

I swivel around to face him. "Shut. Up." I bite out the words, my shoulders rising almost to my ears, with my hands clenched at my sides. I've never wanted to deck someone so badly before, but Kit? He fucking deserves it. He's a disrespectful asshole and he *hurt* my girl with his words and actions, and clearly he doesn't find anything fucking wrong with it.

He raises his hands innocently, a towel dangling from one hand as he prepares to head to a shower. "I'm just speaking the truth, man. What do you see in her? I mean, a one-time thing, sure. I tapped that. But to enjoy my sloppy seconds over and over again? Man, Abel, you don't have to stoop to that level."

Red.

Red descends over my vision like a curtain closing and an inhuman growl erupts out of my throat. Before my brain can process what I'm doing my body launches at Kit and his eyes widen in shock a moment before I collide with him, tackling him to the ground.

My fist rears back and into his face, over and over.

"Don't fucking talk about her like that!" I yell as he punches me back.

We're scrambling over one another trying to get the upper hand.

Suddenly, a whistle blows and we jump apart because we both know what it means.

Coach.

"What are you ladies doing? Break up this ridiculous catfight and get your Goddamn showers so I can go home. This is not fucking *Gossip Girl*. Keep your shit in check or both of you are sitting out the next game!"

"But Coach—" I start, wanting to explain myself.

He holds up a hand. "Never expected to see this kind of shit from you, Russo. Have to say, I'm disappointed. Thought you were better than letting petty locker room talk get to you. And you," he points a finger in Kit's face, "watch yourself. Being on this team is a privilege."

Coach stomps back to his office, and I look around facing all the guys.

Laurent gives me a sympathetic look because he knows I don't lose my shit like this.

"Keep your mouth shut," I mutter under my breath to Kit.

I swear I hear him say *I hope you suffer*, but when I turn back around his head is hidden in his locker.

This has been the day from hell. Parking my truck, I grab my shit and head inside. I want to change my clothes and crash, but not before I talk to Lou.

When I open the door the apartment is dark. Her car was in the lot, but it's possible one of her friends picked her up.

Turning on the lights I search for a note but find none.

"Lou? Are you home? You feeling okay?"

Nothing.

I venture to my left to her room, pushing the door open with the palm of my hand.

I find her buried under the covers, just the top of her messy blonde hair peeking out.

"Lou," I breathe out, "I really think you should go to the doctor if you're this sick."

She sits up so fast it's like something out of the *Exorcist* and I jump a step back.

"The fact you don't know what's wrong with me says a lot."

"Whoa." I raise my hands. "What the hell is going on?"

"Ask your side piece." She lies back down, her voice becoming muffled by all the blankets.

"My side piece? What the fuck are you talking about?"

"Danika showed up. She got her panties she left here last weekend."

Last weekend? Danika? Panties?

"Are you fucking with me?"

She sits up again and if looks could kill I'd be dead right now. "Don't play dumb with me. I'm not stupid."

"Lou," I plead, fanning my hands in a placating gesture. "I have no fucking idea what you're talking about. Danika hasn't been here since that day after I moved in, and I didn't have sex with her."

"Whatever." She flops down. "Lies are ugly and I can't look at you right now."

"You seriously think I slept with Danika last weekend? I mean, fuck, Lou. It seems pretty damn obvious to me and anyone who knows me that I'm crazy about you. You're all I think about. I've *never* touched Danika. Never."

"I don't believe you. I know what I saw."

Hurt flares inside me, my chest actually aching. "You have to be fucking messing with me right now."

"I'm serious as a heart attack."

I yank the covers off her and she glares but I'm tired of arguing with a pile of blankets.

"You mean to tell me you believe some catty ass girl over the guy who ... the guy who..." I exhale a breath, in complete disbelief that it's this moment where I have to confess how I feel. "Over the guy who loves you more than anything in the world. I didn't expect you, Lou, or plan for you. It just happened and I fell hard. I think I've proven that in my words and actions, and the fact you'd believe *Danika* over *me* is fucking maddening."

"I know what I saw!" she shouts, her face turning red.

"What did you see?" I yell back, my tone not angry, just desperate.

"She got her nasty ass lacy thong from your room!"

"Did you see her get it from my room?"

This has to be some cruel joke. I've never fucking touched Danika. I don't want to, not now, not even then.

Her eyes look lost for a moment and then she stutters. "Y-Yes."

I shake my head rapidly back and forth. "I didn't touch her."

"I don't believe you." Those words again. They're like a punch delivered straight to my heart. After everything, the girl I love doesn't believe me. I know it all comes down to how she's been treated in the past, but it doesn't make me feel any better. "I want you to go."

"Go?" I repeat in disbelief.

"Leave, please." Her tone is soft, begging, and it breaks my fucking heart even more.

I believe in fighting for what I want, what I believe, but I know I won't get anywhere with her the way she's acting right now.

"Fine." My shoulders slouch in defeat, my head bowing. I head toward her door and stop, glancing back, to find her gathering the blankets up and around her once more. "You might not believe me, but I'm telling you the truth. I never touched her, never would. I hope by the time you realize that it isn't too late for us."

Her bottom lip trembles and she covers her face with the blankets.

Gathering a bag with my stuff, I leave behind the first girl I've ever loved and a piece of my heart with her.

CHAPTER TWENTY-NINE

Lou

The incessant banging on the door wakes me from a deep sleep. I pop my head out of my burrow of covers like some sort of underground mole or something.

The knocking continues and it doesn't help the headache pulsing behind my eyes. I've barely eaten in two whole days and my body is clearly begging for me to fuel it.

Pushing off the mountain of covers I stand up and thrust my feet into my slippers, gathering my robe around my body.

Padding into the living space, I swing the door open and find Miranda and Tanner standing outside of it.

Miranda pushes past me inside before I can even utter a word.

Tanner gives a sympathetic shrug and follows suit.

"What are you guys doing here?"

"What are you doing missing two days of classes?" she counters, tossing her purse on the couch and planting her hands on her hips. "No guy is worth all this pouting. It's disgusting. Have you seen yourself? Or *smelled* yourself?"

I sniff inconspicuously at my shoulder, near my armpit.

Oh, nasty.

"Mhmm," she hums. "It's bad. I also think there's way more going on here than we know."

"What are you talking about?"

"You haven't seen it?" Her eyes narrow and she grabs her purse, digging through it. "It's all over campus."

Locating her phone she hands it to me.

"What am I supposed to do with this?"

"There's a video." Finally Tanner speaks.

"A video?" My brain automatically goes to a sex tape

starring Danika and Abel. "No, thanks. I don't want to see this."

I thrust the phone back to Miranda and she shakes her head. "No, girl. Watch it."

Exhaling a sigh, I start the video. I can tell it's in a locker room and two guys are going at it, throwing punches like they mean business. A coach steps in and when the guys break apart I see it's Abel and Kit.

"Apparently happened yesterday." Miranda takes her phone back from me before I can rewatch it.

"I don't understand what this means?"

"All I know is Kit and Danika have been spending an awful lot of time together. They're both snakes in the grass if you ask me. The hiss, hiss motherfucker type if you know what I mean."

"Um..." I hesitate, my eyes bouncing from Miranda to Tanner who looks just as lost as I am, though mildly amused.

"I need to investigate this. I'm going to need a disguise and then change the batteries in my walkie-talkies." She taps her lips in thought. "Possibly some rope if he tries to fight me." Tanner's eyes widen and bounce to me. "And a quiet place to hold him for questioning."

"What the hell are you planning?" Tanner blurts, looking like he's ready to run out the door.

"Well, something is clearly amiss here. As much as I'd

love to nut-punch Abel for hurting my girl, I'm not sure he's the problem."

"Miranda! You're supposed to take my side!"

"You didn't see him moping around campus today or that Danika chick following him like a dog in heat." My expression sours. "He didn't pay her any attention."

"It doesn't matter. What he does isn't my business."

"Sometimes I want to slap you. I get it, Lou. You've been hurt. I have been too. It happens. It's part of life. Without the sting of hurt we wouldn't appreciate the high of happiness. Not everything is rainbows, sunshine, and unicorn farts. But Abel," she shrugs, giving me a sheepish look since she knows she's pissing me off, "I see the way he looks at you and I don't believe he did this. If I'm wrong, I'll still punch him in the nuts for you."

I give a small laugh at the visual. "You can do whatever you want, Miranda. But I know what I saw."

Her eyes slide to Tanner. "You ready to kidnap a football player?"

"No," he squeaks.

"That's okay. I'll get you ready."

Tanner gives me a pleading look, but I can't save him, not when Miranda is on a warpath.

She grabs her bag and takes Tanner by the arm, tugging him out of the apartment.

I want to think she's kidding about kidnapping Kit, but with Miranda I can't quite be sure.

CHAPTER THIRTY

Abel

"Can you hold Cristian?"

It's a question, but one I don't get to answer as the screaming baby is planted into my arms. My sister races to the oven to pull out whatever meal it is she's prepared.

I rock Cris in my arms, trying to soothe him, but the way his mouth keeps opening and closing I know he wants a boob, which I definitely can't help him with.

I could fix him a bottle, but I know my sister only likes him to have a bottle if she's not around, so the poor little guy is just going to have to wait.

"G, I could've done that." She flits around the kitchen gathering plates like a madwoman. Her in-laws are coming into town and it's the first time they've seen the baby. My sister always goes into a panic when her husband's parents come, but I don't understand why. They're cool people.

"No, no. It needs to be perfect."

She starts cutting perfect squares of the lasagna she prepared and placing them exactly in the center of the plates.

"The baby, G. He's hungry." She gives a small whimper of panic, eyeing the clock. "I can give him a bottle, but I know you're not crazy about—"

"Yes, please, God. Give him the damn bottle."

"Okay, okay."

I fix a bottle and then leave my psychotic sister behind because she's making my head spin just watching her.

My brother-in-law, Leo, left two hours ago for the airport so he's due home with his parents any minute.

I join Matty and Bells upstairs in his room, where my sister sequestered them so they couldn't drag out any more toys.

"Mommy's being mean." Bella pouts, clutching her lovey close.

"Your mom's stressed. Sometimes when people are stressed they act mean, but they don't mean anything by it. I promise."

She frowns, but then shrugs. Kids are cool like that. They don't let things eat away at them the way adults do.

"Will you play dinosaurs with us?" Matty holds up a dinosaur that looks like Cera from *The Land Before Time*—that's the extent of my dinosaur knowledge.

"As soon as Cristian eats I will."

Bella grabs a dinosaur and makes a *rawr* noise, pretending to eat the one Matty holds.

Cris slurps greedily at his bottle and I have to keep pulling it away from him before he drinks it too quickly. Once he's finished, I burp him and grab the rocker from my sister's bedroom, carrying it into Matty's room so I can put Cristian in it and play with the other two.

It's hard balancing my time between the three kids. I can't possibly imagine how my sister feels. Two feels like a good solid number to me. Then you're not outnumbered.

We haven't played with the dinos for long when the alarm chirps signaling the garage door opening.

"Kids!" My sister calls up. "Grandma and Grandpa are here!"

The kids drop their toys where they are and run out

of the room, leaving me behind like they don't care about me at all.

"Feel the love guys." I know they can't hear me, but I joke anyway.

Picking up the discarded dinosaurs, I dump them in Matteo's toy box so things aren't a complete disaster when Giulia comes up later.

"All right, little man, ready to meet your grandparents?"

I pick up Cristian and carry him downstairs. As soon as I reach the bottom of the steps, my sister comes out of nowhere, sweeping the baby from my arms.

"And this is Cristian." Already she's headed in the direction of the dining room and I'm left standing in her whirlwind. "Abel! Come say hi!"

"The Kraken beckons," I mutter to myself.

God, I miss Lou. If she were here, she'd be as amused as I am about my sister.

When I showed up telling my sis I needed to stay a few days she wanted to know what happened with Lou. I asked her how she knew anything was going on between the two of us and that's when she told me she caught us on her security cameras snuggling. After I told her what happened, she advised me to give Lou time, that sometimes women are overly sensitive and she'll come around. That might be true, but it's fucking hurtful for her to not believe me from the start.

Venturing into the formal dining room, I greet Leo's parents, giving them each a hug before we all sit down to eat.

I have to suppress my laughter at the extravagant table set up, because my sister didn't even do this for Thanksgiving last year. My dad drove down and we all ate mostly around the TV so we could watch football. But tonight she has a tablecloth draped over the table along with actual place settings I've only seen in movies before. There are even tall candles she has lit with the chandelier above dimmed.

"I've never eaten in the almost-dark." She kicks my leg with the point of her heel and I try not to groan. That shit hurt.

"We're having a nice meal. I know you're not used to that kind of thing at school."

"Sure I am. I make my own meals, always very healthy and delicious, I just don't eat in the dark."

"Abel," she hisses, leaning over her plate of food ready to lunge across and murder me.

Leo's parents laugh.

"We're so happy to be able to visit. We don't get to spend enough time with family," his mom, Leanne, says with a kind smile directed at my sister.

G's shoulders relax slightly. "We're really happy to have you."

The rest of the meal goes smoothly and I volunteer to

clean up the dishes. My sister is letting me crash on her couch while her in-laws are in. It's the least I can do.

It's getting late so Leo and Giulia get the kids in bed while his parents head to bed too, tired after their flight.

G comes down grabbing a sippy cup for Bells and hesitates in the family room.

"You look sad."

I shrug, fanning a blanket over the couch. "I'm hurt. I think sadness is a secondary response to being hurt."

"Lou's a good girl. You're my brother, so I'm always going to take your side, but if you really care about her you shouldn't give up so easily. If a love isn't worth fighting for, it isn't worth keeping."

Her words ring true, and I know she's the one worth fighting for, but I also know in the state she's in, fighting will only push her further away from me.

Grabbing the pillow I toss it on the couch. "Sweet dreams."

Giulia gives me a sympathetic smile and pats my shoulder as she passes me. "The sweetest."

CHAPTER THIRTY-ONE

Lou

I haven't seen or spoken to Abel in nearly a week. I can tell he's been by the apartment to grab some more things, but either it's been a coincidence or he's strategically avoiding me.

Striding across campus toward my parked car, my phone starts ringing.

I ignore the annoying sound, letting it go to voicemail. More than likely it's a bored ass telemarketer and I'm not in the mood to troll their ass.

As soon as the call ends, it starts up again and I reluctantly dig out my phone, swiping to answer when I see Miranda's name flashing on the screen along with a goofy picture of us.

"Where are you?"

"Near the theater, headed to my car."

"Don't do that! I'm going to get you, fucker!"

"Do what? Get me, why?"

"Not you, him."

"Him, who?"

"That's not important. Just get over here."

"I don't even know where you are."

"Near the cafeteria. You can't miss us. Hurry."

I hear some grunts and groans, her breath heavy. I swear I catch Tanner mutter something in the background. Ending the call, I abandon my plan to go home and sulk, crossing to the other side of campus, out of my way, to find Miranda.

I see the cafeteria in the distance and—

"Oh, my fucking God." I don't ever run, but I do then. "What are you doing?" I scream at Miranda.

Somehow she has the giant, muscled, wall of a man, Kit, sprawled on the ground in a hold that I think I've only seen on WWE.

"Tap out, motherfucker. Tap. Out." She taunts him.

Who the hell is my best friend? Should I be scared? Is she secretly a wrestler?

"Let me go, psycho!" He tries to get away from her and I'm beyond impressed that he can't.

Tanner stands to the side looking mildly afraid and unsure what to do.

"Uh ... Miranda. What are you doing?"

My best friend notices my presence and grimaces as she tightens her hold on Kit.

"Tell her you slimy worm. Tell her what you guys did."

"Let me go. I'm calling the cops."

She tightens her hold and he yelps. "No, you won't. What are you going to tell them? The big bad asshole football player got beat up by a girl?"

"All right, all right. I'll talk to her. Let me up."

She leans over his body. "Tap. Out."

"Are you fucking kidding me?"

"I said, tap out. You're not very good at following directions? You know what they say about small brains?"

"No?"

"Small brain, small peen."

"Bitch," he hisses, but he does actually tap his hand against the ground.

She releases him and points two fingers at her eyes and then him. "Run and I'll catch you."

Tanner eyes me and mouths, "I'm scared of her."

"Someone explain what's going on here." I cross my arms over my chest, waiting for some sort of clarification on what I've witnessed.

Miranda points an accusatory finger at Kit. "Speak, peasant."

Kit gathers himself to a standing position and I swear he winces in pain like his knee hurts. I might feel bad for the guy if he wasn't such an asshole. There's a bruise on his cheek, but after seeing the locker room video I know that's courtesy of Abel.

Kit clears his throat, glaring at me like *I'm* the one who tackled him to the ground.

Dude, it's not my fault you got bested by a girl.

Miranda kicks the back of his shin and his knee buckles slightly.

"My God, woman," he cries, glaring at her.

"You're taking too long." Her head cocks to the side and she crosses her arms over her chest. One foot taps restlessly against the sidewalk in a *tick tock* gesture.

Kit reluctantly looks at me once more, his eyes drop to the ground and back up repeatedly.

"Danika and I were pissed off about you and Abel being together so we devised a plan."

What? WHAT?

"A plan?"

"To break you up."

Oh my God, if Miranda doesn't kill him I might, and

then I'll hunt down that dark-haired Victoria Secret model wannabe.

"Why would you guys want to break us up?" I glare at him, trying not to reach out and strangle his thick neck.

"Danika wanted Abel, but I wanted her."

"I ... what? How does that make any sense?"

Miranda hisses under her breath, "Like I said, small brain equals small peen."

"We hooked up a few times, but she was always lusting after Russo. I thought if she got it out of her system she'd see I'm better for her."

"You two are definitely meant to be." I honestly can't believe what I'm hearing. "So, what happened exactly?"

He shrugs, glaring around at the three of us. I don't know why he's so pissed off considering this whole thing is his fault.

"We made a plan for her to show up at your place when we knew Abel wasn't around and make it look like she left her underwear there."

"But she didn't?"

"No." He shakes his head. His eyes dart to Miranda and she jolts forward like she's going to get him and the guy actually jumps like he's scared. I feel like laughing, which is a pretty great feeling after the last week and few days I've had.

"Elaborate, Bitch Boy." Miranda purses her lips at him, her eyes nothing but slits.

"Jesus Christ, all right." Wringing his hands together the same way Matteo does when I scold him he exhales a breath. "The panties were in her purse, they were never in his room."

I flashback to her visit and close my eyes in pain, because I'm a fucking idiot. I didn't follow her to his room, so it made it easy enough for her to pull out the thong from her purse while she was in there and leave with it clasped in her hand. I remember how nervous she seemed and how her story changed from Saturday to Sunday. She was never there at all and I...

I made a big fucking mistake.

"Poor Abel."

I feel tears well in my eyes, because I hurt the guy I love by letting my insecurities get to me. I've been so much better about not letting stuff get to me, but some scars are deeper than others. My past with guys has burned me and I let it blind me to the one, brilliant, man who wants me for me and nothing more.

"You guys are assholes." I kick him in the knee and he falls forward, kneeling in front of me. Grabbing his chin in my hand I stare into his eyes. "I like it when my inferiors kneel. You're one of the worst mistakes of my life, but that's all you'll ever be. A blip in my life, someone I won't even remember one day. But me? You'll never forget me, because girls like me are hard to find."

Letting him go I shove him away and stalk off.

"Where are you going?" Miranda calls after me.

Turning around to face her, I walk backward. "To make a plan to get my man back."

She exchanges a look with Tanner, and both grin. "We're coming, too."

They hurry to catch up to me and I sling an arm around each of their shoulders.

"We're the three best friends anyone could have," I sing-song, quoting *The Hangover*.

They laugh, hugging me as we walk.

Kit stands behind us, completely forgotten.

CHAPTER THIRTY-TWO

Lou

"What are you wearing?"

I stare at Miranda dressed in head to toe black. Black long sleeve shirt, black jeans, black combat boots. I half-expect her to pull out a black mask burglars wear.

She looks down at her ensemble. "What's wrong with this? I'm trying to be incognito."

"Exactly. We can't show up to a football game with

you dressed for mourning. We need team spirit. Go home, change, and come back for me."

She appraises me, still in my robe. "Thank God, I was little worried you thought going naked would be a good way to get your roommate back."

I roll my eyes. "Shoo, go! We don't have much time."

"Don't you have something I can borrow?"

"Are you kidding me? I'm going to steal Abel's shirt. I have no school spirit and I would normally never be setting foot at a game except I know how much football means to him and I need to apologize in a big way."

"I mean, I'm all for this plan, it means I get to use my walkie-talkies, but I still think you should consider using sex to apologize. It'd be much easier."

"Miranda." I expel a breath. "I'll have plenty of time for make-up sex later. Right now, I need you to scrounge up some team spirit and not look like one of Charlie's Angel's."

"Fine, fine. I'm going. I'll text you when I'm back."

I close the door behind her, and dash to the shower. I've squandered most of my time away wondering if this plan is totally insane and trying to finish cross-stitching my mother's birthday present.

Happy fucking birthday you old broad my current design reads.

Yeah, it's rude and crass, but it's a *joke* and my mom knows that. We've always had the kind of mother-daughter relationship where we pick on each other. I'm also going to get her a spa day so she can get a massage and be pampered. She deserves it.

After shaving every inch of my body—which is not something I do on the daily, or even weekly—I lather and wash my hair. Out of the shower, I pluck my eyebrows, prep my skin and apply makeup.

Sneaking into Abel's room, as if he's going to catch me in the act, I take the shirt I need and hack it with a pair of scissors until it's a crop-top.

I'll buy him a new one. I'm not a total monster.

Frankly, I'm just thankful it's still here. A lot of his clothes are gone and I know from Giulia that he's been staying there. I could tell she was a little irritated with me on the phone, but also surprisingly understanding. When I called her yesterday to fill her in on my plan, she sounded back to her normal self and was completely ecstatic to help me win her brother back.

I dress in the newly cut crop-top, a pair of high-rise jeans, and red cowboy boots. I wanted pink ones but they only came in kid size, so I bought the red ones instead. Fixing my hair into two space buns with two loose pieces framing my face I assess my appearance in the mirror.

"Looking hot, Lou." I shoot myself finger guns in the mirror and wink. If you won't flirt with yourself, how do you expect anyone else to do it?

My phone vibrates on top of my comforter and I grab it.

Miranda: I'm waiting out front, biotch. Don't make me wait too long. I'm hangry now SINCE YOU MADE ME GO HOME AND CHANGE.

Me: WHY DIDN'T YOU EAT WHILE YOU WERE THERE? WE ARE ON A MISSION HERE. I DON'T HAVE TIME FOR YOUR HUNGRY BITCHINESS.

Miranda: It's a football game. There's a concession stand. I'll eat there.

Rolling my eyes, I stuff my phone in my back pocket, grab a cardigan in case it gets chilly, and swipe one of Abel's protein bars on my way out.

In front of my building, Miranda sits in her car waiting with the windows rolled down.

"Get in, loser! We have a football player to snare. I hope your vagina is secretly a Venus flytrap."

I bust out laughing as I open the passenger door and climb in beside her. "Here, eat this." I pass her the bar as I buckle myself in.

"What's this?" She stares at the bar as if it's personally offended her.

"It's a protein bar. Eat it. You're not you when you're hungry."

"I told you I'm eating at the game."

"Nope, no you aren't." I shake my head adamantly. "I need my wing woman, remember?"

She rolls her eyes. "The things I do for you." She rips open the protein bar and takes a massive bite as she pulls into traffic. "It's not like I can't eat and perform my duties at the same time, but fine, whatever you want."

"You're a true friend. I'll reward you with pizza and dessert at a later date."

"Mhmm," she hums, brushing crumbs off her top before they can fall into the crater between her boobs to be lost until the end of time. "You owe me and I'll be calling to collect."

When we arrive at the stadium, the lot is already packed and Miranda whines as we're forced to park far enough away she declares we'll be walking a mile. She's probably not wrong.

We follow the flow of the crowd and students dressed in our school colors of red and blue. Many sport paint smears across their face and even their chests. It seems too cold to me to be bare-chested but the guys act like they're used to it.

"Wow, people go all out for this," Miranda muses, her eyes darting around.

Like me, she's never been bothered to attend.

We pay for the tickets, entering the stadium. I stand there in shock for a moment because I'm not quite prepared for the vastness of everything and the nearly full seats. This is a small college town and I never expected to see *this*. It makes me beyond nervous for what I have planned, considering I need to sneak onto the field.

Grabbing Miranda's hand I pull her along with me.

"Where are we going?" She struggles to pull her hand out of mine, digging her feet into the ground, but when I'm determined I can't be stopped.

"Can't you just be a good friend and follow along?"

I don't wait for her answer and tighten my hold so she can't get away. I scan the field, looking for the bench where the guys will sit when they're not playing. I don't know much about football, but I do know that.

"Come on, down here," I direct, but Miranda has no choice but to follow me since I hold her hand hostage.

Taking the stairs down to the asphalt in front of the field I find a spot hidden in shadow.

Perfect.

I sit down, wiggling my ass on the uncomfortable hard surface. My extra padding is going to come in handy tonight.

"This is the worst." Miranda glares at me and the dirty ground before reluctantly parking her butt beside me. "Remind me to *never* agree to any of your favors ever again. I'm pretty sure I could've come up with a much better plan than this. How do you think you're going to get on the field anyway?"

"Do you have what I need?" I bypass her question,

because frankly I don't know. We're going to have to improvise this plan.

She rolls her eyes. "What kind of friend would I be if I *didn't* agree to do you a favor?" She fights a smile around her retort and passes me the backpack she had slung over her shoulder.

I inspect it, finding that she did manage to get everything I asked for.

Grinning evilly, I stretch out my legs and wait for the game to begin.

We're hidden well enough away into the shadows I don't think Abel will spot me, besides he's not expecting me and with this kind of crowd it's pretty difficult to notice anyone in particular. It's nothing but a sea of red and blue.

Twenty minutes later, the lights in the stadium dim and the crowd goes eerily quiet.

"What's happening?" Miranda hisses under her breath, grabbing my hand like she's afraid we're about to be sucked into the darkness by some psychotic killer. She ought to know by now I'll throw her to the wolves and make a break for it. No way am I getting murdered with her.

Taking my hand back, I whisper, "I don't know, but stop acting like a scaredy cat. It's *football*."

Music blares suddenly and Miranda jumps. I resist the urge to roll my eyes, even though she wouldn't see even if I did. The girl can tackle a two-hundred pound football player to the ground but is afraid of this.

The lights flash off and on rapidly before bursting back on completely and blinding me.

"Jesus Christ." I slap my hands over my eyes to shield them.

Jesus is probably shaking his head right now wishing I'd stop using his name in instances like this and instead be a little more humble and get on my knees to pray.

I only get on my knees for far more fun and interesting activities. At least when it comes to Abel.

Names and stats are called out as the guys run onto the field. They jump around and bump each other's chests, clearly pumped for the game to start.

Abel is announced, number 27, and he strolls onto the field grinning from ear to ear. His helmet is clasped in his hand and he pumps it in the air a few times. The crowd cheers and I see the way he lights up, absorbing every second of it and reveling in the crowd chanting his name.

My heart aches to be near him. I'm angry at myself for letting my doubts get the best of me. I should've trusted him and believed him from the start. He'd never lied to me before. But lessons like these are important ones to learn. If he forgives me, this is one I'll never make again.

My phone buzzes in my pocket and I pull it out.

Tanner: Where are you guys?

Instead of trying to text our location I call him and give him details.

"Be there in a minute."

Hanging up, my eyes find Abel standing with his teammates. Their backs are to the crowd and they're talking together. My eyes take in the wide broadness of his shoulder pads, tapering down to his narrow waist, and settling on his firm bitable ass.

It's probably totally wrong of me checking him out like this after how I acted, but I can't help myself. He's hot and he's mine.

Or he was.

God, I hope he still is.

If I ruined this ... Kit might be forgettable but Abel isn't. I would never forgive myself for losing him.

Miranda knocks her shoulder into mine. "You're drooling." She pretends to wipe the corner of my mouth.

"I'm allowed to *look*," I defend jokingly and she laughs. Rifling through the backpack again I sit back and tilt my head toward her. "This is dumb, isn't it?" I bite my lip as doubt creeps in. "Maybe I should just say sorry like a normal person?"

"Who cares if it's stupid? Life is all about dumb, irresponsible choices. They make for a good laugh later in life. Besides, when has doubt ever stopped you from doing anything? You're weird—in a good way—and a normal boring apology isn't you."

"True dat," I respond in my best Kourtney Kardashian impression.

A heavy breath is exhaled and we both find Tanner approaching. "It took me for-fucking-ever to find you guys, but this is definitely easier than trying to find you in that massive crowd." He eyes the stadium with fear, then his eyes drop to the ground and he makes a face at the dirty asphalt before sitting down beside Miranda.

"Glad you found us." I lean around Miranda and give him a smile.

"Wouldn't miss this." He grins back. "Anything to help you."

The game starts and it turns out to not be as dull as I imagined. In fact, I find myself getting a little *too* into it. I'll never let Abel know this tidbit of information or it'll be held against me forever.

Watching the clock, I wait for it to get closer to halftime. As the time ticks down I grab the bag and smile conspiratorially with Miranda. "Showtime."

Doing a forward roll, pretending I'm a spy and this is an undercover operation, I sneak around staying low. I know I look ridiculous, and I'm not hiding at all, but this is part of the fun.

Miranda walks behind me muttering under her breath about how crazy I am.

If she wasn't the same way she wouldn't be friends with me.

Tanner looks nervous, but doesn't say anything.

My heart pounds in my chest and I feel nerves skyrocket through me.

"This is a bad idea," I blurt, coming to a sudden stop so Miranda plows into the back of me.

"Jesus," she curses, righting herself from a stumble. Moving in front, she levels me with a glare. "I didn't go to five different stores for you to chicken out. You also didn't put this much effort into your hair, makeup, and clothes to decide not to do this. This isn't like you. You never stop to think about the consequences, you just do it. I admire your ability to take risks and put yourself out there. It's one of the reasons I love you and you're my best friend."

I sniffle, pretending to wipe away a tear. "I knew you loved me."

I go to hug her and she swats my open arms away. "No hugging until the mission is complete." Giving a small laugh, I nod. "Now let me grab the walkie-talkies."

"And I'm chopped liver," Tanner grumbles good-naturedly. "She might not hug you but I will."

"Aw." I dive into his open arms. "Fate led us to the same table at Griffin's and now you can't get rid of me."

He laughs, releasing me. "Wouldn't dream of it, Lou."

Fate, I realize, is what led me to Abel.

If ass-hat Jamie hadn't raised rent costs I would've never needed a roommate and Abel and I would've never met.

I was angry at the time, but it's because I didn't understand what was in store for me.

I didn't trust fate this one time, when I was actually about to gain the person who completes me.

Miranda dives into the backpack, rifling through the contents. Grabbing a walkie-talkie she passes one to me and pulls out another for Tanner she must've bought.

"They're already set to the right channel," she informs us, straightening back up and extending the bag to me.

"You remember what you need to do?"

She huffs a breath. "Do I look like a fucking amateur to you?"

"You?"

Tanner nods. "You made me memorize it. Miranda is going to take care of hi-jacking the music and I'll get the other thing."

"Exactly." Holding out my fist for them to bump, I struggle to hide my grin, but finally it breaks free. "Game on."

We head in opposite directions and I look at the clock, seeing less than a minute until halftime.

My heart races erratically because I know I'm about

to put myself on display for not only our entire school, but the opposing team as well.

All in the name of love. Get this shizz done and get your man back.

I get into position, ready to run onto the field when it's time. Security might pull me off the field before I accomplish my goal, but I have to try.

Seconds count down and as it gets closer to zero my anxiety grows. I might be quirky, and say weird things, but I'm not the type to put myself on the line like this.

Please be worth it. Please forgive me.

"Get ready, chick. Shit's about to go down. Over." Miranda's voice comes across the walkie-talkie.

"Mic good? Over."

"You're all linked up. Just have to turn it on. Over."

I'm lucky Miranda is beyond smart when it comes to multiple things. Since I'm crashing the field, I felt it was important for the crowd to hear exactly what's going on. They'll also hear his rejection if he can't forgive me for not believing him, but it's less than I deserve to have hundreds of people, maybe thousands, be witness to my failure.

"All good here. Over." Tanner.

My heart beats impossibly fast and I wonder if I might pass out before this happens.

Unfortunately, or I guess fortunately, I don't.

The clock hits halftime and Miranda's voice echoes

across the stadium before the teams can head for the locker room.

"Ladies and gentlemen, we have a very special performance for you this evening. Hey, you! Yeah, cheerleader? Sit your ass down. You're not performing. You too band peeps. Sit tight. Capiche?" You can hear her clear her throat before she continues. "Yo, number twenty-seven in the Hornets jersey, stay where you are."

Abel looks around in confusion, taking off his helmet. His face and hair are drenched in sweat, but I swear he's sexier than I've ever seen him. I'm really regretting this being my first football game, but hopefully I can make up for it.

The walkie-talkie chirps and I know that's the signal she's about to start the music.

The background music to *Mickey* by Toni Basil begins to play and I hop over the fence, somehow managing to do it one try—probably thanks to the adrenaline—and the crowd yells. Abel's head swivels and his eyes light on me.

His team is behind him and the opposing team is closing in but I see him and only him.

Stopping right in front of him, pom-poms that I dug out of the backpack in hand, I begin to sing along to the song.

"*Oh, Abel you're so kind, you're so kind you fulfill my life. Hey, Abel. Hey, Abel.*"

His shocked expression quickly turns to a grin.

He waves someone away and I wonder if it's security trying to get me or something else.

Reaching my further improvised chorus I sing, *"You've been gone all week and that makes me sad. I thought you lied, but it was me who had it wrong. Why did I fight fate when it's you that I want? I'm sorry. Oh, Abel, I'm sorry. Forgive me."*

The song wraps up and I'm left standing in front of him, pom-poms dangling loosely from my hands. I feel so incredibly small in this moment, like one touch of wind could knock me over.

I've never felt so raw as I do standing before the guy I love begging for forgiveness.

"I love you." The words are laced with so much of my heart it's impossible not to hear the truth in them. "I let fear dictate me and I didn't believe you when I should have. You're the one I want. Today, tomorrow, ten years from now. It's you. I want to argue about Starburst flavors, annoy you with the Jonas Brothers, and pretend to like football for your sake." He gives a small laugh, his brown eyes twinkling. "I'm sorry for believing others over you. I'm sorry for not trusting you when you've given me no reason to believe otherwise. I'm sorry for not talking to you. I'm just really sorry and I hope you can forgive me."

His smile grows and he rubs his lips together, trying

to hide it. "You mean to tell me, you put together this whole song and dance routine, plus got my nephew and niece involved just to apologize?"

I look over my shoulder and find Tanner with Giulia, Leo, and the kids. Cristian is strapped to Giulia's chest but the two kids stand in front holding homemade posters that beg for Uncle Abie to forgive Lou.

"I needed a backup plan. You'd have to forgive me for the kids' sake." Tears well in my eyes at the same time laughter bubbles out of my throat.

He grabs my face in his hands. "Silly girl, all you had to say was sorry and I would've forgiven you. I didn't need this, though I might've enjoyed forcing you to eat a yellow Starburst as a consolation." He winks.

"Never."

"The day I met you I didn't know that the crazy girl who spoke of fate on the phone would change my life like you have. You're the thing I've been waiting for that I didn't even know I needed until I had it. I was hurt, and I needed time to cool off, but like someone wise once told me, if a love isn't worth fighting for it isn't worth keeping, and Lou?"

"Y-Yeah?" I hesitate, staring up at him.

"I would fight through hell and back for you."

I swear the entire crowd *awws*.

With those words he takes my lips with his, giving me the kiss of a lifetime.

Over the loudspeaker I hear Miranda scream, "That's my girl!"

The crowd, and even both football teams still on the field, all cheer.

The kiss seems to go on forever.

Breaking apart, Abel presses his forehead to mine. "Still desperately seeking a roommate? It seems I'm in need of one since I got kicked out."

I grab his jersey in my fist and pull him closer. "I'm seeking so much more."

He kisses me again and I know this is only the beginning.

EPILOGUE

#1
Lou
Five Years Later

"Why are we here?" I stare around at the darkened university stadium, the site of my epic apology and a place that later came to feel very much like us.

"You ask too many questions, Blondie."

"You've been acting weird," I accuse as we take the stairs down to the field. There's something glowing on the field, but I'm not sure what since he brought me into the stadium near the top. "Are we even allowed to be here?"

"Since when do you abide by the rules?" Abel grins at me.

"Since I became a respectable journalist."

"Mhmm." He gives me a conspiratorial smile.

We reach the field and I find hundreds of candles already lit. In the center of them is a pile of pink Starbursts and I bust out laughing as he guides me into the center of them.

"Did you buy me a lifetime supply of Starbursts?"

He drops to one knee, still holding my hand but his other delves into his pocket.

"Oh my God." My free hand flies to my mouth.

Maybe the whole field thing, candles, and Starbursts should've tipped me off but I've learned over the years Abel is very romantic and sentimental.

"No, but I want *you* for a lifetime."

Holy shit.

He lets go of my hand to open the ring box and my jaw drops at the beautiful pink diamond ring resting inside.

IT'S PINK! My brain screams at me.

"I've spent years loving you and I know I'm going to love you for the rest of my life, but I want to call you my wife. You're my other half, Lou. My sweetest dream brought to life. Will you marry me?"

I tackle him to the ground, kissing him until I can't breathe.

He chuckles as I roll off of him onto the pile of pink Starbursts. "Is that a yes?"

"That's a hell yes!" I scream, throwing my hands in the air.

He goes to grab the ring from the box but it's gone.

"Oh, fuck." He pats his hands around frantically, looking for the ring. Locating it in the grass, he wipes it clean.

"Ready for this, Blondie? This means a wedding, kids, growing old, and always arguing over who's right and who's wrong until our dying breath."

"Stop trying to scare me. I already said yes." I hold out my hand and he slides the ring onto my left ring finger. It looks like it's always belonged there.

Wrapping my arms around his body I hug and kiss him.

Who could've guessed one small ad would change my entire life?

"Here's to forever, Mr. Popular." I pull away, wiping my lipstick from his mouth.

He shakes his head. "No."

"No?" I raise a brow. "Are we already arguing two minutes after we got engaged?"

He tucks a piece of hair behind my ear like he always does.

"I said no, because here's to *now*. Forever will come."

My smile spreads. "To now, and the forever that will come."

EPILOGUE

#2
Lou
Five Years After That

Entering the zoo gates, I feel a sense of nostalgia wash over me. I haven't set foot here in ten years. It seems apt that it's happening again now.

"See the monkeys, Sawyer." I point out the silly acting monkeys to my two-year-old son, lifting him into my arms. He bangs his small fist into the glass and I grasp his tiny hand in mine. "No, sweetie, don't do that. We don't want to scare the monkeys."

"Monkeys!" he cries, throwing his hands in the air and I laugh, darting my head away when he nearly smacks me in the face.

Sawyer Abel Russo is the spitting image of his dad, except with my blue eyes. He's perfect in every way, so perfect in fact, we decided to have two more—well, one more, the third wasn't expected or planned for at all. Definitely not this soon at least.

"Be good for mommy." Abel bends and kisses the top of Sawyer's head. "I know you're wild like she is, but she's carrying your brother or sister."

Abel's large hand splays across my belly that Sawyer's legs dangle over. Our nine-month-old daughter, Sophia Louise, is strapped to his chest, giggling and kicking her legs wildly.

I'm fourteen weeks along with our next and even though we agreed on two and then to see how we handled that before we considered adding another ... well, fate, the pesky bitch that she is, loves to interfere with our lives and I was surprised to find myself pregnant with our third.

It's entirely Abel's fault, though. He can't keep his hands off of me.

It seems appropriate for us, though. We're chaotic and

full of life, why shouldn't we have a whole brood of children to chase after?

After standing watching the monkeys for a bit, I put Sawyer back in his stroller as we explore more of the zoo.

We near the snake exhibit and a wistful smile spreads across my face.

"Would you like a picture?" A zoo employee asks and we both turn toward the sound of the voice.

No.

I don't know if she recognizes us, but it's the same woman who told us ten years ago we had a beautiful family.

Only then it wasn't ours.

Abel and I exchange a look of disbelief and one word is communicated between us.

Fate.

Again and again that words appears in our life. I can't not believe in it, not when the evidence is always staring me in the face.

"Thank you, ma'am. We'd love that."

He pulls out his phone and turns the camera on, handing it to her.

I pick up Sawyer from his stroller for the photo-op and Abel and I stand in the exact same spot we did all those years ago, only this time the zoo employee doesn't have to tell me to stand close to my husband.

"Smile."

We do.

The flash goes off and I see stars as Abel takes his phone back.

We stand there looking at the photo, thinking of the one we took with his niece and nephews who are now fifteen, thirteen, and ten.

"We were always meant to end up here, weren't we?" He gazes at me with so much love and awe that if I wasn't already pregnant I'm pretty sure I'd be getting pregnant tonight.

"Always."

Through Starbursts, Jonas Brothers, crepes, fancy cookies, football games, and so much more, we made it to today, tomorrow, and every day after.

ACKNOWLEDGMENTS

It takes a village to write a book, and I'm so beyond grateful for the village I've created.

Barbara and Kellen, you're always there to take my book to the next level. You cheer me on when I'm feeling down or doubting my words. I love the friendship we've created and can't wait for all the goodness that is yet to come.

Emily Wittig, thank you for creating this gorgeous cover. I told you abs aren't my thing but I wanted to try something different for this cover and you delivered in creating something I absolutely love. Props to you. I can't wait until I can squeeze you again.

To my beta readers Raquel and Stefanie thank you for all the hard work you put in on my books. It's so appreciated and never doubt your roll in the stories I create.

Regina Bartley, I miss your face like crazy. You're the bestest author friend ever and we seriously need to start our sprints up again.

Sara and Wendi, thank you for your unwavering friendship, support, and laughs. I hope one day we have a Fab Four get-together with us and Barbara. ApollyCon 2020? Let's make this happen, ladies.

To you, Dear Reader, whether you've read all of my books or are just starting with this one thank you. Without readers, authors are nothing, each book you buy, review you leave, makes a huge difference in my life. I appreciate every message and comment I receive from you guys. It truly makes my whole day, and I'm beyond blessed to be able to live my dream.

Until the next one.

XoXo,

Micalea

ALSO BY MICALEA SMELTZER

The Wildflower Duet

The Confidence of Wildflowers

The Resurrection of Wildflowers

The Boys Series

Bad Boys Break Hearts

Nice Guys Don't Win

Real Players Never Lose

Good Guys Don't Lie

Broken Boys Can't Love

Second Chances Standalone Series

Unraveling

Undeniable

Trace + Olivia Series

Finding Olivia

Chasing Olivia

Tempting Rowan

Saving Tatum

Willow Creek Series

Last To Know

Never Too Late

In Your Heart

Take A Chance

Willow Creek Box Set

Always Too Late Short Story

Willow Creek Bonus Content

Home For Christmas

Light in the Dark Series

Rae of Sunshine

When Stars Collide

Dark Hearts

When Constellations Form

Broken Hearts

Stars & Constellations Bundle

Standalones

Beauty in the Ashes

<u>Bring Me Back</u>

<u>The Other Side of Tomorrow</u>

<u>Desperately Seeking Roommate</u>

<u>Desperately Seeking Landlord</u>

<u>Whatever Happens</u>

<u>Sweet Dandelion</u>

<u>Say When</u>

<u>The Road That Leads To Us</u>

The Game Plan

www.ingramcontent.com/pod-product-compliance
Lightning Source LLC
LaVergne TN
LVHW030315070526
838199LV00069B/6474